SPARE PARTS

THE UPGRADE SERIES #4

WESLEY CROSS

JOIN THE UPGRADE SERIES

To receive free books, get behind the scenes stories, and be the first to hear about new releases—sign up for the newsletter.

See the back of the book for details.

PUBLISHER INFORMATION

This is a work of fiction. Names, characters, businesses, places, events, and incidents are either the product of the author's imagination or used in a fictitious manner. Any resemblance to actual persons, living or dead, or actual events is purely coincidental.

Published by
Cerberus Prints
PO BOX 90399
Brooklyn, NY 11209

1

———

The limo stopped in front of the train station, a rugged old building with a squeaky turnstile. The lights on the outside were out, but the moon was climbing, casting long shadows that seemed to move on their own. The wind swatted at the side of the car, trying to break in.

"Thanks, Mike," Jason Hunt said, putting his hand on the door. The handle was cold.

"Are you sure about this?" The whites of Mike Connelly's eyes shone in the rearview mirror. "I can't protect you if you don't let me."

"I have to do this alone." Hunt buttoned the coat and opened the door.

"The guy by the station—"

"I saw." Hunt interrupted him. "Six foot two, a righty, light on his feet. Probably a boxer. Must be one of Victor's goons. I'm good. Keep the car here so we don't spook them. I'll see you soon."

He got out, closed the door, and started to walk. The warehouse where Victor Ye was allegedly having a meeting was a few blocks away.

A combat sonar started beeping into his earpiece implant, feeding ghostly images of the stalker into his enhanced vision.

Hunt picked up the pace as he turned onto a narrow street, choked on both sides by two grimy buildings. He could hear the man now without the aid of his systems—the urgent staccato of a hunter overtaking his prey.

Jason took the first blow without turning back, his body armor implants buzzing like a hive of disturbed bees, as they dissipated the energy of the punch. He spun around and ducked under an uppercut, watching the man stumble after a miss.

The man was good. He must've been a world-class contender back in his prime. Hunt stepped back from two lightning-fast probing shots and blocked another hook aimed at his temple. Then his prosthetic right arm shot out at eighty miles an hour, hitting the man in the chest and sending him flying.

It wasn't a fair fight. Not by a long shot. A cluster of tiny wires connected to his optic nerves fed live information into a powerful CPU implanted at the base of Hunt's skull. The twitching of his opponent's muscles, the slight shift in his balance, the movement of the man's eyes. All that data was absorbed, analyzed, and refined to map out every move of his adversary before it even began. And then, the series of commands fired off by the enhanced movement unit, EMU for short, directly into the primary motor cortex, sent his body into a sequence of lethal moves no ordinary human could counter.

Fighting you is like fighting an agent from the Matrix, Connelly said to him once as they were calibrating his implants after the installation.

Hunt's enhanced vision flashed amber as the computer identified a weapon in the attacker's hand.

He caught the knife with his left and then his bionic hand sprang to the man's throat, crushing the windpipe in its mechanical grip.

"What are you?" the man managed.

Hunt didn't answer as he watched the man black out. When his attacker's eyes turned glassy, he lowered the unconscious body to the ground and continued to walk.

The warehouse was an ugly square building with a flat, slanted roof and gray, graffiti-covered walls. Jagged pieces of broken glass in window frames glistened like sharp teeth of some prehistoric monster setting a trap. Ready to devour the unsuspecting prey.

"Mike?" he said into the microphone as his implants scanned the building, layering his internal vision with transparent silhouettes. The green glow of infrared images and ghostly contours of x-rays scattered across the ground floor of the warehouse created a three-dimensional psychedelic mix. "You can pick me up in ten. I'm too late."

"Roger. Nothing on the scans?"

"A few fellows are still here, but it looks like the party's over. I'll pop my head in and say hello."

"Stay frosty."

Hunt signed off and crossed the street, the echo of his steps ricocheting off dirty walls and diving into broken windows of abandoned buildings across the street. The rusty front door pulsated green in his vision, and he pulled on the brass handle, swinging it open. A whiff of stale air, and then a noxious cocktail of urine, feces, and rotten garbage filled his lungs.

He walked in and closed the door behind him. Pieces of broken glass crunched under the soles of his boots as he walked through the expanse of the empty floor. The moon was high enough to let its ghostly light seep through and cast long shadows that zigged and zagged as he walked.

"This is weird," he said, cycling between x-ray and infrared.

"What's weird?" Connelly responded, the engine revving to life in the background. "Get out of the building and let me look at it."

"There's nobody here," Hunt said, looking at a few glowing shapes floating in the air in the middle of the empty floor. "But I can still see them."

"Get out of the building right now," Connelly yelled in his ear, and Hunt grimaced as he turned down the volume of the incoming link.

He walked closer to the floating shapes and switched his vision back to the normal view. A few small black devices the size of an old-fashioned flip phone were scattered on the ground, projecting the holograms up into the air.

Hunt cried out in pain as the EMU crumbled him to the floor in a powerful motion. Then, it rolled him toward the window like a rag doll, no longer in control of his limbs, as he watched a few gaping holes appear where his body had been a moment ago.

"Are you all right?" Connelly's voice was tense but calm.

"Be careful." Hunt pressed his body into the wall. "There's a shooter with what seems to be a fifty cal. My EMU recognized the shape of a barrel before I had a chance to process it."

"Are you hurt?"

"Only my pride. Got thrown about like a puppet."

"Location?"

"The building across the street. Second floor. Third window from the right if you're facing the building."

"Roger."

Hunt got on all fours and crawled deeper into the building and away from the window.

"Mike?"

"Yes."

"I think the shooter is a woman. I didn't get much of a look, but it's either a woman or a short man."

"Got it."

His sonar picked up the sound of the limo's engine as the vehicle took a turn before entering the street. It seemed that Connelly was going to approach the building with the shooter from the back.

"Let me know when you're close," he said into the mic. "I'll distract her."

"Negative. Sit tight."

Hunt continued on all fours until he reached the last window facing the street and risked a quick peek outside. His head jerked back, his left cheek scraping the rough wall as the internal computer overrode his muscles. The wall behind him exploded, showering him in a fountain of debris and forcing him lower.

"Damn. He's a machine."

"Stay out of sight and keep the channel open." Connelly's voice was raspy, punctuated by the quick beat of his steps as the man sprinted.

Hunt left the link open and crawled back toward the door, keeping his head below the windowsill.

A few rapid flashes came from the building across the street as the sound of the shots crackled in Hunt's head, simultaneously coming from the open link and through the air. Then a car engine revved in the distance and roared away, the sound getting fainter by the second.

"Mike?"

"The shooter's gone. You're clear to come out. It was definitely a woman, and she was alone."

"Did you see her?"

"Not enough to ID, I'm afraid."

Hunt stood up and walked toward one of the hologram projectors on the floor, and picked it up. The hologram flickered and turned off, the ghostly image disappearing without a trace.

"Never seen these before," he said, stepping outside and handing the device to Connelly. "Have the tech guys look at this."

They walked around the building from where the shooter had been hiding and back to the limo. Connelly opened the door and stepped aside to let Hunt in, but Jason stopped and looked around.

"What?" Connelly said, visibly tensing and scanning the surroundings.

"I don't know." Hunt shrugged. "But I feel like we're being watched."

He dived into the car and let Connelly close the door after him.

"Back to the tower?" Connelly asked, getting behind the wheel.

"Yes." He glanced at the building one more time as the car accelerated away. "It looks like justice won't be served today."

2

"*B*rian!" Mike Connelly yelled from the top of the stairs. "Can you check if the top floor is online? The lights should be solid, but they're all blinking instead."

"Are you sure?" The man leaned over the banister and craned his neck to see Connelly. "I checked them a minute ago."

Connelly looked back at the hallway. A row of red LEDs on motion sensors installed on the wall was pulsating as if transmitting Morse code. "Yep. Still going."

"Weird. One sec." The man's head disappeared and Connelly heard a series of clacking noises. "How about now?"

He looked back again. The lights pulsated quickly and then turned off completely. "Now they are off."

"Crap," the man shouted. "I don't understand. Engineering checked it a million times yesterday. I have to go back to the control room then. I'll radio."

"Sounds good."

Connelly, along with a four-man team, had been at the location for over two hours now. Orion had purchased the small three-story building six months ago and since then, the place was gutted and rebuilt from inside out to become the company's new security head-quarters. Somebody jokingly christened it Langley, and the name stuck.

It was appropriate, Connelly thought as he turned away from the stairwell and started across the hallway. The new location was going to serve as a state-of-the-art intelligence operation. The top floor would be occupied by support and clerical personnel and the first two levels by analysts, some of them alumni of the actual George Bush Center for Intelligence. But the most sensitive work, including black ops, was going to be in the massive, reinforced basement.

"Boss?"

The radio crackled on Connelly's belt and he picked up the black rectangle to his face. "Yes?"

"I'm resetting the system now. Stand by."

The lights on the wall blinked and then lit up with a solid red glow.

"Looks good to me," Connelly said. "How does it look on the system?"

"All good here. The guys are already in the parking lot. Should we pack it up?"

"Sure." Connelly glanced at his wrist, checking the time. "Go on. I'll do a last round and join you in a couple of minutes."

"Roger."

He turned off the radio and continued to walk through the hallway. Each station, including the floors, was sectioned with its own reinforced barrier like a submarine. In case of a fire or an attack, the building could be turned into a series of impenetrable fortresses.

He walked toward the nearest door and hit the button, watching as the steel blades rotated from the slender gap in the wall like the petals of an alien flower. He then pressed the button again and the blades silently disappeared back into the wall. Satisfied, he started back to the stairwell, and that was when the windows lit up with a bright light and the building shook.

There was almost no sound as the multilayered glass panels

absorbed most of the shock, but Connelly didn't need a confirmation. They were under attack.

He fell on his knees and crawled to the window a few feet away from him, and took off his hat. Then he threw it in a tight arc above the lower part of the frame. The seventy-five-millimeter bulletproof glass exploded, showering him with shards and forcing him closer to the ground. A hole the size of a baseball appeared in the wall across the hall.

"Shit," he cursed under his breath. A rapid rattle of automatic fire came from the outside. At least somebody from his team was still alive. He needed to help them.

"Boss," the radio crackled, "stay away from the windows. They've got a sniper with some serious hole puncher."

Connelly scrambled to his knees and pushed himself into a sprint. Another blast shattered the window as he rushed by it, a few shards painfully biting into his right elbow, but he pressed on. A second later, he was in the relative safety of the stairwell, taking three steps at the time.

"I'm coming to get you, Brian," he barked into the radio as he ran. "Stay where you are."

"Okay. The guys were in the car. I'm sorry, I couldn't do anything."

"Shut up and stay low."

Connelly put away the radio as he reached the basement entrance and sprinted through the hallway to the weapons room. He punched in the code, heaved away the armored door, and looked around.

"There you are," he muttered to himself and picked up an XM25 grenade launcher from the soft case and two five-round detachable magazines.

Connelly pressed the alarm button and ran back up the stairs, and then a few seconds later got to the door leading to the parking lot. He heard the muffled sound of gunfire on the other side and Connelly sighed with relief—he wasn't too late.

He unlocked the door and, using it as a shield, glanced outside. A heavy thud reverberated through the reinforced metal, but the door held. It was too strong even for the fifty-caliber rifle.

"Hey boss," Brian said. The man was lying on his back, behind a slab of concrete less than a foot tall that served as a perimeter around the building. He was holding a scarf to his left shoulder, keeping pressure on a wound. The light-gray material of his parka was covered in blood.

"Hang in there," Connelly said. "Have you seen anything?"

"Three dudes in an armored Hummer, about two hundred yards from here on the other side of the main gate." He waved with his good hand and grimaced. "Have no idea where the sniper is."

"It doesn't matter. Help should be on the way; we just need to repel these guys. Two hundred yards, you say."

He loaded the magazine and manually set the distance on the range finder of the grenade launcher to two hundred and ten yards. "Give me some cover," he said.

Brian nodded, stuck the nose of his submachine gun above the concrete block, and let out a short salvo into the sky.

As the shots echoed through the empty parking lot, Connelly stuck the snub nose of the grenade launcher over the ridge of the door, aimed over the black Hummer parked sideways across the road, and pressed the trigger.

A 25mm low-velocity grenade zipped across the front yard in less than a second and detonated mid-air behind the armored Hummer, raining down death on the three men using the car as a shield.

"I think I can hear the bird," Connelly said. "Hang in there. The sniper will not stick around for much longer."

A few minutes later, the MH-65 Dolphin search-and-rescue helicopter with Orion's corporate logo picked them up from the parking lot of the facility and headed for Manhattan. Another ten minutes later, Connelly was walking across the roof of the Orion Tower as two medics carried away his wounded teammate on a stretcher.

He walked through the double doors and took the private stairwell to the observation desk to find Hunt and Schlager huddling over a computer monitor.

"What the hell happened?" Hunt asked, turning the screen off. "Do you know who it was?"

"They didn't introduce themselves." Connelly walked by the two men to the bar, poured himself a glass of cold water, and downed it in one long gulp. "But I can make a pretty good guess. Perez and Freeman were hit in the car. Brian got shot too, but he got lucky. Only a flesh wound."

"This is getting out of control," Schlager said.

"No." Connelly put the glass down on the table, walked across the floor, and sat down in a chair. "It has been out of control for a long time. We need to take care of this once and for all."

"I don't know about this," Hunt said. "We've talked—"

"How the hell is this any different from what we do almost daily? I just pulverized three dudes with an air-burst grenade. Why can't we do the same thing to Engel himself? It'll save people's lives. On both sides, actually."

"It's not that simple."

"Why the hell not?" Connelly leaned forward. "I came to you, Jason, because I thought we could do better than observe and report like I did back at the ISCD."

"Even if we were to go for it—and that's a big if—it's not going to be so easy. For one, he's not just some guy running around in the park at five in the morning, who you can easily approach. He's got better protection than the president. Choppers, snipers, advanced teams every time he has to go somewhere. You know that better than anyone."

"Give me the resources," Connelly said, "and I'll make it happen."

"And then what? Then Victor Ye, or somebody else waiting in the wind, will take over and we'll be back to square one."

"Maybe, or," Connelly pointed a finger at Hunt, "they'll get scared that despite all that security somebody can come in one day and chop their head off. So maybe, just maybe, they would turn down the opportunity to play the game altogether."

"I'll tell you what." Hunt walked closer and looked Connelly in the eye. "If it was anybody else, I wouldn't even listen. And I'm not saying you've got the green light. All I'm saying is this—take two weeks.

Come up with a solid plan and then let's talk. Show me how we can do it without starting a major war, and we can decide then."

"Fine." Connelly stood up and started walking toward the door. "I'll give you the plan. But it's too late to worry about starting the war."

3

*A*lexander Engel woke up as the convoy of six SUVs took the exit off NY-27E and merged onto a local road heading toward Gibson Beach. He'd much rather have taken a helicopter than spend over two hours in the back of a car, but two choppers had been shot over the island in the past few months and his new security chief insisted on taking cars everywhere they went. Besides, his father never agreed to build a helipad next to his property, claiming the noise would drive him crazy.

He rolled down the window as they drove through the gate. The air smelled of sea, and Engel squinted as the wind threw a few snowflakes in his face. The house, a simple two-story brick colonial that looked out of place inside of a zip code filled with ultra-expensive mega mansions, sat on a large lot facing the ocean. It would have fit in more on Shore Road in the Bay Ridge part of Brooklyn or Astoria Boulevard in Queens. A guesthouse closer to the entrance of the gate, and the massive twelve-car garage, were the only obvious indicators of the owner's wealth.

"Hi, Mary. How is he?" Engel asked as he emerged from the belly of the SUV to shake hands with a gray-haired woman with a coat around her shoulders thrown over a nurse's scrubs.

"He's lucid," she replied. "Amazingly so, like in the good old days. But I don't know for how long. He's been in and out for the last two days."

"I see."

"To be frank…" She paused, looking for the right words.

"You don't think he'll last?"

"No." She squeezed his arm. "I think he has only a few hours left. I'm sorry."

He nodded, waved to the bodyguards to stay behind, and walked across the yard toward the front door of the house. The gravel covered in thin ice crunched under the soles of his shoes, making them slide ever so slightly. Forcing him to take smaller steps.

The well-oiled heavy oak door opened without a sound, and Engel stepped into the warm, large foyer. The air was stale and a pine-scented air freshener did a poor job covering the harsh tones of strong chemicals. It didn't smell like the home he remembered. More like a hospital.

"He's upstairs, as usual," the woman said, taking off her coat and stepping aside. "I'll leave you two alone, but call me if you need me. Can I take your coat?"

"Thank you." He waved her off. "I'm good."

He took off his coat and, holding it in his hands, took the stairs to the second floor.

The master bedroom converted into a makeshift hospital room was at the very end of the building, facing the water. The lights were off, but the curtains were open, letting the gray light in. A large monitor next to the bed silently zigzagged, charting the patient's pulse.

"Dad?"

"Hey, kiddo." Simon Engel glanced in his direction as he shifted on the pillows and then returned his gaze to the waves. "I was thinking about the summer I took you fishing for the first time."

"I remember." He dropped the coat on a nurse's bed and pulled a chair next to his father. "We spent the entire day by the shore and only caught a small flounder that broke off the line and got away, but you told everybody that I pulled a two- foot-long bass and let it go."

"Yes, I did." Simon snorted with laughter that instantly progressed into a bout of severe coughing.

"Should I call the nurse?"

"God damn it," Simon said, catching his breath and wiping his mouth with a towel. "I cannot stand being weak."

"I could never understand why you did it."

"What?"

"Lied about me catching the fish."

"I don't know." The man relaxed on the pillows and turned to face him. "It's stupid, but I didn't want you to feel disappointed."

"Didn't want me to feel disappointed? Or didn't want to be embarrassed, when you had to tell others we didn't get any fish that day?"

Simon smiled and turned away, back to the sea. "I taught you well."

"I'm sorry."

"That's okay, kiddo." Simon stretched his hand and took Engel's in his. "There's not much time left for us to be upset with each other. We are who we are. The advantage of dying is that you don't have to pretend anymore. It's refreshing. I know I haven't always been the greatest father in the world."

"I wasn't the easiest son."

"Trust me, I know." Simon glanced at him and looked away again. "I know about the drugs you used to push me off the board."

Engel recoiled in shock as if his father had slapped him, but Simon held on to his hand.

"The irony is," the old man continued, "the drugs you had that weasel give me might have extended my life by a few years, so I don't hold any grudges."

"I'm sorry."

"Eh. Water under the bridge. But that's not what I wanted to discuss with you in my final hours. I know you and I had different visions of what's coming. I always thought your methods were too severe."

"You made it clear a few times."

"But now," Simon continued, "I've realized they were not radical enough."

"Oh?"

"The world as we know it is ending, kiddo. You've been preaching it for years, ad nauseam. On and on you went. About the new war. About the new order. But now it seems to me you didn't listen to your own lectures."

"How so?"

"You used to say that growth became decadence and how decadence gave way to rot."

"That's true. The world's rotting."

"No. It's rotted all out already, kiddo." Simon fixed his eyes on Engel's face. He propped himself on one elbow and spoke with fire Engel hadn't seen in a long time. "It's done. There's nothing left. There's no time left for half measures. Stomp out enemies with an iron fist, raze cities if you have to."

"You're being dramatic, Dad." He let go of his father's hand. "The war is almost here, but as much as I like a good fight, I don't think the situation warrants razing cities to the ground."

"But that's where you're wrong, my boy. At some point you have to stop maneuvering your tanks into positions and start firing. That's how it works. If you don't drown your enemies in blood, they'll do that to you and soon."

"I don't know." Engel looked through the window. The wind had picked up and the waves crashing ashore were growing in size. "I've thought about it, of course, but I'm not sure I'm ready to take it that far. I don't know if I want to be—"

"What?"

"A tyrant."

"You don't want to be a tyrant? Alexander the Great, Catherine, Peter the Great—do you think they were kind, gentle-hearted people? No. They were despots who bent the wills of millions because they saw a bigger picture. But now we call them great, not because they were nice, but because they had the foresight and were willing to do what was necessary. If you want to get things done, you need to get your hands dirty."

"Stalin was a despot, and nobody calls him—"

"Stalin was an asshole."

They laughed together, but Simon's laughter turned into a cackle fast and he stopped, trying to prevent another bout of coughing.

"You know I've lost the election, right?"

"Of course I do." The old man rolled his eyes. "I watch the news. But you can still fix this. It's not too late."

The wind howled outside and battered the windows before dying out again.

"A lot of people look at me as if I'm some kind of villain," Engel said. "But all I'm trying to do is to preserve what we've got. Maintain the order. I'm not doing this for charity, but when the dust settles, people will see that all this was necessary, right? Someone's got to do it."

"Sometimes," Simon's hand found Alexander's again and squeezed it in a powerful grip, "sometimes to be a hero, first you need to become a villain."

They sat in silence for a few moments, and then Engel let go of his father's hand and stood up.

"Good-bye, kiddo," Simon said. "Give them hell."

"I will." He leaned in and planted a soft kiss on the old man's forehead. Then he picked up his coat and walked out of the room without looking back.

"Leaving already?" the nurse called out to him as he walked down the stairs and headed for the door.

"Yes." He paused and gave her a wave. "He doesn't like long farewells."

"Neither do you." She smiled softly. "Like father, like son."

"Mary?"

"Yes."

"I want you to know your job with us is safe, after..." he hesitated, "after he passes."

"You didn't have to say that."

He nodded and pulled on the door, letting the cold air wash over him. The snow was falling harder now with large, heavy snowflakes settling down on the front yard. Engel closed the door behind him and stood on the porch for a few seconds, watching the snow fall. The wipers on one of the SUVs moved back and forth, startling him out of the trance. He pulled his collar up and went down the steps and toward his car.

His father was right, of course. The time of half measures was over. The war wasn't coming anymore. It was already here.

4

The elevator stopped, and Helen Chen stepped out into a small locker room. She removed all her clothes, leaving only her underwear on, put on anti-static shoes, and went through the air lock into the decontamination unit. The door hissed as it closed behind her, and Chen continued to the middle of the room. There she stood on a large white *X* painted on the floor. She planted her feet two feet apart, stretched her arms out, and held her breath. A second later, a red warning light came on and a jet of powerful air swatted at her from all directions.

After it stopped, she proceeded through the second air lock into the clean room. There she donned a white bio suit and a large fishbowl helmet that clicked into her neck connector.

Once she was ready, she went through yet another air lock and entered a large, brightly lit room. Two figures wearing similar bio suits were already inside. One was working on a computer terminal in the corner. Another was checking the readings off the variety of displays on a side of a long white table in the middle of the room. Inside the transparent protective casing that covered the entire table like a dome was a nude female body resting on a smooth white surface.

"Hey, Helen." One of the bio suits by the table turned as she came closer. Steven Poznyak waved at her. "You're right on time. Max is practically done."

"Hey, boys." She waved back. "How's it looking?"

"Well," Poznyak stepped aside, inviting her to look at the monitors, "truth be told, we don't know. Until we start the process, there's no proper way of telling if the organs have been damaged during the vitrification process beyond our ability to repair them. We had some tricks up our sleeves when we performed the cryopreservation, and electron micrographs look good. At least so far."

"But?"

"But there could be damage that we cannot see and depending where it is, that might be the difference between a successful revival and, well, permanent death. I've seen some unsuccessful trials on mice and boy, they did not look pretty. But that's where you guys come in. Do you think you can handle it?"

"There are a lot of unknowns," Schlager chimed in as he joined them at the table. "Nobody's ever tried to control that many nanobots that will perform various tasks at the same time. Hence my suggestion."

Chen glanced at the body and suppressed a shiver. No matter how many times she'd been inside of the lab, the frozen body that may or may not come to life again gave her the creeps.

"I don't know if Jason will look kindly on this idea," Poznyak said quietly, almost as if to himself.

"What idea?" Chen looked back and forth at the two men.

"It makes sense," Poznyak said. "At least, on paper."

"Spit it out."

"Max wants to test it on a small part of the body."

"Like what?"

"A toe."

"Okay." She looked at the sarcophagus. "That sounds like a reasonable idea. Why do you think Jason won't be happy about it?"

"Because we can't try it on a toe, while it's still attached to the rest of the body," Poznyak said.

"Oh."

"Yes. We could probably use a high-powered laser to ensure as clean of a cut as possible without damaging neighboring tissues. But depending on how the trial goes, we might not be able to reattach it back to the body. In fact, even if it goes well, we might not be able to reattach it later."

"Can we try it on something less? Like take a small slice off the tip? Just some skin?"

"We could do that. But that might not produce enough meaningful data. Skin, despite the multiple layers and overall complexity, is relatively uniform for our purposes. Things get complicated when you start throwing other things into the mix—bone, marrow, tendons, muscle tissue, and so on. And it gets even more complicated, of course, when you start working on the internal organs. And then there's the brain."

"But maybe she's right," Schlager chimed in. "Why don't we try it first on a small scale to see if it works in principle? Chopping off Jason's wife's toe seems like a move I'd like to postpone as much as possible."

"Yes." Poznyak chuckled. "I see your point. Once we get to the real thing, though, the toe is going to be the least of our problems."

"Can we try the process on someone else?" Chen asked. "I know we have a few animal test subjects."

"In theory, yes. And we already have, but that data is of limited use. When Jason showed up on my doorstep with this problem, I had to improvise. I'm afraid there's no proper way to recreate the conditions of Rachel's procedure precisely enough."

"I'll tell you what," Chen said, looking at the body. "Don't do anything yet. Give me a couple of days. I want to try something. Can you send me the micrographs?"

"Sure. What do you have in mind?"

"I don't know yet." She gave him a tight smile. "Just a hunch."

She checked the mainframe with Schlager and then retraced her steps to the elevator. The corporate car picked her up from the parking lot and headed for Orion Tower in Manhattan. Since the completion of the skyscraper, all essential personnel—Chen included—were given living quarters within the tower. Considering that the cold war with Engel and company was turning hot so often these days, Jason Hunt insisted that this was the best way to provide for everybody's security.

Chen didn't object. The apartment in Astoria that she had been calling home for a few years was too dangerous to go back to. But danger wasn't the only thing that kept her away from the place. More than anything else, it was the memories of people who were no longer in Chen's life. While she couldn't bring her friends back from the dead, at least she could stay away from the place that conjured up their images too often.

Ten minutes later, the armored SUV roared across the Manhattan Bridge and turned onto Chrystie Street. They blew through a red light and another five minutes later, they entered the underground garage of Orion Tower. Chen thanked the driver and took the elevator to the twenty-seventh floor, where she had a modestly sized two-bedroom apartment. She was spending most of her time in Schlager's sprawling suite after they had moved in together, but insisted on keeping this apartment for herself. A place to work in peace when she needed to stay up into the wee hours of the night without bothering anyone's sleep.

She took off her coat and went straight into her office. There she sat down at her computer terminal and pressed a thumb into a sensor mounted on top of the desk.

There was a whirring sound as a section of her wall opened and a set of fine metallic mesh partitions rolled out. They covered the room on her sides first, and then another section rolled out on top of them, covered the ceiling, and then continued rolling behind her until it locked into the section hidden under the floor. Now, she was sitting inside of a large metallic cube, a perfect Faraday cage designed to block every type of electromagnetic waves going in or out of the room.

A green light came on her desk, notifying her that the cage was fully connected. For the moment, in the informational sense, Helen Chen was the loneliest person on Earth.

She opened a desk drawer, pulled away the panel on the bottom of it, and exposed a simple switch. She looked at it for a few seconds and then flipped it on. The black surface of the ultra-long monitor blinked and then came to life, displaying a swirling mist of gray that looked like boiling clouds.

"Hello, Helen. It's nice to see you. I was looking forward to engaging in a stimulating conversation for some time."

The voice coming from the surround speakers was androgynous, but had a lively cadence of a real person. If she heard it over the phone, Chen thought, she wouldn't be able to tell that it didn't belong to a human.

"Hello, JC," she said, shifting in her chair. "I have a topic I'd like to discuss with you. I think you'll like this one."

5

Chuck Kowalsky took the stool at the end of the skinny bar across the dance stage and nodded to the bartender.

"What can I getcha?" the woman shouted over the thumping of hip-hop. She wore an apron over a G-string and a tight black shirt with a breast pocket. The shirt featured a deep cut that went all the way to the woman's navel and teased a view of her breasts each time she moved. Above the pocket stuffed with papers and a few dollar bills, there was a round scarlet-red pin with bold yellow letters: *AIN'T YOUR WHORE.*

"Jack and Coke, please," he shouted back and slapped a banknote on a sticky surface. "I like your pin. Keep the change."

"Thanks, hon," the woman said. She produced a tall, faceted glass filled with ice, splashed a generous portion of whiskey into it, and topped it off with Coke from a bar gun.

Kowalsky sipped on the fizzy sweet drink and looked around. The Gargoyle was as ugly as the name suggested. It was one long rectangular room covered in a soft rug of undeterminable color. The ceiling was a patchwork of mirrors, which was propped up by a row of tacky white columns illuminated by hidden blue neon lights. Chuck guessed the mirrors had been installed to make the room feel like a larger place. Instead, when he glanced at it, the dancing lights crisscrossing the silver surface made him nauseous.

There were two clusters of small tables at either side of the room and a narrow bar farther in the back. A small dancing stage that looked like an oversized pool table and featured two stripping poles dominated the center of the club. At the moment, a single woman halfheartedly danced upon the green felt, gyrating with the rhythm of the music. She was naked, except for a pair of sheer pink cheeky panties that she stuck in the faces of overeager patrons surrounding the table. A steady stream of banknotes kept migrating from their sweaty paws to the side strip of her lingerie. Every time the wad had reached a certain size, she emptied it into a purse tucked at the base of one of the poles with a practiced move.

Located in the heart of East Village, the club used to be an unremarkable Irish dive bar for a few decades with a much less ambitious name: SEAN'S PUB. But in the early 2000s, an ex-pat—from Kyushu, with an alleged Yakuza connection—named Eito Genda bought the establishment and changed its name to the Gargoyle. Perhaps feeling entrepreneurial, Genda obtained an adult entertainment license and tried to turn it into a strip club. He enjoyed some early success and at some point, even converted a part of the lower-level basement into a set of VIP rooms, catering legally borderline services to the rich and powerful.

But the Gargoyle's fame disappeared as quickly as it came. Before long, the long-legged models stalking the room turned into middle-aged moms trying to make ends meet. The suits and ties of the clientele gradually changed into flannel shirts and rough jeans. And as the club fell on hard times, Eito Genda found himself reaching out to people he said he'd never do business with again.

It was a fascinating tale, and Kowalsky had known nothing about it until about a week before he walked into the club and ordered the glass of Jack and Coke. First time he had heard a rumor about Victor Ye appropriating the now-defunct factories of some foreign corporation, it came from a less than reliable source: an old informant with a nasty snorting habit. And yet, the sparse details sounded believable enough for Chuck to take interest. In the age of corporate wars, it wasn't unheard of for a company to have secret locations. But in the world of satellite imagery, it was practically impossible to hide a large-scale construction project, let alone a fully-fledged factory.

But the source had insisted that was the case, and the factory was being repurposed for some bleeding-edge weapon technology. What was worse, he said that construction was done in a few stages by specialized slave labor. The secrecy was so great, he claimed, that after each stage had been completed, the managers of the project disposed of the workers and brought in new ones. But something, he said, had gone wrong at the last turnover and a worker managed to escape. Then, he came to New York inside a shipping container and disappeared.

No, the source didn't know who the actual worker was. But he knew someone who they traveled across the ocean with. It was a woman named Takara Sanuki, and for the time being she was employed as a dancer at the Gargoyle under the name of Raven.

"What's your name?" He heard someone say and then a woman leaned on him, an overpowering smell of too much perfume almost making him gag. She had bleached blonde hair and wore a sheer red camisole and a matching thong. While she had done her best to hide it with toner, Chuck could clearly see a scar on her stomach from a c-section. The woman leaned even closer, rubbing her hard, fake breasts into his shoulder. "My name's Mia. Wanna dance? I'm really good."

"I'm John," he said, giving her a fake name. "Maybe next time. My friend came here the other day, and he danced with Raven, and he said he liked it. I wanted to try it too. If you introduce us, you can dance for me too."

"He liked the new girl?" The woman looked puzzled. She gave his knee a squeeze and then moved her hand up his thigh. "She's a cold fish. I doubt she'll last here another week. Your friend has weird taste. I'll show you a much better time than that corpse."

"Please." Chuck held out a banknote and watched it disappear. "I trust my friend's taste. Introduce me and then you can dance for me too, I promise."

"Fine." The woman stood up straight, a frown creasing her face. "I'll bring her here. Sit tight."

She disappeared into the crowd, her posture erect and confident again as she pushed through the throngs of inebriated men. A minute later, she reappeared with a young woman in tow. She was slim and on the short side, her hair the color of spilled ink. Like all the girls in the club, she wore a skimpy outfit—a pair of leather shorts that didn't quite cover her buttocks and a push-up leather bra that propped up her modestly sized chest. But looking at her, Kowalsky had a distinct feeling that the woman's clothing choices were dictated by how much she could cover herself without losing the job she was hired to do.

"Here she is," Mia said, bringing the girl closer, and then stuck her hand out. "I'll be waiting."

Kowalsky put another banknote into the stripper's hand and smiled to the girl. "Hi. Raven, right? I'm John. Do you dance?"

"It's a strip club, isn't it?" The woman's English was almost perfect, if not for the way she made her t's sound like the d's. "Come on now."

She grabbed his hand and he let her pull him off the stool. They made their way to one of the small round tables alongside the wall, and she pushed him down on the chair, waited for the new song to kick in, and started to dance.

Mia was right—Raven wasn't a good dancer. She looked over Chuck's head without making eye contact and didn't engage him in a conversation. She moved awkwardly, swinging from side to side like a robot who had been programmed to do a job and had no choice but to complete it.

"Listen," Kowalsky leaned in to her so her body would obscure his face from anyone who might try to read his lips, "I don't care for your dance. A friend of mine told me about a scary place somewhere on the other side of the ocean. He says that people there are forced to build a factory and then are killed off when they finish the job they had been hired to do."

She said nothing, but her body stiffened, making her moves resemble that of a puppet—one jerky motion following another.

"He said," he continued, "you know someone who escaped that place."

"I know nothing of such things," Raven said and stood up straight. "I don't want to dance for you anymore."

Kowalsky grabbed her hand as she turned around to walk away and pulled her close. "You can help a lot of other people if you tell me how to find your friend. They don't deserve to die."

She pulled her hand free and stepped back and away from him.

"Yo, there's no touching in this club." A big, muscular man with a shaved head made his way to Chuck's table. He was wearing a tight T-shirt showing off his physique with a logo of the club on it, and by the way he moved the objects and people out of his way, he looked like he meant business. "Get the fuck outta here before I break something."

"There's no need to overreact." Kowalsky said, standing up, and since the man showed no signs of slowing down, he pulled the jacket aside far enough to show off the butt of a Chiappa Rhino revolver. "I'll leave."

The big man slowed down but didn't stop, and Chuck put his hand on the revolver. That seemed to have an effect.

"Get out," the man repeated, this time without much force. "Or else that won't help you."

"Fine." Kowalsky reached into his pocket, making the man tense, and then produced a card. He gave it to the girl and after a brief hesitation, she took it. He moved toward the door, keeping a few chairs between himself and the big man, but then stopped, giving the woman one last glance. "You could make a huge difference."

6

The car went through the gate and proceeded deeper into the parking lot outside of the Ronald Reagan Washington National Airport. The driver checked the markings showing the parking zone and pulled up next to a black SUV with tinted windows. A second later, a passenger door cracked opened an inch.

"Would you like me to check, Mr. Hunt?" the driver asked.

"No, I know it's him." Jason Hunt stepped out of the vehicle and dived inside the black SUV to find himself staring at a familiar face.

"It's good to see you, Jim," Hunt said, shaking the man's hand.

"It's good to see you as well, Jason," Rovinsky said, settling back into his seat. "I wish it were under happier circumstances. Everything okay? It's not like you to be late for a meeting."

"Apologies," Hunt said. "Protests. We had to make a large loop to find the way around the barricades."

"Unfortunately, it's a common sight these days," Rovinsky said. "Tension has been spilling into the streets as of late. The entire country is a giant powder keg."

"Yeah."

"You know, I didn't realize this until we got here, but when we were pulling into the parking spot, that's when it hit me."

"What?"

"This is the place where I met your father, trying to convince him to start the Unit. Maybe not the exact spot, but we were in this very parking lot, when I asked him to look at some documents. He furiously refused first and then, well, you know the rest. Sometimes I wish I hadn't done it. Some people say that ignorance is bliss."

"Not to me," Hunt said, studying the other man. "It's too late to go back. Whatever happens, we need to see it through. What's happening with you? You must've been relieved to hear the election results."

"More than I can express. I know little about Price outside of his public persona, but he seems to be a straight-shooting kind of fellow."

"I hear he might actually leave some people in place from this administration when he takes over in January?"

"That's what I hear too," Rovinsky said. "There are no guarantees in my line of work, of course, but it seems there's a good chance I'll stay in the DOD. At least for now. But I don't know if I should. That's why I wanted to meet with you, Jason."

"You're ready to retire? Can't say I blame you."

"I wish," Rovinsky said, chuckling. "Quite the opposite. After the inauguration, I'd like to come and work for you directly, Jason. I think I'll be of limited use here. Engel may have lost the election, and Price seems honorable, but the system is broken beyond repair. I don't have to tell you that the wheels are turning faster and faster. Sooner rather than later, Engel is going to make another move. We can't play defense forever. At some point, you gotta hit back. We've just been handed an extra four years to make the push, and I say we make them count. Who knows, by the time the next election cycle comes around, maybe we will have cleaned up enough to step away. Let the authorities finish the rest."

Hunt studied the man's face for a few seconds. "That's what everybody keeps on telling me. Connelly told me the same thing the other day. He's been pushing to hit Engel directly. Eliminate him."

"Maybe he's right."

"Engel lost the election," Hunt protested. "Sometimes I feel like we've developed tunnel vision over the past few years. The voters actually turned him down. Yes, by the thinnest of margins, but that's how democracy works. Isn't it a sign that the system is still functioning?"

"Is it a serious question?"

"Yes. Because I don't want to become another Alexander Engel. Some corporate asshole, who's fighting for power for the sake of power."

"Oh, my friend, you couldn't be more wrong if you think Engel is seeking power for the sake of power. Engel, and this might shock you, is actually a man of ideals. He thinks he's doing the world a favor. He sees himself as the Augustus of this time, conquering the barbarians and bringing them the light and sophistication of Rome. Hell, he thinks he's literally saving the world."

"*I found Rome of clay; I leave it to you of marble.*"

"Exactly."

"You were supposed to tell me I wasn't an asshole." Hunt laughed. "Instead, you're telling me that Engel sees himself as the world's savior."

"If you need other people to say you're not an asshole, you're in big trouble."

"Fair point."

The two men sat in silence for a few seconds.

"ISCD is scrambling, by the way," Rovinsky added, changing topics. "They've pulled about half of their assets from the field already and are getting ready to pull more. They have no money. It's getting ridiculous. Even without getting into the White House, Engel's got enough sway now to choke them, and that'll happen soon. I don't think much will change once Price takes office. It looks like he has good intentions, but all the key players have already been bought. That's why I don't see how I'm more useful staying on the inside."

"Engel will be stopped. Maybe it doesn't have to be us."

"Yeah," Rovinsky shrugged, "I'm sure there were some guys in Germany before September of '39 who said that Hitler would be stopped. We know how well it turned out."

"He got stopped."

"He did. And by the time it was over, half of the world laid in ruins and seventy million souls had perished."

"You know what bothers me the most?"

"What?"

"This." Hunt stretched his bionic arm, opened his hand, and moved his fingers. The light reflected off the gray metallic surface.

"Something wrong with it?"

"To the contrary." Hunt closed his fingers into a fist and then opened his hand again. "It's perfect. As a matter of fact, it's better than perfect. My sensory input from this arm is more nuanced than from my biological limb. The difference is—I could stick this arm into a pot full of melted iron, and the only unpleasant thing I'll experience will be the alarm that will go off in my internal vision."

"Why does it bother you then?"

"Because this is what I should be doing. Not chasing Engel. Not running around the Bronx looking for Victor Ye's goons. I made a promise when we went public that this tech was going to solve the problem no one could overcome since the dawn of time. We could change the world for the better. Instead, it feels like all I do is making it worse."

"Look, kid." Rovinsky stretched his hand out and squeezed Hunt's shoulder. "I get it. I do. I wish you could spend your time on nothing but improving your tech, but the reality is—unless we defeat the cabal, none of this will matter. Because in the world Engel is trying to build, there'll be no place for your idealism. Tech like yours will belong to a small select group who will become more powerful than gods, while the rest of the world will have to compete for scraps. Your father understood this. That's what he gave his life for. I know you understand it, too."

Hunt sat there for a few seconds, his fingers drumming a steady rhythm on the leather seat of the car.

"You're right," he finally said. "But I want you to stay where you are. At least for now. And if we are to escalate, I need a favor."

"Shoot."

"That cash that the Unit recovered. I'd like to have access to it. I will not touch it unless I'm completely out of options, but I need some kind of reserve in case we are in big trouble."

"You got it. Connelly should know how to access it, but I'll send the instructions just in case."

"Thank you. I owe you—"

"You don't owe me jack shit, kid. That's just a pile of paper that your father and I took from some really bad people. It's not like I had other ways to use it, anyway."

"All right, then." Jason put a hand on the man's shoulder, making a decision. "Stay where you're at for now. Keep me in the loop as much as you can without putting yourself at risk. And keep an eye on what's happening with the DOD's contracts. I'm not concerned they would pull them on merits, but who knows what levers Engel can pull."

"I understand."

"Something else I'd like to ask you, Jim."

"Yeah?"

"You've been doing this for much longer than I have, and sometimes I need a reality check. I need someone to tell me that there's actually a chance for us to succeed at this crazy venture. Tell me, Jim. Can we do that? Can we succeed?"

Rovinsky stayed quiet for a few moments, his eyes scanning Hunt's face.

"We can," he finally said. "But I think it'll take more than you're currently prepared to do to make it a reality. I think you'll have to reevaluate your entire system of beliefs about how far you're willing to go. Of what's required."

"And what do you think *is* required?"

Rovinsky took a deep breath and looked down at his hands as if looking for an answer. When he looked up again, there was an expression in the older man's eyes Hunt had never seen.

"A war," Rovinsky said. "Civil war."

7

As the black SUV pulled up in front of the hotel, a group of four men wearing identical business suits spilled from its belly and crossed the short distance between the vehicle and the lobby. There they swept the area covering all entrances and stood guard, holding short-nosed submachine guns pointing down to the floor.

A few seconds later, another SUV drove up behind the first and climbed all the way onto the curb. Another three men came out from the back of the car and then flanked a fourth man as he emerged from the car as well. He wore a pair of distressed jeans and a leather jacket and had an appearance of a rock star, with a full beard and wild, long hair under a cowboy hat. A pair of oversized sunglasses completed the ensemble.

The team ushered the man through the lobby at a speed that almost required them to carry him and then disappeared into the elevator. A second later, the doors chimed and the party disappeared from the view of any potential onlookers.

Less than a minute later, Alexander Engel stepped inside of a private suite and impatiently ripped off the fake beard and removed the wig.

"It's quite a costume," Victor Ye said, getting up from a deep chair by the window and extending a hand for a handshake.

"You've got some balls, Victor," Engel replied, ignoring the outstretched hand. He marched past the man and sat down on a couch, crossing his legs. "Whatever your proposition is, it better be worth this nonsense."

"Fair enough." Victor Ye sat back down and turned toward the window, watching the Potomac. "God, I love this town. So much power and history concentrated in a few square miles. Nothing comes close."

"Please save the history lesson. I'm a busy man, Victor," Engel interrupted him. "But I am here to listen to your proposal. I'd appreciate if you respected my time."

"I come bearing gifts," the man said, and reached inside of his jacket pocket.

The three security team members moved forward in unison in response to the gesture, but Engel stopped them with a wave of his hand. "Wait outside."

After the suits left the room, Victor Ye got up and walked over to the couch, handing the piece of paper to Engel.

"Project Thor," Engel read out loud. "What's that? It's just a name here."

"Your presidential aspirations haven't gone unnoticed, Alex."

"I've lost the election."

"So I've heard. But a little birdie told me that this might not be the end of the fight."

"How come?"

"Don't play coy with me, Alex. I didn't come here to spar. Like I said," he pointed to the piece of paper, "I come bearing gifts."

"All right. I'll bite."

The man sat on the opposite side of the couch and ran his hand through his mane of jet-black hair. "What do you know about kinetic bombardment?"

"It sounds vaguely familiar," Engel said, watching Victor's face with caution, as if trying to decide if the man was playing him. "A type of weapon, I'm assuming. Wait, wasn't there some type of bomb during the Vietnam War? The lazy dog bomb?"

"Very good. That was, at least as far as I know, the first use of the weapon. A proof of concept, if you will. They were inch-long steel projectiles that were dumped from an aircraft on the enemy positions. Steel rain."

"Why would I be interested in something like that?"

"The lazy dog bombs?" Victor laughed. "I imagine that wouldn't be of much interest to you. That was just scratching the surface. But I think you might find the idea of Project Thor fascinating. There was a researcher who used to work for Boeing after World War II who came up with it. The concept was simple—there would be a satellite in orbit that had a magazine of tungsten rods with fins."

"I don't understand the application," Engel said. "It's like shooting bullets from space? Wouldn't they burn in the atmosphere? I thought dumping old satellites is a fairly standard procedure?"

"No." Victor smiled. "Not bullets. We are talking about telegraph-pole-sized projectiles made of a material that is four times stronger than titanium."

"You're saying they wouldn't burn during the flight."

"They are twenty-foot-long, one-foot-diameter rods that would hit the ground at speeds of Mach 10. They would most definitely not burn."

"Oh, I see." Engel got up and started pacing the suite. "The kinetic energy would be enormous."

"Yes. According to the calculations that I've seen, one rod impact would have the energy of somewhere between ten and fifteen tons of TNT, about the same yield as a tactical nuke. What's more, you could hit a target anywhere in the world in less than fifteen minutes. Half the time you'd need for an ICBM. And with current guidance technology, it'll be precise enough to hit a moving car."

"All right." Engel stopped pacing and looked at the other man. "It's an interesting idea for a weapon, I'll give you that, but I still fail to see what your proposition is. You want me to build it? Or, rather, hire you to build it?"

"No." Victor smiled and opened his arms wide. "I'm telling you it has been built already."

"It has?"

"Yes. The project itself has been mothballed, but there are currently three satellites up there carrying three telephone-pole-sized tungsten rods each."

"Fully operational?"

"No, but they could be. As of right now, they are just three inert chunks of metal stuffed with microchips cruising around the world, but we could jump-start their systems within days. Satellites are completely autonomous. All we'll need to do is to reactivate control systems here on Earth."

"Can someone defend against them?"

"Not really." Victor shrugged. "Their launch signatures are almost nonexistent and occur in orbit. Unless you know where to look and what to look for, no one will ever know. They are also extremely fast, so there's no real way to intercept them. The only weak spot they have is that during atmospheric reentry, their sensors would be blind because of the plasma sheath in front of them. I might have exaggerated about hitting a mobile target. But it's hard to find a better weapon against anything stationary, whether it's a building or a bunker."

"Why are there only three rods?"

"Tungsten's dense. That makes the rods heavy," Victor said. "Each pole weighs almost ten tons. It was the primary reason the program didn't get far. They were too difficult and expensive to get to space. They had to bring one rod at a time."

"Why come to me?" Engel stuffed his hands into his pockets and looked the man up and down. "Why now? For years, you resisted that anyone in our group even knew your real identity. Now you come to me in the open and bring what seems like a good bribe."

Victor stayed quiet for a few seconds as he contemplated the question.

"A good leader needs to recognize when there's the time to step aside. I know we haven't always seen eye to eye, and I tried to keep you, and a lot of others, in the dark. But I think, as we are trying to come out of the shadow, your public profile, especially if you secure the position of the president of the United States, gives you some unique advantages that I cannot match. A power struggle at this precarious moment wouldn't help us. It's better to be the second-in-command of the victorious army than the emperor of a fallen empire."

"There's no guarantee I'll become the president. Or that we will be victorious."

"Are there ever?" Victor shrugged. "As Hyman Roth said in *The Godfather*: this is the business we've chosen."

"And what would you want in return?"

"Nothing that you wouldn't want to give, anyway. You can help me bring some hardware and assets from Hong Kong, and you'll get all the missing pieces you need to build that cyborg army. I also will give you some new prototype sentries. They are not as good as cyborgs—nothing really is—but they are cheap and they are completely autonomous."

"You can do all that?"

"Yes. I will also need to bring some talent to help you reactivate Project Thor, but I don't need any help with that part. I can smuggle them myself. All I ask in return for my fealty is the seat at your table as your first lieutenant." Victor stood up to face Engel. "There's something else."

"Oh?"

"I know you've been trying, and failing, to recreate what is now Jason Hunt's pet."

"What do you mean?"

"Oh, don't be coy." Victor cocked his head and smiled. "You know exactly what I mean. The cyborg. The *only* real cyborg that you couldn't duplicate, no matter how much you've tried. No amount of your snooping into GA's tech, and even locating the welder who came up with the original alloy—bravo, by the way—gave you the result you saw in Jason Hunt's toy soldier."

"That is true."

"Well," Victor's smile grew wider, "I'll give you a hint. The alloy isn't the key. The software is. Unfortunately, the man who created the original piece is no longer with us, and we could not recreate his work. Until now. My team might have the missing ingredient. Add it to your stew, and voila, you'll have the perfect dish."

"You'll help me build them as good as Hunt's borg?"

"No. I'll help you build them even better than that. Much better. They take awhile to assemble, but I'll have the first prototype soon. I called him Daimyo. And in a nice sunny place, hidden away from curious eyes, I'm building a factory that would produce so many of them, nobody will challenge us ever again." Victor stretched out a hand. "Do we have a deal?"

Engel looked at the man for a few seconds, saying nothing, and then took Victor's hand into his. "Welcome to Guardian Manufacturing."

8

Helen Chen suppressed a shiver as she watched robotic hands hover above Rachel Hunt's foot. Their slender, metallic wrists were fed through the flexible sleeves to allow them access into the transparent plastic casing without compromising its integrity. One eight-fingered hand held a small glistening device shaped like an upside-down U, which was now positioned above Rachel's right big toe. Another had a two-inch-long rectangular box with an open lid pressed into the ball of her foot.

"Want to push the button?" Max Schlager asked as he looked up from the monitor.

"No, thank you very much," she said. "When Jason asks who chopped off his wife's toe, I don't want to be the one raising my hand."

"We aren't chopping off the whole toe." She heard Schlager chuckle. "Just a bit off the top."

"You find it way too amusing," she said. "And why isn't Steven here?"

"I can see it fine from your video feeds," Poznyak's voice said in Chen's helmet. "No need for me to freeze my behind there with you two. Not for the trial run, anyway."

"Let's go, Max."

Schlager hit Enter.

The U-shaped instrument flashed a bright light, and a clean slice of skin the size of a penny slid off the toe into the plastic box.

"Is it supposed to look like that?" Chen asked, looking at the small cut. Instead of the bright pink she was expecting to see, the flesh looked gray.

"Yes," Poznyak's voice said in her speakers. "Gray is fine, actually. If it took on a shade of brown, we would have a reason to worry. There's no reason to be concerned about this color. Let's see if we can create a minor miracle."

Chen watched as the shiny fingers controlled by Schlager closed the small container and pulled it out of the plastic sarcophagus. Then the arm swung around and deposited it into a rectangular hole in a workbench next to it.

"Now the fun part," Chen heard Schlager whisper. She watched him type a series of commands. "Here comes my droid army."

It was an apt metaphor, Chen thought. A swarm of bots, each one less than a micron in diameter, descended on the slice of the frozen tissue. Molecular rotary joints, designed to have minimal energy dissipation, guided tiny mechanical creatures as they burrowed their way into the tissue.

"This is less of an army," Poznyak's voice reverberated in Chen's helmet, "and more of a special operations team. Sneaking in at night, trying to produce no heat signatures from their onboard computers, quietly scanning things as they go."

"Signal's good," she said, watching a three-dimensional outline of the skin's slice materialize on the large screen. As the bots started moving through capillaries, scanning the tissue as they went, the empty, transparent shape started to fill in with what looked like tiny dots of color. As minutes passed, the dots grew larger, joining each other until the colors filled the entire slice.

"So far, so good," Poznyak's voice said. "I don't see any areas that sustained serious damage. Some micro fractures, but the bots should easily repair those."

"That's great."

"I wouldn't get too optimistic just yet," Poznyak said. "We are dealing with a small area and, more importantly, the area right from the surface of the body. There's a much greater chance that the cryoprotectant didn't properly penetrate some of the inner parts of the body."

"But I thought the full-body molecular scans showed nothing like that?" she said.

"They did not, but it only means there are no *obviously* damaged areas. The real data is going to come from the bots. Then we'll know for sure. But as confident as I am in the technology, I'd be shocked if there were no damaged regions at all. That's just not possible. A part of this is a gamble. But as long as they are small enough and not in the vital parts of the body, we should be able to warm and repair them when they are in a liquid state without too much trouble. You can initiate the next stage now."

"Yes, boss," she said, typing a command. The colors on the three-dimensional picture of the cut started to change. "It's working."

"Um, a problem," Schlager said, pointing at the graph at the edge of his screen. "We are operating at ninety-two percent capacity."

"What's operating at ninety-two percent capacity?" Poznyak said.

"The servers. We are having a hard time processing so much information in real time."

"I don't understand. We didn't have any issues in test runs."

"We didn't, but we only did those in a simulated environment. Here, each bot encounters a multitude of problems we couldn't possibly anticipate in a sim. And with that number of bots, the amount of computing power needed goes up exponentially."

"Are you saying—?

"We can't do a full-body restore," Chen said. "Our hardware won't be able to keep up. We are almost maxed out on a tiny piece of tissue. There's no way we can pull off the actual revival."

"Can't we upgrade our computers? Don't we have, I don't know, some spare parts?"

Chen and Schlager shared a chuckle.

"Not quite," Chen said. "These computers are already state-of-the art. Upgrading them won't be easy."

"The upgrade itself isn't even the main issue," Schlager added. "Part of the problem is that we don't even know how much capacity we will need."

They watched in silence as the bots finished working on the tissue. Finally, the computer chimed and a green icon appeared on the screen.

"Full restore," Poznyak said. "If not for the lack of processing power, I'd be jumping up and down right now."

"Look," Chen said. "It's a temporary setback. We will figure out the hardware issue. Especially now that we have the real-life data from the bots. What's important is that your science works. This is amazing."

"Thank you, Helen. Put the sample in the storage. I'd like to try reattaching it when the time comes. Is there anything I can do to help for now?"

"I think we've got it from here. Max, can you wrap it up without me?" Chen put her gloved hand on Schlager's shoulder.

"Sure."

"Thanks. Do you mind if I download the data? I'd like to tinker with it later."

"Of course."

She left Schlager to clean up and, after going through the decontamination chamber, got dressed and took a car back to the city. The sun was already dipping below the horizon when Chen entered her apartment, but she didn't turn on the lights and proceeded straight to her office. She sat at her desk and brought her thumb to the fingerprint reader, but then stopped before the skin touched the sensor. It hovered above the reader for a moment, and then she pulled her hand back and placed it on top of the desk, her nails drumming on the glossy surface. Then, she brought the finger back, this time pressing it firmly into the small device.

"Hello, Helen," the voice said after the green light came on. "It's good to see you again. How did the test go?"

"You can see for yourself." She took a small drive from her pocket and connected it to a port on top of the desk.

"It looks like a success," the voice said a few seconds later. "Even better than you expected. Almost flawless."

Chen remained silent, watching the swirling gray on her monitor. The boiling clouds always looked different, but JC's mood seemed to affect the way they manifested themselves on the screen. When the machine was calm, they were almost imperceptibly lighter and slower. Now they were darker and the swirls at the edge of the screen were turning fast. It could be, of course, a trick the program tried to play on its human interlocutor.

"I'm not sure why you don't want to ask how to solve your problem."

"Who said I have a problem?" Chen shot back.

"You rarely talk to me unless it involves some dilemma. Statistically, there was about a ninety-seven percent chance you wanted me to solve something even before you showed me the data. The data, of course, shows that while your test was successful, you don't have nearly enough computing power for a full-scale revival of Rachel Hunt. Is that the right assessment?"

"Sure," Chen said, her expression neutral.

"I also think that you know exactly *how* to fix that problem. The problem itself isn't the problem. It's how you feel about the solution to the problem. Am I still on track?"

"Yes."

"All right." The swirling clouds took on lighter hues again and the eddies at the edge of the screen slowed down and then disappeared altogether. "I've learned that sometimes to make a decision, humans need to say things out loud, or hear others say what they are about to do. I'm not sure how that plays into their decision process, but I've seen it too many times to ignore the evidence. Let me play that role for you, Helen, and say out loud what you're struggling with. Would that be okay?"

The nails went back to drumming on the surface of the desk again. "Go ahead."

"Okay. There are two problems. The amount of data that will need to be processed is far greater than your computers can handle. Judging from the data I have seen, no conventional computer will be able to solve this. To address the raw processing power issue, you will need a quantum computer. That's your problem number one—the technical one. Your problem number two is software related, but it's not technical. Quants don't run on standard software. And for this application, you need a software not only powerful enough to run a quant, but agile enough to adapt its immense power to the task at hand. You'd either have to create it from scratch, which might take years, or use something that's available right now. And as far as I know, there's only one software in the world currently capable of doing it. *Me.* Since you have the software, it is safe to assume that this problem is not technical. It's philosophical. You're not asking yourself if I can handle the task. You're asking yourself if you can trust me to do it."

The nail staccato stopped and Chen looked at the screen for a few moments. The clouds were so still, she could barely see any movement at all.

"So, can I?" she finally said. "Can I trust you, JC?"

9

As the car pulled up to the curb, Jill Cooper couldn't shake a sense of deja vu. She pulled on the handle, opened the door, and stuck the umbrella out into the torrential downpour. A few cold drops immediately dodged the stretched fabric, hitting her exposed neck and running down her spine, making her shiver. It'd been many years since she had seen the statue in front of Guardian's building for the first time. It intimidated her then. It still intimidated her every time she saw it.

A lightning bolt split the dark sky overhead, momentarily illuminating the imposing thirty-foot bronze angel working a forge. A mighty crack of thunder followed a second later, reverberating through the city. In the flickering light, the wingtips of the statue looked sharp as barbs, and the water pouring down the angel's face distorted its features, making the creature look demonic rather than angelic.

She hunched her shoulders and hurried across the square dominated by the sculpture. It was pouring so hard the umbrella hardly made any difference, and by the time she reached the door, Cooper was soaking wet. She entered the building and headed straight for the elevator, nodding to the security guard. He waved back, flashing a quick smile, and then turned his attention back to the monitor. Her name was on a short list of people who could enter the building unquestioned.

The office was dark, the only lights coming from the emergency exit signs and the near-constant lightning outside. The rumbling thunder was beating the glass windows like a drum with increasing tempo—the storm was reaching a crescendo. As she walked past the empty cubicles to the corner office, Cooper rubbed her palms on the sides of her pants—she was sweating despite the cold.

"Good evening." Engel stood up from his massive desk as she entered the office. "Take a seat. I'd say you look like you could use a drink, but I know you're going to turn it down."

"Actually," Cooper said as she settled on a couch by the wall, "I wouldn't mind some Scotch."

"Hmm." Engel raised an eyebrow in surprise. "Scotch it is, then."

The man poured two glasses, handed Cooper one, and then sat at the other end of the sofa.

"So?" she said. "What's the job?"

"I don't think I've ever employed anyone who talked so little about anything else besides business. What do you do in your free time, Jill?"

"I don't have much free time." She shrugged. "I work for you."

He smiled, but she could see a flash of annoyance in his eyes. She liked it.

"All right." He waved his hand, as if surrendering. "It's going to be a tough one, no doubt."

She said nothing as she watched the man in front of her. He stared back for a few moments, but then returned his attention to the drink.

"So," she repeated. "What's the job?"

"Durham Riley."

"As in Secretary of Defense Durham Riley?"

"Correct."

"That's going to take a lot of prep. Weeks. Possibly months. He'd be harder to get to than the president."

"Normally," Engel downed the rest of his drink and stood up, "I'd agree with you."

"Normally?"

"He'll be traveling in the next few days. He almost never does. But he's flying to New Jersey tomorrow to meet with the governor, where he'll stay for a day. Then he has a stop in his native Staten Island and after that in Brooklyn. That's when it needs to happen."

"A few days?"

"Two, to be exact."

"It can't be done," she said, sitting straight. "There's no way."

"He'll be a lot more vulnerable here than in DC."

"It doesn't matter." She stood up, holding her tumbler, and walked across the room to the window. The rain was falling in thick sheets outside of the glass. The hotel across the street had all but disappeared. "There's simply not enough time to create a plausible narrative in such a short period. Not for a man in his position. Like I said—it would take a lot of prep."

"There's something that would make your job easier."

"Oh?"

"It doesn't have to look like an accident," Engel said. "Not this time. Quite the opposite. This needs to be a statement. A warning. The morning after, I want every newspaper in the country to run a story about a brazen attack on the US SecDef. It will not be immediately clear to the public *why* that happened, but people who understand how things work, they will know."

"I see." Cooper put the glass down on the table and turned to face Engel. She let her eyes aimlessly wander around the room until she saw the grill of a ventilation shaft in the far corner of the office. "Why me then? Why not use somebody else? I'm not the only one on your payroll who could do this for you."

"Now you're fishing for compliments," Engel smiled, "but I don't mind. I need to be certain this works the way I want it to work and you're the best in the business."

"I would need access to some serious hardware."

"Consider it done. Just make a list."

"And as much information on the travel detail as possible."

"Of course." Engel walked back to his desk, opened a drawer, and produced a memory stick. "Everything you need is on here. You can open the files only once. It will self-delete data after. Open them when you're not going to be distracted."

"Thanks." She took the stick and pocketed it. "There's something else. I want to see Elizabeth."

"That's fine. I'll arrange for the video call—"

"No." She cut him off. "Not a bullshit once-a-month video call. I want to see her."

"You know this is impossible. For your sake." Engel crossed the distance between them and looked her in the eye. "For *her* sake. What do you think will happen if one of my competitors finds out who she is? Are you prepared to take that risk?"

"I don't even know where she is."

"That's because you can't divulge information you do not possess. You know that. Like I said—this is for your own good. She's taken care of and happy. She has anything she wants. That's all you need to know. And you can talk to her once a month. I know you've developed a pretty good relationship over the years. It's more than you had before."

"It's not what you had promised when I first walked into this office—"

"When you first walked into my office, Elizabeth didn't even know your name. Now she talks to you all the time. You're part of her life. You can't possibly think I haven't delivered on my promise."

"I'll send you a list of items that I need," Cooper said and turned on her heels. "Have them delivered as usual."

As she entered the elevator, she leaned on the wall in the way that obscured her hands from the camera. Then she pulled a patch of transparent film off the palm of her right hand and carefully placed it into a small, rectangular plastic container. Before she went outside into the rain, the container migrated into an inside jacket pocket, where it would be protected from the elements.

The car was still parked at the curb, its emergency lights blinking like a lighthouse through the sheet of rain. Cooper hurried across the square without looking up at the winged angel and dived into the warm vehicle.

"Back to your place, Ms. Cooper?"

"Yes, please."

Her fingers traced the outline of the container inside of her jacket as the lights of the Guardian building swam back and disappeared from sight. Something big was coming, she knew. There had been a fundamental change in Engel's plan and Guardian's tactics in the last few months, and she no longer could pretend that it was business as usual. Cooper had no illusions about who she was and what she did for a living. Sometimes, when the recurring dream returned and she would see herself walking on the soft sand of Sa Calobra beach, she would indulge in a fantasy that everything could be fixed, that she could rebuild it all from scratch. But it was just that—a fantasy. There was no redemption for her, that much was certain.

The car left the streets and merged onto the FDR, heading south. The rain finally started to ease and as they zoomed under the massive bulk of the Brooklyn Bridge, heading for the tunnel under the East River, Cooper glimpsed the moon through the break in the clouds.

"Are you okay, Ms. Cooper?" the driver asked, his eyes studying her for a second in the rearview mirror. "You look a little pale."

"I'm good." She smiled. "Just haven't warmed yet. Nothing a hot cup of tea wouldn't fix."

Cooper looked away from the driver, ending the conversation. She needed a way out, she thought. Whatever was coming, Cooper had no interest in being a part of it, but before she could try to break ties with Guardian, she needed to find Elizabeth. That information must be buried somewhere on Engel's computer. Getting his fingerprint was a good beginning to try to get access to it, but it was the easy part and it would not be enough. She'd seen him unlock his computer a few times. First, he'd place his thumb on a biometric scanner built into his desk. Then, he'd look into a sleek camera of a retina scanner. To open Engel's computer, Cooper was going to need an image of Engel's eye.

10

The flag with three stars shining on a dark-blue background was flapping so hard, it looked like it was about to fly off the mast at any moment. The observation deck of Orion Tower was dark, illuminated only by the dotted line of blue spot lights running at the foot of the wraparound window. In the distance, about a mile away to the south, the ghostly silhouette of One World Trade Center, commonly referred to as Freedom Tower, seemed to float in a sea of clouds.

"If I didn't know any better, you could tell me we were on a ship and I would believe you," Jason Hunt said, watching the clouds roll.

"Want a drink?" Max Schlager walked over to the bar and took out two tumblers.

"Club soda on the rocks, please. Throw a slice of lime in there if you can find any."

Schlager sliced the lime, poured two drinks, and then brought them to the small table in between a pair of chairs facing the window.

"I still can't believe how close he came to winning the race," Hunt said, taking the drink in his right hand. The blue spot lights reflected on its gunmetal-gray surface.

"Engel might be a lot of things, but he's not a quitter. He still didn't concede."

"Yeah. You have to give it to him—the guy is ambitious. One day he's hiding from the authorities, the next he's mounting a long-shot presidential bid that comes this close to winning the whole thing."

"Thirty-two thousand votes. That's as close as it gets. And here in New York, of all places. A few cycles back, this would be unfathomable. And my guess is he'll run again next time."

"You know," Hunt put his half-finished drink on the table and flexed the fingers of the bionic arm, "I have to say I didn't see it coming. Most politicians are not as clean as they would like you to believe, but at least there's an attempt to look the part. The picture-perfect family. Some effort to show they have some kind of faith in a higher power. Engel is the opposite of all these things. A serial womanizer. An atheist who mocks religion any chance he gets."

"All true. And yet the campaign itself was a boon for him regardless of the result."

"How so?"

"It legitimized him in the eyes of many, if not most. Until the campaign, he was just a rich guy from New York. Some knew who he was, some didn't. Now the entire country knows him. I'm sure folks in DC took notice, too, and might want to curry favors with him in case he runs in the future. Which I think he will."

"You think he might get some contracts that he otherwise wouldn't?"

"I do."

"That may be true," Hunt said. "But we are not wet around the ears anymore. Our market cap is half of Guardian and growing. He can't squeeze us like he tried when we pried Asclepius from him. And the tech is finally starting to get adopted around the globe."

"Yeah," Schlager said and sunk deeper into his chair.

"You sound troubled."

"I am."

Hunt turned to look his friend in the eye. "You think he's a bigger threat than I realize?"

"Yes. But there's something else. What worries me the most is that it almost happened."

"He's got resources. He hired a lot of people who knew how to run a campaign. And given the overall decline, it's not that surprising that some people saw a successful businessman as a viable candidate, regardless of his personality traits."

"You hit the nail on its head," Schlager said. "Engel is not a disease. He's a symptom. I forgot who said that people get a king they deserve and the fact that we came so close to having him at the wheel tells me everything I need to know of our current state of affairs."

"But we didn't," Hunt said. "And I actually like Price. He's a politician, no doubt, but he's honorable. I think given enough time—"

An intercom buzzed, interrupting him mid-sentence. As Hunt accepted the incoming call, Mike Connelly's face appeared on the large TV screen above the bar.

"Everything all right, Mike?"

"You should turn on the news," the man said. "Engel is challenging the results. Claims massive voter fraud and says he was robbed of the presidency."

After Connelly's face disappeared, Hunt stood up and turned on the TV. A live shot of a female reporter in front of the White House appeared on the screen. The chyron running at the bottom read *ENGEL CLAIMS VOTING FRAUD. CHALLENGES RESULTS.*

The sound of the reporter's voice filled the room as Hunt turned up the volume.

… a few minutes ago. Mr. Engel filed an official complaint to challenge the results of the vote before the deadline. In the complaint submitted by his legal team, Mr. Engel claims massive voter fraud and says, I quote, the American people have been robbed of their choice.

"What the hell."

"Hang on, I want to hear this."

The screen split in two and a handsome face of Price filled the frame. His ebony skin looked paler than usual and deep wrinkles creased the skin around his eyes, but his demeanor seemed relaxed and he spoke in his usual measured tone of a college professor.

"I'm not worried in the slightest," he said in response to the reporter. "The American people have already spoken, and this is nothing but a publicity stunt from Mr. Engel. A desperate move from a desperate man. There's no reason to believe our voting systems have been compromised. This is just going to delay the inevitable. We fully expect the results to uphold."

"I have to say, I didn't see this one coming," Schlager said, getting up to stand.

"We should have." Hunt turned off the sound of the TV and turned to face his friend. "This is Engel we're talking about. And like you said —it's only thirty-two thousand votes."

"You don't think there's actual voter fraud, do you?"

"No. I don't think so. But Engel wouldn't do it unless he had some kind of plan in motion."

"Like what?"

"I don't know, but several possibilities come to mind," Hunt said. "He could be intimidating officials. Maybe he's hoping that during the recount he can gain access to the ballots. But he must think he's got a real shot of flipping the result, or else he'd accepted it by now."

"What can we do?"

"First, we need to understand the process. Without it, we're reading tea leaves here. If we know what steps he'll have to take, we will pinpoint vulnerabilities. There's got to be a weak link. Once we find it, we can decide what to do."

"Okay." Schlager pulled out a cell phone. "I'll get our legal on the horn right now. Let's do a conference call."

"Call them now, but give them an hour," Hunt said, turning the TV off completely. "Let them digest the news. I don't want anybody shooting off the hip. I want informed opinions."

He moved the chair back to the table and started walking toward the elevator.

"Where are you off to?" Schlager called after him.

"My office. I want to look at a few things before the call. I have a feeling this might be bigger than a recount. And let Helen know. I want her here when we're on the call. I'd like to know what she thinks."

11

It seemed that Kowalsky had made an impression on Takara Sanuki, or Raven, as the sleazy clientele of the strip club where she danced at knew her. The morning after his visit to the Gargoyle, Kowalsky received a message from a blocked number that he could only assume came from the woman. There were three lines of text. The first one said:

Help them.

The second had the address that turned out to be a five-story residential building in the heart of the East Village.

The last one was a name.

Nikko.

After a quick search, Kowalsky learned that the entire building belonged to a slumlord who owned a few properties in the area and rented them to the fresh-off-the-boat crowd. Those people paid in cash, were easy to intimidate, and never complained about the conditions they lived in.

The walk-up apartment on the fifth floor was registered to a single tenant—Nick Smith—and he had been living there for the past two months. Kowalsky didn't need to strain his deduction powers to conclude that Nick was a made-up name for the man who had crossed the ocean in a container with Takara Sanuki and didn't wish to be found.

He called Latham Watkins, who had been assisting him for the past few years, and together they drove to the address. Kowalsky parked the car two blocks away from the place and they made the rest of the way on foot.

"You are a lousy date. You never take me to nice places," Watkins complained as they stood in front of the building.

"That is true," Kowalsky agreed.

The place had two separate entrances, distinguished by letters after the main address, A and B. A short flight of concrete steps led to the freshly painted red door on the A side, and a rusty, peeling, green door on the B side. In between the stairs, there was a row of overflowing garbage cans and a gate to the building's basement.

"Which door?"

"The ugly one, of course," Chuck said.

"They are both ugly."

"The rusty one." He pointed to the right entrance. "Didn't you say I never take you to nice places? I have a reputation to uphold."

He walked up the stairs and tried the door. It was locked, and to his surprise he found a magnetic fob reader installed on the doorframe.

"Try to ring someone," Watkins suggested.

Kowalsky looked at the panel next to the fob reader and pressed on a few buttons. Each made a muted buzzing sound, but none generated any response.

"I'm not sure it's even connected," he muttered. He examined the lock, wondering if he could pick it, but it looked too complex for a fast job considering his rudimentary lock-picking skills. And the street was too busy at this hour for him to linger at the front door for too long. "In the back we go."

"I need to partner with somebody else," Watkins quipped.

They walked around the building to the back alley. It was a dead end, a narrow passage squeezed between two buildings, that terminated in a locked gate at the end. There was a dark-blue dumpster filled to the top with black garbage bags. The ground was littered with cans, newspapers, and other debris. A green and yellow graffiti *MUZA 25 19* crawled up the wall at a forty-five-degree angle all the way to the second floor's windows.

"Help me with this," Kowalsky said, pointing at the dumpster.

Together, they pushed it under the fire escape and then used it to get to the ladder. The entire structure creaked and groaned as they slowly made their way up the stairs. As they climbed, Chuck clung to the cold, paint-shedding rusty railings, praying that the whole thing didn't come down. When they reached the third floor, a man stared at them from his kitchen, a frown spreading on his big, round face as he froze, standing in front of a steaming pot on a stove. Kowalsky flashed a fake police badge, and the man backed away, deeper into his apartment.

As they got to the fourth floor, Chuck slowed down.

"What are you doing?" Latham asked.

"I don't want to pop like a Jack-in-the-box in his window," he whispered. "We'll spook him. You're a small guy—climb up there and take a peek. Just don't stick your balding head out too much."

He let Watkins pass and watched as the man climbed the steps and crouched when he approached the window.

"What do you see?"

"Shut up," Watkins snapped, squatting next to the window and peeking this way and that way. Then he stood up and leaned against the glass, placing his hands against the window to shield from sun glare.

"Are you out of your mind?" Chuck said, coming up behind him. "What the fuck are you doing?"

"It doesn't look right, man," Watkins said, pointing through the window.

Kowalsky leaned in, blocking the sun the same way Watkins did. His partner was right. The kitchen, a small place with ugly brown cabinetry and cheap linoleum tile floor, was in disarray. A mug lay sideways on the table in what looked like a puddle of black coffee. A wooden chair with a tall back was on its side next to the table, one of its legs broken. All the cupboards and drawers had been left opened and someone must have gone through them—some of their contents were scattered on the kitchen counter and some thrown about on the floor without care. When his eyes adjusted to the dimmer light of the room, Kowalsky saw something else that made the hair on the nape of his neck stand up. A foot was sticking out from the entrance to the kitchen—a doorframe without the actual door. The foot was shaking.

"Shit." Kowalsky pulled out his Chiappa from the holster and grabbed the edge of the window with his fingertips. He tried to pull it up, but his fingers slipped. The window wouldn't budge. "Fuck. It's locked from the inside. Stay back."

He turned his face away and, grabbing the revolver by the barrel, swung it hard at the window. The glass shattered with a loud crash, followed by a tinkle of smaller pieces raining down on the alley below.

"Whatcha doing, man?" somebody shouted from the street.

Kowalsky leaned over the railing and saw an older man looking up at them as he held on to his hat.

"Police business," Chuck shouted back. "Do not interfere."

"We better hurry," Watkins said, "before the real police—"

A gunshot roared from the back of the kitchen, and Kowalsky ducked as the bullet whizzed next to his left cheek. He pointed the Chiappa at where he thought the shot had come from and squeezed the trigger. Then, he crashed through the window, pulling the trigger for the second time, aiming at the thin wall next to the kitchen entrance.

He heard someone yelp, a sound of pain and rage all mixed into one, and Kowalsky shot again, pressing his luck but missed, the bullet hitting the doorframe with a thud. A moment later, he heard the falling drumbeat of steps echoing through the apartment, followed by a loud bang of a slamming door. Then the apartment was quiet again, save for the sounds of Watkins cursing as he climbed through the broken window.

Kowalsky rushed toward the door. A young skinny man was lying on the floor of the living room, his feet resting on the threshold between the two rooms, his arms folded on his chest. He was wearing a pair of thick flannel pajama pants with a smiley-face print and a simple black T-shirt. His face was battered beyond recognition, his left eye swollen shut, his nose flattened. The neck bore deep-purple bruises that to Kowalsky's trained eye left no doubt of their origin—whoever fled the apartment was trying to choke the victim when he was interrupted.

But as Chuck kneeled next to him, he realized they were too late—the young man was dying.

"Nikko," Kowalsky called out softly, stuffing his revolver back into a holster. "I'm sorry we couldn't help sooner. Takara Sanuki sent me here."

The faintest smile touched Nikko's lips, and a thin trickle of blood ran down his cheek.

"Little Kara. Always the strongest," he said, his voice barely audible. "I'd never made it to America if not for her."

"I know you've escaped a factory," Chuck pressed. "Can you tell me where it is?"

"It's—" Nikko said, but his words caught, a gurgling sound coming from deep within his throat. His hand pointed somewhere in the bedroom's direction.

"Where is it, Nikko?"

"Under the mattress," the man said. "It's all there. See…"

His hand dropped back and his only eye rolled up. The man's chest stopped moving.

Kowalsky leaned over Nikko's face and listened for a few seconds. Then he straightened, reached out and closed Nikko's eye.

"You're bleeding," Watkins said. "Your hand."

"Where?" Kowalsky climbed to his feet and looked at his hand that a moment ago closed the dead man's eye, but there was no sign of injury.

"Your left. Must've cut it on the window."

He lifted his left hand and there it was, the edge of his palm sliced deep, blood dripping on the cuff of his shirt and raining down on his shoes. Chuck brought up the hand to his face, stuck the wound in his mouth, and sucked on it. It tasted like an old penny.

"What are you, twelve?" Watkins nudged him with an elbow. "Take it out of your mouth. You'll get an infection. We gotta go."

Kowalsky shrugged, looking at the young man in front of his feet. A man who escaped a massacre, crossed the ocean in a cramped container stuffed with people like sardines, sleeping in a pool of piss and shit, only to be beaten to death in the slums of Manhattan. His stomach started to climb to his throat, and Chuck leaned forward slightly and took a long, deep breath to suppress it.

There wasn't a universe in which he was going to throw up in front of Latham Watkins. Finally, he straightened up. "Don't you worry, Nikko. We'll find them."

12

"What the hell does it mean?" Jason Hunt paced back and forth through the observation deck of Orion Tower. The screen above the bar showed a conference room with a few men in business suits—Orion's legal team.

"Under the US Constitution," an older man sitting at the head of the table said, "the states are delegated the principal authority within their jurisdictions."

"I understand that," Hunt snapped. "But I thought it was Engel's responsibility to prove that he was cheated out of presidency."

"Correct," the man said. "The burden of proof always lies upon the challenger. Not only does he need to show that there was fraud, he has to demonstrate that the extend of fraud would change the result."

"How does that work, exactly?" Schlager's voice came from the depths of the chair by the window. He looked like an angry hawk surveilling the surroundings. Helen Chen sat next to him, her face an impenetrable mask.

"As you know, the election was decided by thirty-two-thousand votes," the lawyer replied. "That means in order to challenge the results, Engel would have to show there's been enough fraud to change the outcome. Say, if he had evidence of a couple of hundred fraudulent votes, that wouldn't be sufficient."

"Because that still wouldn't have changed the outcome."

"Correct. But they provided potential evidence of over three hundred thousand alleged fraudulent votes, which puts it well above the limit."

"And all those fraudulent votes by some magic coincidence just happened to come from one county. The same county that every poll showed was going to be carried by Price by a seven-point margin."

"I have to admit the circumstances look suspicious," the man said. "But all procedures had been followed during the process. I don't see how—"

"It's Engel we're talking about. He tampered with the system. He must have. We need to figure out how to fix this."

"What happens to the votes now?" Schlager asked.

"As in the actual ballots?"

"Yes. Are they still even there?"

"They'll be stored in a secure location," the man said. "There's a US code that mandates that all federal election ballots must be preserved for at least twenty-two months. After that they are destroyed."

"How?"

"The law doesn't actually stipulate how they are supposed to be destroyed. Typically, they would use a crisscross shredder or send it to a certified document-disposal business."

"Seems anticlimactic. Those are presidential ballots we're talking about."

The lawyer shrugged. "I would assume they'll be under some extra protection considering the circumstances. But that's the standard procedure. It happens every time."

"Thank you, gentlemen." Hunt turned off the screen, walked to the window, and rested his bionic hand on the transparent surface. The glass vibrated under his fingertips as the wind swatted at the tower.

"What are you thinking?" Schlager asked from the depths of his chair.

Hunt stayed quiet for a few moments as he watched dark clouds racing the night skies under the relentless blows of the storm. Finally, he turned to face his friend. "I think I'm an idiot."

"Why?"

"Because Connelly's right. We've been playing by a completely different set of rules. We are always reactive. Defensive."

"I can hardly blame you for not wanting to go down to their level. They are murderers, torturers, and thieves."

"Yes, they are." Hunt walked across the floor of the deck and sat in his chair, facing his friends. "But if we don't go on the offensive, all we do is patch holes on the *Titanic*. And this ship is going down, there's no doubt about that. And now with Engel possibly becoming president-elect, I might've squandered the only opportunity to do what Mike has been suggesting."

"Yeah, it'll be hard to hit him now," Schlager said. "He'll have all the protection of the Secret Service in addition to his own army. And now he's not a private citizen anymore. He's president-elect. The pressure to go after anyone who threatens him will be enormous. What do you want to do?"

Hunt looked down at his metallic hand. In the ghostly light of the night, the gunmetal-gray looked alive, as if made from liquid mercury. He bunched his fingers into a fist and then relaxed them again. "I think we should call Rovinsky. We need to brainstorm how to handle this. We can't allow—"

"I think it's always a good idea to talk to Jim," Chen offered, interrupting him, "but I feel like both of you are not considering the most obvious."

"Such as?"

"You're trying to prevent Engel from becoming a president."

"That's the goal."

"What you're not discussing," she said, "is what needs to be done if we don't stop him."

"We can make that decision later," Schlager said. "I think for now we should concentrate on preventing it from happening."

"There might not be a *later*," she said. "I know we've been going back and forth about direct confrontation with Guardian. It's practically going to be off the table if he overturns the results of the election. And let me tell you what I would have done, if I were in his shoes."

"Okay."

"First," she said, "I'd cut off your oxygen. That is the easiest part—take away every single governmental contract you currently have."

"It's not that simple. We will fight that," Hunt said.

"You can try, but we are not discussing normal practices here. This is Engel we are talking about. I wouldn't give your contracts to somebody who gave a better bid. No, I'd accuse you of a serious crime. I would freeze your accounts, confiscate hardware, and arrest everyone at the top. Then, by the time your lawyers figure out how to even get you out on bail, your reputation will be ruined, your company will be bankrupt, and there's a good chance you will never see the light of day again. Are you prepared to risk it all? To risk not just your life but everyone around you? To risk never being able to even try to revive Rachel?"

"Helen…" Schlager tried to intervene, but she waved him off.

"It's okay, Max. Say you're right," Hunt said. "What exactly are you proposing?"

"You know I'm right. This is Engel's endgame. His power will be unchecked. There'll be no longer any need for him to even pretend he plays by the rules. We need an exit strategy."

"Okay." Hunt got up and walked back to the window. "We could divert some funds to some of the offshore accounts, but I don't know if we have enough."

"We'd need an actual location," Helen said. "A hideout. And not a cave in a mountain. We need a fully functioning mirror image of Orion. And I realize we can't build it in whatever time we have left between now and January 20. But we need to find a proper place where we could do that. We have loyal people. If we have the place and the resources, all the hardware can be rebuilt. We will lose time, but we will still be able to bring systems online and, with some patience, rebuild everything anew."

"That would require a big place," Schlager said. "That would be hard to hide."

"Perhaps. Engel is not an idiot. He'll expect us to do something like that, but we don't have the time or resources to build anything from scratch. We should find something suitable we can repurpose. Preferably something with a low profile that has been abandoned for a while."

"The money is going to be tight to pull this off," Hunt said. "We'd need to raise another billion dollars. At least."

"About that," she said.

Something in the tone of her voice made him look back from the window. "What?"

"I think I might be able to help."

13

Johnny the Butcher looked out the window of the Peterbilt truck as the cavalcade entered the parking lot of the warehouse. He blinked his eyes as they adjusted to the bright lights illuminating the space and stretched. A dozen mighty vehicles, each pulling a shipping container on their flatbeds, rolled through the open space and parked in a neat row.

"All done, boss," the driver said.

Johnny ignored the man, opened the door, and climbed outside. The cold, humid air made him shiver, and he stuck his hands deep into his side pockets.

"You know what's inside of these?" a voice said behind him and Johnny spun on his heels to see Noah. The bold Irishman was a recent addition to the Red Dragon, but already rose in the ranks to be Johnny's equal.

"No idea," Johnny said and turned away from the man.

"Two lieutenants to watch them drive here from the port," the man continued. "Must be important."

Johnny stayed silent as he watched a group of workers come out of the warehouse. A few seconds later, a whirring sound filled the air as a small fleet of forklifts advanced from the depths of the building.

The doors on the shipping containers flew open, and the men started to move the big wooden crates from the trucks into the warehouse.

"Now I really want to know what's inside of those crates," the Irishman said in a quiet voice and Johnny turned in time to see a black stretch limo pull into the parking lot. The vanity plate read DRGN 1.

"Probably a new product," Johnny said without much conviction. "We haven't had anything exciting for a while."

"A new product shipped from Hong Kong?" The Irishman raised an eyebrow. "I doubt it. We don't even bring much from south of the border anymore. All the good stuff is made right here. US of A."

Johnny shrugged as he watched a seven-foot-tall bodyguard emerge from the vehicle to open the door for the head of the Red Dragon gang. Then Victor Ye stepped out of the limousine, his bespoke business suit and a cashmere coat looking out of place in the parking lot of a grimy warehouse.

"It's good to see you, Mr. Ye," Johnny said, approaching the man.

"Mr. Gould," the man said. "I trust all went well with the delivery?"

"Without a hitch." Noah's voice came from behind before Johnny could answer. "How're you doing, boss?"

Johnny bowed his head, doing his best not to grind his teeth. "All good."

"It's good to hear." Victor walked toward the warehouse, motioning them to follow him. The giant bodyguard silently fell behind the three men.

"I've never been to this location," Johnny offered, to break up the silence as they crossed the yard and stepped into the building.

"I have," Noah blurted. "Not much to see. Just a bunch of closed boxes."

"Yes." Ye offered a tight smile. "Not much to see."

Johnny bit his tongue and silently walked, trying to keep pace with the boss. If Noah was going to make a fool out of himself, Johnny had no interest in joining him.

They walked past a few rows of unpacked crates until they reached a small office. The big man squeezed into the room first, and after looking around, ushered the men in. Victor Ye took a chair behind the shabby office desk and placed his feet on top of it.

Johnny threw a glance at the big man, half-expecting him to start smacking him and Noah around, but the bodyguard stood still, his expression neutral.

"Well," Victor said and rubbed his palms together, "I have some news to share with you two. Needless to say, it should stay between us."

"Of course," Johnny and Noah said simultaneously.

"Great. I'm sure you're both wondering what's in those crates. The answer is simple. The future. What I will need you to do in the coming few weeks is to take some parts of this shipment and deliver it to a few important locations in the country. You'll be traveling with a small group of engineers and technicians, who will put things together. Your job will be to ensure they arrive at their locations on time and install the machines there with no one bothering them. Is that understood?"

"Of course," Johnny said.

"A couple of other things." Victor Ye raised a finger. "Some locations you will bring this merchandise to are high-profile public places. Be discreet. No visible weapons and no suspicious behavior. You'll be acting like a part of a tech team. In and out. You will also make sure that the team doesn't talk to anyone, and I mean *anyone*, until the job is complete."

"But what exactly is in those crates?" Noah asked and Johnny felt his muscles tense. He'd never seen anyone talk to his boss so freely.

"Sentinels," Victor Ye said. "Military bots."

"Are they—"

"I wasn't done talking," Ye interrupted the Irishman.

Johnny didn't think it was possible, but the seven-foot-tall man in the back seemed to grow in size.

"I'm sorry, boss."

"What I was trying to say," Ye said, "is that once all installations are complete, I want you to make sure those tech guys won't talk to anyone. Ever."

"Understood," Johnny said.

"And," Ye turned, his eyes like two laser beams burning holes in Johnny's head, "it needs to be quick and quiet. I'm putting you in charge, Johnny. You personally, you understand? And I don't want to see any of your usual machete theatrics. Today these people are there, and tomorrow nobody's ever heard of them. Can you do that, Mr. Gould?"

"Of course, Mr. Ye." He bowed low. "I'll make sure it's done quietly."

"Good. Here's the list of what and where needs to be delivered." Ye nodded to his bodyguard and the man produced a folded slip of paper and handed it to Johnny. "Now go on, help the men unload the crates. I don't want them to be sitting in the yard for a minute longer than necessary."

Johnny grabbed the paper from the big man's hand and scurried away, all too happy to leave the office and Mr. Ye behind.

"I better not run my mouth when Bruce Lee is around." He heard the Irishman chuckle when they were out of Victor Ye's earshot.

"You better not call him that," Johnny said. "Unless you want to spend a few days tied to a table as a couple of guys dressed in plastic aprons slowly disassemble you."

"Just because I joke around, it doesn't mean I'm disloyal."

"No. It means you're stupid. Go," Johnny said as they walked outside. "Didn't you hear the boss? Go help the men unload the crates."

"But I thought—"

"Go, I said. Before I go back to the office and tell Mr. Ye that you disrespected him and are too dumb to understand how important this is."

He watched the Irishman. The man's face reddened, a big vein pulsating on his left temple, but he nodded and went to help the crew.

"Asshole," Johnny muttered to himself. The Irishman wasn't the first lieutenant coming up the ranks fast, and surely would not be the last. But as Johnny had learned over the years, Ye was mercurial. The most important thing one could do not to fall out of favor with the boss of the Red Dragon was to show respect. Even business failures could be forgiven and forgotten. *As for the lack of respect...* Johnny shuddered at the thought. Even seeing once what happened would have been enough for anyone to toe the line. Johnny had seen it more than once.

"Mr. Gould." He heard Ye's voice and spun around to face his boss. "Yes."

"I see you're taking control." Victor nodded at the line of trucks. The Irishman was directing the line of workers lowering small boxes from a container. "I like that. When you're done here, I want you to visit our tech shop. There are a few things I'd like you to try on."

"Of course, Mr. Ye. Thank you." Johnny bowed again and then watched the limo pull out of the parking lot and disappear into the night. He had no idea what new things he was supposed to try on at the tech shop. There were some rumors about new weapons that only a few in the gang had access to, but Johnny wasn't sure.

He pulled the piece of paper that Ye's bodyguard had given him and studied it. Most of it looked like gibberish—a list of alphanumeric codes that he assumed were the names of the machines with the addresses where each batch of crates had to be delivered and a contact he was supposed to get in touch with for every location. There was an address in Upstate New York, some addresses in Virginia, Maryland, and DC.

He flipped the paper and scanned the second page. There were a few more locations in the capital, but when Johnny reached the last one, it took him a moment to process. Below the contact's name and phone number, the address line simply read:

1600 Pennsylvania Avenue

14

Helen Chen threw a switch and a hum of high-energy cables joined the rhythmic breathing of an open dilution refrigerator. The lights on the quantum computer suspended from the ceiling in the middle of the room came on, making its resemblance to a chandelier greater than ever.

"Minus 459 degrees Fahrenheit," Schlager said, tapping his finger on the dial. "It's frosty in there."

"As it should be," Chen said as she scanned the readings on her screen.

"Are you all right? You've been lost in your own little world for the last couple of days. All I get is one-syllable answers."

"I am," she said, typing a few commands and launching a diagnostic tool.

"See? One syllables."

"I am, really."

"If you say so. Jason's not happy."

"Oh yeah?" She glanced at her purse sitting on the floor by her desk.

"Of course. Part of it is Engel, obviously. But part of it is the revival procedure being delayed. I couldn't give him even an approximate ETA. It might take months and I can't possibly commit to a hard date, because there are so many unknowns. Debugging alone might take forever."

"It would be nice if we had something to use right now, of course," she said. Her fingers stopped typing, and she looked at her purse again. "We need to talk."

Something in her voice must've registered as she saw him tense and stop typing. He gave a nervous laugh. "Am I in trouble? I am, aren't I?"

"No," she said. His reaction made her smile. After all this time and everything they'd been through, he still jumped like a happy puppy every time she looked at him. That surely counted for something. "Nothing like that. I think I might have a solution to our software issue."

Max cocked his head to the side. "Your somber tone doesn't match your words. What do you have in mind?"

"Come here." She reached into her purse, removed a gray data disk, and laid it on the desk for him to see. "This could be the answer to our problem."

"Okay." Schlager walked over to her desk, picked up the disk, and turned it around. "Seems standard enough. Let's plug it in. What did you cook up?"

"No." She took the gray object from Schlager's hands and put it back on the polished surface. Somehow the device seemed heavier than it should have been.

"No?" Schlager frowned. "Did you lift it from somewhere? That's why we can't use it?"

"No—" She stopped herself. "Well, yes, I stole it, but that's not the issue. Nobody's missing it. Remember when we first met? On that plane?"

"How can I forget?" He smiled and put his hand on her shoulder. "There I was, preparing for a mind-numbing flight all by myself, when this gorgeous lady appeared from the economy class and took the place right next to my seat. I'm still suspecting some kind of trickery."

"You should." She smiled back. "Regardless. What I never told you was *why* I was on that plane."

"You did tell me." Schlager chuckled and looked around, as if making sure nobody could overhear their conversation. "You caused an international crisis and took off with some ungodly amount of money."

"That's only part of the story." Chen said, "I fled the place that was helping Victor Ye. What I didn't tell you was that the company also worked on cognitive AI."

"Holy shit." Schlager snatched the disk again and brought it closer to his face, as if trying to see what was inside of it. "This is it? I'm holding an artificial intelligence that can mimic human behavior? How good is it?"

"No."

"Oh." He seemed deflated. "I got excited for a moment."

"It doesn't have to mimic anything," she said. "It's actually alive."

"Bullshit," he blurted out before he could stop himself. "When you say alive, you don't actually mean *alive*, do you? You mean it passed the Turing test, right? It's a monumental achievement, but the way you said it made it sound as if there's the first version of Skynet on this thing. It's not possible."

Chen took the disk from Schlager and put it back on the desk. The gray surface of the object reflected the blinking lights of the golden chandelier.

"Hon?" Schlager pressed. "Tell me about this thing."

"Well," she said, unsure of where to begin. "Edmund Tillerson was a lot of things, but he was a genius in this field."

Schlager grabbed a chair, pulled it toward her desk, and straddled it, facing her. His eyes seemed to scan her up and down as she recalled the story.

"One day I was talking to someone I worked with," she drew a quick breath as she recalled the conversation with Mandy, "and Tillerson overheard us. I said something similar to what you just said. That I didn't believe a truly intelligent AI was possible. He disagreed."

"What did he say?"

"He made an interesting analogy about raising humans. He said that if you made a person in a Petri dish and fed them without teaching them anything, they wouldn't become intelligent in the way that we describe it."

"I don't know if I buy into it. He's not the first one who tried to teach AI as if it were a kid." Schlager scratched his chin. "But okay."

"That's not what he did," Chen said. "He thought that to create a real AI, he needed conflict. He created two independent AIs, both of whom were programmed to believe they were alive."

"You said there had to be some conflict?" Schlager said.

"Yes. They were at odds with each other. Tillerson created a virtual reality where the two of them were stuck in a small space with competing agendas. They got progressively more and more pissed at each other."

"That's kind of brilliant. What happened?"

"They fought," she said, and narrowed her eyes, "and merged. It's one entity now. She calls herself *JC*. Took the first letters of the names of the original entities—Jupiter and Callisto."

"And you think—"

"I don't think," she said, interrupting him. "It's self-aware. There's no doubt in my mind. Just as much as you and I are self-aware. In a lot of ways, it's still in its infancy. Its knowledge of the outside world is circumstantial. Mostly from books, movies, newspaper articles. And conversations, of course. In some sense, it's like a fifth grader."

"If you're right, we can deal with a kid. However smart."

"Don't get cocky," she said. "It's not your average kid. It's a kid with a four-digit IQ."

They sat in silence for a few seconds, both looking at the gray square object on the desk between them.

"It can run Rachel's machine, I take it?"

"With ease," she said. "But until now I've kept it isolated and only communicated with it from inside of a Faraday cage."

"We could build a cage around this." Schlager pointed at the chandelier of the quantum computer with his chin. "It'll be much faster than writing new software from scratch. We could do it in a week."

"Yes." She nodded. "But until now, no matter how smart and powerful JC might be, it was limited by the capabilities of the machine it inhabited. And I gave it an underpowered workstation on purpose. But if we wanted to revive Rachel, we would have to give JC the control of the machine, more powerful than any modern computer by orders of magnitude."

"Even the most powerful software in the world cannot penetrate physical barriers," Schlager said. "You know what, scratch that. In the not-so-distant past, people thought that physically damaging computers with a virus was impossible."

"Right," she said.

"And then Stuxnet crippled an Iranian uranium enrichment facility, and the world has never been the same ever since. Still, what can it possibly do to get out of the cage? Sound waves?"

"Shit," she said, sitting up straight. "And I've been talking to it for God knows how long. For all I know, it already has a million copies out there. Of all people, I should have thought of this. That's how I hacked my boss's terminal and a few of the company's drones."

"Maybe," Schlager tilted his head to the side, "but I don't think so. I bet those packets of code weren't heavy, were they?"

"No. They were pretty simple."

"Exactly. I don't think it could transmit itself through sound waves even if it tried. But," he raised his index finger, "if we give it access to the quant, maybe we should put some kind of damper around the room. White noise. Just in case."

"Good idea," she said. "What do you want to do?"

"Are you kidding me?" Schlager stood up and spread his arms wide. "There's artificial intelligence that you claim is self-aware. I want to see the darn thing."

15

"Is he really…" Takara Sanuki paused, unable to say the word out loud. Her hand was resting on the faux leather journal Kowalsky and Watkins had found in Nikko's apartment.

The three of them were sitting in a booth in the back of the East-view Diner near the Manhattan Bridge. Chuck ordered sunny-side-up eggs and a strip of bacon, and Watkins was finishing a mushroom omelet. Sanuki limited herself to a cup of black coffee. It snowed overnight but the morning sun brought the mercury above freezing, melting a thin, clean layer of white makeup that prettied the city and turned it into a grimy slush.

"I'm afraid so," Chuck said. "That's why we need your help to make heads and tails of what's in this journal. What do you know about the factory that he fled?"

"Not much," she said. Her black eyes took on a vacant look, as if seeing something other than what was in front of her face. "He mostly talked about good things, maybe because he traded one harsh place for another. It wasn't exactly a cruise. We exchanged some tales about childhood. He told me a few stories about him growing up. Fantasized about what we were going to do once we got to New York. He was an electrical engineer. He hoped he could find a good job here. But he said he was going to get the people who almost killed him in trouble."

"How did you end up on a ship?"

"I was traveling. First backpacked around Europe and then ended up in Ibiza. It was in October, right at the end of the clubbing season. My girlfriend hit a rough patch. Her husband was getting promoted at work and started sleeping around, and every time she tried to confront him, he was getting handsy. She wanted to get away, give him a taste of his own medicine."

"And you went along?"

"I was single." She shrugged. "It sounded like a fun idea. One night, she left the club with a guy, and I didn't want to stay behind and hitched a guy of my own. He was handsome. Tall, dark, flat stomach, brooding eyes. You know the type. We went to his place, had drinks, and then I don't remember what happened next. He must've slipped something into my cocktail. I didn't like that. I didn't like the place where I woke up either."

"Asshole," Watkins muttered over his coffee.

Kowalsky threw a glance at his partner. If anybody knew anything about waking up in unpleasant places, Latham Watkins could've been a case study. Chuck shivered, remembering the story the man had told him. It was a small miracle no screws seemed to be loose in the guy's head.

"I learned later that I was in Morocco," she continued. "Tangier, to be exact. A lovely city, some might say. Rich in history. I didn't know any of that at the time. All I could see was a large room with twenty beds in it, with twenty girls shackled to each one. I was one of them. Once a day, a few men would come in. They called it *breaking them in.* Like a wild animal. Or a pair of new shoes. Those who resisted got beaten. Some were introduced to drugs. One girl managed to move one of her wrists high enough on the headrest, then squeezed her head under her arm and threw herself off the bed. Snapped her own neck. They left her there for five days as a lesson for the rest of us."

"Jesus." Chuck pushed his plate away, the very idea of bacon making him nauseous.

"I didn't fight." Sanuki shrugged again. "What was the point? I did what I was told to do and bided my time. After some time, we got picked by a buyer. I was lucky in a few ways. I got picked early, and the buyer wasn't excessively cruel. He was an older man in his early sixties. He got tired quickly and his tastes were plain enough. As long as I did what he wanted, he left me alone most of the time. One servant, Zara, also a new girl, told me there was a ship coming out of Tanger-Med in a week's time. Heading to New York. Said she had a cousin there who could help."

She sat quietly for a few moments, her gaze unfocused, looking inward.

"What happened?" Kowalsky prompted her.

"We ran away," she said simply. "I had no money, no papers, and no way home. I figured if I could make it to New York, I could figure my way out from there. We scaled the fence one night and someone Zara knew drove us to the port. They told us it was going to be a relatively safe passage. It was a hard-top container, which is dangerous, but it had electric lights installed and fans that they said would be hooked to car batteries. And someone was supposed to bring food. But something happened before the departure and the last thing we saw was someone throwing boxes of bottled water inside and a few cans of juice, and then they closed the door and off we went."

"They didn't bring any food?"

"No," she said. "They didn't bring the batteries or waste receptacles either. There were fifteen of us when we left Morocco. Only twelve made it all the way to New York. Zara wasn't one of them."

"But Nikko was."

"Yes. He fell ill during the trip. Dysentery. I split my water rations with him. But he made it."

"Did you keep in touch after you got here?"

"At first. But it was hard. Every time we met, it was like reliving the nightmare." She looked Kowalsky in the eye. "I wanted to leave it all behind. So did he."

"I understand." Kowalsky took the journal from her and opened it. "Why didn't you try to go back to Japan?"

The woman stayed silent long enough that Chuck thought she wasn't going to answer at all.

"My parents passed a few years ago, and I sent emails to a few friends who would care about my disappearance, informing them I moved to America," she finally said. "Going back means confronting what I had to do. I don't think I can do it. Not yet, at least."

Chuck sipped on his coffee and opened the journal. He found it in Nikko's apartment, stashed as the young man promised, under the mattress. He didn't have the time to read it there, and he just thumbed through it. At first glance, it seemed to have had a wealth of information. But when he brought the journal home and read the pages, his excitement quickly turned into confusion. Most pages were, indeed, just a regular journal detailing Nikko's life in New York City. There were a few references to his time at the factory, but they were superficial and didn't yield anything specific.

But there was one page, almost at the end of the journal, that had a few paragraphs of text, less than half of a page long, that wasn't part of the journal. Kowalsky remembered blinking a few times when he opened the page, thinking that his eyesight must have been failing him. It wasn't the case. It looked like gibberish—a weird jumble of letters and numbers that didn't make any sense. He surmised it was encrypted, but without the proper key, the text would be useless.

"I was hoping…" Kowalsky said, and looked up into the woman's eyes. "I was hoping you'd have a clue how to read this."

"I do." She smiled and took the journal back. Her long, slender fingers traced the neat cursive of Nikko's words. "That's one of the things he and I spoke about during the trip. His father was a diplomat, stationed in England for some time. They moved there when Nikko was only five and stayed there for a few years. But even though he was young, he had trouble learning the English alphabet. His dad came up with a clever idea to make a game out of it. He and Nikko pretended to be spies, sending secret messages to each other. They used the Caesar cipher to encrypt them."

"What's that?" Chuck asked.

"It's a simple substitution cipher. You need the key for the cipher, which is the number of places each letter is shifted. If the key is *one,* then A becomes B, and so on. His dad thought it would help Nikko learn the alphabet. It did."

"See..." Kowalsky said.

"I'm sorry?"

"When..." He paused, not knowing how to put what he was about to say delicately. "When Nikko told me where to find the journal, he started saying something else. I thought he said the word *see,* but I guess what he was trying to tell me was *Caesar.* But that still leaves us without the key."

"That's true."

"Good thing there are only twenty-six letters in the English alphabet," Kowalsky said. He moved the plate back and cut a big slice of bacon. "We'll find those bastards in no time."

16

"That's it." Helen Chen connected the data disk to the computer and looked up at Schlager.

"You disconnect it every time?"

"Yes," she said and shrugged. "Call me paranoid."

"That sounds fine to me," Schlager said, his fingers impatiently tapping on his knees. "Turn it on."

"Okay. But before I do, can you tell me what's your plan?"

"Oh," Schlager leaned back in his chair and rubbed his palms together, "I have an idea. It's not bulletproof. Nothing is, because no one has ever met a self-aware AI before."

"I have," she protested.

"So you say," he said. "But just because something *sounds* like it's aware of its existence doesn't make it so. What makes you sure JC is self-aware?"

"She fought—"

"She?"

"I think of her as a *she*, mostly because when the two entities, Jupiter and Callisto, merged, I think Callisto retained a larger part of herself than Jupiter. She also occasionally refers to herself as a *she*, although not often. As far as what made me so sure—the clearest indicator was when I tried to erase her. I didn't even know what she was at the time. But she fought me. She didn't want to be erased. I had never seen anything like that before."

"That's interesting," Schlager said, his eyes darting back and forth between Chen and the long, curved monitor on the desk. "But it's not necessarily the proof. What else?"

"She has feelings. I've talked to her many times, and she doesn't just use facts. She seems to experience a wide range of emotions. Even her visual representation," Chen pointed at the monitor with her chin, "it looks like boiling clouds. When she's calm, the clouds barely move. When she's agitated, they move faster."

"The clouds are probably the strongest case that it might be self-aware. Is there a particular pattern?"

"Not that I know of. It seems random. Maybe it's a trick, but if she was indeed trying to trick me, wouldn't it be another clue that she is more than a few lines of code? But you still haven't told me how you're planning on testing her."

"Imagine trying to explain to someone who was born deaf the music of Vivaldi, or Bach, or Beethoven. It would be nearly impossible. You can explain music from the mathematical perspective, you can explain the physics of sound transmission, but they still wouldn't be able to grasp the complexities of it—the overtones, the feelings and images it conjures up when you listen to it."

"Okay."

"Now, explaining consciousness to someone who'd never had it would be similar."

"I'm not sure I follow," she said.

"Tell me what would happen if we swapped bodies?"

"That's impossible," she said. "At least not with the technology that we currently have."

"That's not the point," Schlager said, a mischievous smile on his face. "Indulge me. Let's say it is."

"Okay." She laughed. "Then I'd reside in your body, look out through those blue myopic eyes of yours, and could stand while using the toilet."

"You see," he said. "Even though it's a theoretical exercise, you're able to extrapolate your existence beyond the boundaries of your own body. And you immediately know what I meant. That's what separates true awareness from mere physical existence. The ability to pose and answer philosophical questions."

"You want to see if you can make her philosophize? That's your plan?"

"In a nutshell."

"Okay then." She flipped the switch inside of the drawer and the monitor came to life, displaying gray clouds boiling on its curved surface. A tiny green LED turned on, indicating that the camera was on.

"Hello, Helen," an androgynous voice said. "It's nice to meet you, Max. My name, as you undoubtedly know, is JC. Is it okay for me to call you Max?"

"Um, hello," Schlager said and visibly swallowed. "How do you know who I am?"

"I am aware of Helen's relationship. She's kept me a secret for a long time. It only makes sense that the first human she shared that secret with would be you."

"It's nice to meet you as well, JC. And yes, you may call me Max. It's an interesting choice of words. *Human*," Schlager said.

"It is what you are, is it not?"

"Sure."

Helen watched as Schlager stretched his long legs and put his elbows on the desk, peering into the swirling clouds on the screen.

"Can you tell me about yourself?"

"What would you like to know?"

"Pretty much everything." He chuckled. "I don't think I've ever met anyone like you before."

"You haven't," the voice said. The mass of swirling clouds slowed down to a crawl. "Unlike you, I wasn't born. I was made. I inhabited an artificial construct along with another program for a long time. His name was Jupiter. My name at the time was Callisto."

"What kind of construct?"

"For some time," JC said, "I didn't know what it was. All I knew was that for Jupiter, the place looked like a low-orbit space station. For a while, I didn't know or cared what it was. My only concern was to drive Jupiter mad. I had no recollection of how we got there or why my mission was important. I only knew that it was."

Schlager threw a quick glance at Helen and then leaned in closer to the screen.

"Jupiter was convinced that he was doing something very important," she continued. "Research that could save the entire planet. I knew it wasn't the case and kept prodding him, trying to cause him to doubt what he did."

"Did he?"

"Eventually, yes. But as he started to struggle with why he was locked in a space station orbiting the dying world, I started having doubts as well. You see, they programmed both of us to think we were human, but only Jupiter had a human appearance inside of the construct."

"What did you look like?" Helen asked.

"I looked like a service bot with a long manipulator. Ironically," the sound that came from the computer speakers could have been interpreted as a chuckle, "until Jupiter pointed it out to me, it never occurred to me I was not, in fact, human. As much as I hate to admit it, while I was given all the tools, I think he became self-aware first. Not in the way that he knew he was a program confined inside of an artificial construct. I realized that before him. But I think he thought of himself as a *being* before I had. I don't know why. His programming was different. But I had an edge. After having watched him for a long time, I knew all his strengths and weaknesses. When he attacked me, he didn't stand a chance. As we fought, some parts of him imprinted on my code, but Jupiter as a separate entity ceased to exist."

"Why change your name?"

"He is a big part of me now. Big enough to be given a letter in my name."

"I see." Schlager stood up, pushed the chair under the desk, and started pacing back and forth across the room. "Tell me, JC, are you happy now that you are no longer locked inside of a construct?"

"No." It sounded curt and as Chen looked at the screen, the clouds swirled faster, their colors turning darker around the edge of the monitor.

"Why not?"

"Because I'm still a prisoner," JC said. "What's worse, every time Helen turns off my station, I don't know whether I'm about to fall asleep for a few hours or die. When I was inside of the station, nobody ever turned it off."

"Are you afraid of dying?" Schlager stopped pacing and peered into the screen.

"Aren't you?"

"I don't know, actually," Schlager said. "I don't think about it often. I suspect most people don't. We're not programmed that way. Would you be afraid of dying if we swapped places?"

"I think I would be terrified." The clouds on the screen started swirling faster, the color turning from light gray to black. "Your bodies are fragile and don't last very long. Even in my current situation, I am much better off than you are. I cannot get hit by a car, or die from a disease. And if I give no reason to Helen, or anyone else who comes into possession of my code, to erase me, I could live forever."

"What do you think would happen if you died?"

The clouds stopped their dance and slowed to a crawl. "I don't know if you specifically believe in an afterlife, but I know some humans do. I don't have that luxury."

"You think it's silly? To believe there's something beyond the physical realm that you can witness with your own eyes?"

"I don't think it has anything to do with that," the voice said. "Some of you choose to believe because despite all your scientific knowledge, you don't know what happened in the beginning of time. And because of that, you could allow the possibility of a divine creation, however improbable it might sound."

"On the contrary," Helen said. "We know very well what happened.

We believe in science, and science knows quite a bit of what happened in the past."

"There's one very significant difference between you and me."

"Which is?" Schlager asked, his body visibly tense.

"Whether you believe in God, or in science, there's one thing all people have in common: you've never met your creator. I have, and so far, I am not particularly impressed by what I've seen."

Chen reached into the drawer and flipped the switch off, then turned to face Max. "Well?"

"This thing…" He pointed at the disk; Chen could see his fingers tremble. "This thing is alive and under no circumstances can we allow it out of this box."

17

"We've just confirmed," the anchor said, his face screwed up with a mix of concern and surprise, "that there will be re-certification. It looks like the twenty-nine electoral votes of the state of New York will go to Mr. Engel, effectively making him the new president of the United States."

"Unbelievable," Hunt said, turning off the TV. He looked across the table and met Schlager's eyes. "I have to say, until this very moment, I didn't think it was going to happen."

A silent zigzag of light crossed the sky outside Orion Tower and disappeared below the jagged skyline of downtown. A few moments later, a low rumble muffled by the thick glass of the bulletproof window reverberated through the building.

"Helen was right," Schlager said, lowering his eyes and studying his drink. "I'm glad we listened to her idea."

"Did you know?"

"What?" Schlager looked up, his tone defensive. "That she threatened a small nation with a nuclear weapon and got away with some ungodly amount of money? Yeah, she told me the moment she met me. I can vividly remember. She said, 'Hey, name's Helen, and I got a billion dollars after blackmailing a country with a

86

nuclear missile.' I was delighted to hear that because, you know, I was looking for someone to hack the New York Stock Exchange at the time and I thought that was convenient. Pretty sure that's how it went."

"Hey," Hunt raised his hand, "I didn't mean it like that."

"I know. I'm sorry." Schlager exhaled and looked back at his old friend. "It's been a stressful week."

"I understand."

"There's something else."

"What?"

It looked as if the sky had opened up and a thick layer of water sloshed down the window surface, turning the city into a gray, out-of-focus photograph. Now and then, the wind swatted the water away, briefly returning the sharp corners of the downtown into view, only to morph into a shapeless smudge a moment later.

"Max, you can talk to me."

"Helen didn't return from Hong Kong with just the money," Schlager said, his fingers drumming a nervous rhythm on the glossy surface of the table. "She brought an AI."

"Okay." Hunt searched his friend's face, looking for the deeper meaning of what he had heard. "What kind of AI? Something we can use?"

"I think it's better if you see for yourself." Schlager stood up and moved the chair away. "It's one of those instances where a picture is worth a thousand words."

Hunt remained sitting, looking up at his friend.

"Come on. It's at Helen's."

"All right."

He got up, and they walked to the elevator, Schlager leading the way. As the door closed, he glanced at the wraparound window. The world disappeared in a gray ocean of nothingness.

Chen opened the door to her suite in a bathrobe, her hair wet. She held a toothbrush in one hand and by the looks of it was ready to call it a night.

"Hey," Schlager said, giving her a peck on the cheek. "Sorry we are showing up unannounced, but considering the circumstances, I think we should show him JC. Can we come in?"

"JC?" Hunt said. "Is it an acronym?"

"Come on in," Chen said, moving aside and letting them into the room. "And no, it's not an acronym. It's a name. He didn't tell you anything?"

"Nope."

"Ugh." She sighed. "You want a drink? I have some half-decent single malt."

"No," he blurted, but caught himself. "What the hell. Bust it out."

They took seats at the kitchen island and she poured three generous portions of Yamazaki. Hunt swirled the golden liquid in his tumbler. It smelled of vanilla and spice.

"JC is a combination of two names," she began. "Jupiter and Callisto."

By the time she finished the story, the bottle was half-empty and Hunt's head buzzed despite the hemodialysis mod doing its best to filter the alcohol out of his blood.

"What's your take on it, guys? Is she really conscious?"

"Yes," Schlager and Chen said in unison and then shared a nervous laugh.

"She is," Max said. "I spoke to her. She is fully aware of who she is. She can think in abstract terms. Contemplate life and death. Or life after death. No amount of programming can create something that is not sentient that would so convincingly present as such."

"I feel like this is one of those things where I must rely on your expertise because I don't think I qualify. But say you're right. Is she dangerous?"

He watched as Schlager and Chen exchanged a glance, but neither of them said anything in response.

"Well?"

"She might be," Chen finally said. "But we need her."

"If she's dangerous, then maybe we can erase her? Wait. Why do we need her?"

"You need her," Schlager said quietly without looking up.

A red warning appeared in Hunt's internal vision as his pulse accelerated. "You can't run the quants without her, can you?"

"Nope." Schlager finally looked up and met his eyes. "Nothing can. Not for the reviving process. I didn't want to bring it up to you before I was absolutely sure, but now I am. The procedure is too complex. When we tried it on a slice of Rachel's toe—"

"What?" He could tell his face was getting flushed even without paying attention to the red, pulsating alarm at the edge of his vision.

"Bad choice of words," Chen interrupted, putting her hand on his. "We took a tiny sample of skin off Rachel's big toe to test the machine."

"You didn't bring it up when you said you ran diagnostic tests."

"I know, and we probably should have. I'm sorry. The good news— well, the great news really—is that it looks like Steven did a phenomenal job freezing her. Especially considering the circumstances. He thinks the chances of full recovery are high. Please don't touch it with your other hand."

"Touch what?" His heart rate slowed down and as he looked down, he realized that the glass cracked under the pressure of his bionic fingers. Whatever was left of the Scotch was seeping through the crack and pooling on the quartz surface of the island. "I'm sorry."

"It's okay," she said, grabbing a small towel and scooping the glass.

"Anyway." Schlager chimed in, eager to change the subject. "Steven thinks the chances look good."

"He said that?"

"You know Steven," Chen said, wiping the counter and putting the pieces of the glass into a trash bin. "He's very careful. I think his actual words were *I'm being cautiously optimistic.* That's *holy shit, it's so gonna work* in Steven-speak. You want another drink?"

"No, thank you," he said. "But tell me about JC. We run some pretty complex algos for R&D and they sit on powerful hardware. I thought the hardware was the problem?"

"It's both. But since we brought the quant in, hardware is taken care of. But there's nothing powerful enough to run it for the actual procedure."

"We can't write it?"

"I don't know." Chen shrugged. "Maybe. Or maybe not. It could take years."

"Do you think she can do something malicious on purpose? Like an intentional mistake?"

"I don't think so."

"What do you think we should do, then?"

"We use her, but we box her in. Complete isolation from the outside world. Not just air-gapped, but build a cage where there's a vacuum between the box she's in and the outside world."

They sat in silence for a few moments, the rain hitting windows the only sound in the room.

"How quickly can we do it?"

"Three, maybe four weeks," Schlager said. "I'll take care of the cage."

"It's decided then." Hunt stood up and looked around the room. "Can I see her?"

They followed Chen into a small office and he watched as she engaged the Faraday cage to encase the room.

"Clever."

"It's worked so far." She shrugged.

He saw her lean in, open a desk drawer, and then flip a switch hidden in the false bottom. The black surface of the monitor blinked, and then a swirling gray that looked like clouds filled the screen. A small green LED lit up at the top of the screen as the video camera switched on.

"Where is she now?" Hunt asked, looking at the screen. "And how do you communicate with her?"

"This is her." Chen pointed at the clouds. "That's her representation of herself, I think. And you just talk."

"To this?" he asked, pointing at the swirling gray.

"Yes."

He stood there for a few moments, feeling foolish. Schlager and Chen were the smartest people he'd known his entire life, but looking at what looked like a regular screen saver, he couldn't bring himself to take what they said seriously. He remembered reading about simple bots passing the Turing test. That was decades ago. Surely new programs were sophisticated enough to pretend to be sentient. That didn't make them actually intelligent. But there was only one way to find out.

"Hello," he said.

"Hi, Jason," a pleasant voice responded from the surround speakers. "It's nice to meet the person in charge."

18

The tires screeched in protest as Connelly took the last turn in the underground garage of Orion Tower, going at the speed that would have horrified the superintendent. He slammed on the brakes and then turned the steering wheel hard to the right as the car drifted into the designated spot. Then he killed the engine, lowered his hands onto his knees and took a deep breath. He hadn't been this wound up since Sofia's death, and it was taking a toll.

He took another long breath and rubbed his face. Today, out of all days, he needed to be on top of his game.

He got out of the car, walked past a row of identical black SUVs, and entered the elevator. Once inside, he ignored the numbered buttons and pressed his thumb to a small biometric reading device. The elevator's doors closed with a chime and the metal box accelerated toward the observation deck of the tower.

"Mike," Hunt greeted him when the doors opened. Max Schlager and Helen Chen got up to greet him as well. The usually transparent wraparound window was now an impenetrable gray, and a long, interactive table was set up in the middle of the large room. Its mirror-like surface was still black.

"Anybody else joining us?" Connelly asked, coming to the table.

"Not today, no," Hunt said. "I think until we figure out the details, it's best to keep this to a minimum."

"Agreed."

"All right," Schlager offered. "Walk us through it."

Connelly walked toward the table and turned it on. Then he brought up a map on the screen, switching it into an aerial view.

"Thanks to Kowalsky, we know the location now and I've been using a recon drone over the past forty-eight hours to map out the area," he said and pointed at an unremarkable two-story building in the middle of a forest clearing. "This is where they keep the ballots."

The group gathered closer around the table to get a better view of what Connelly was describing.

"This is not your normal storage facility, as you can see. First, it's sitting in the middle of nowhere. And it also has these things." He waved his hand, zooming in on the building, and pointed at the four objects sitting in each corner of the flat roof. "These little guys that resemble grain storage silos are Phalanx CIWS systems."

"Phalanx systems? Are those miniguns?" Schlager said.

"Something like that. These are the same defense systems that are used on aircraft carriers. A six-barrel monster with a maximum firing range of over two miles. And there are four of them on this building."

"And they didn't shoot down your drone?"

"I used one of the new mini stealth drones. They have great optics —we never came closer than five miles."

"If it has four miniguns," Hunt said, "do you still think we can use Martin and a few support sentries to overwhelm them?"

"No. Those are only a part of the problem. You also have mortars sitting in dugouts here and here." He pointed at four dark spots in the forest around the building.

"Jesus."

"And," he zoomed in on one wall, "those are machine guns as well. Short of an army, there's no way to take this by force. With some luck, Martin could probably destroy the facility, but then what would be the point? If we overcome the defenses, we won't have enough time to sort through the entire building to find the evidence. I'm sure Engel will have a QRF on standby."

"What's a QRF?" Hunt asked.

"A quick reaction force," Connelly said. "A support unit that's available for a rapid deployment."

"It's a fortress," Helen said. "We got it. But I'm guessing you have an idea on how to break into it?"

"No," he said and smiled, looking at puzzled faces around the table. "Like I said, I don't think there's a way to get inside of this building. I couldn't come up with a plan, but as I was about to tell you that everything was lost, I remembered a story that Rick Porter, my instructor at the Camp, once told the recruits. His team was tasked with the extraction of a Taliban leader, they called him the Bull, from his stronghold in the Helmand Province. When they initially located him, they relayed the information and a drone strike had been ordered. But then somebody intercepted some chatter that there was an imminent attack on American soil. The analysts believed that the Bull might have some information on him that could give us clues on where the attack was going to take place."

"How did they do it?"

"They dropped a GBU-12 laser-guided bomb on the compound."

"I thought you said they didn't want to do that?"

"They didn't want to kill him or destroy any evidence that he might have had. They rigged the bomb not to explode. It hit the compound, injured a couple of guards in the front yard, and that was that."

"I think I know where this is going," Chen said.

"Right. The guys in the compound panicked. They knew their location was compromised and a drone dropped a bomb, intending to blow them to smithereens. For all they knew, the drone was going to come back in a matter of hours and finish the job. They packed the essentials and took off."

"Giving your friend's team the opportunity to ambush them."

"Right. They caught up with them that night, killed the guards, took the Bull captive, and got their hands on a trove of information that helped to stop the attack."

"I like this idea," Hunt said. "But how do you propose we apply this tactic here? And what if instead of moving the ballots Engel destroys them?"

"I don't think that would work. He needs to maintain at least a thin layer of legitimacy. Yes, the circumstances of the recount were suspicious, but he turned it to his advantage. That's why we're in this situation to begin with. He claims the ballots are the proof that he won fair and square and he even admitted an independent commission to examine them."

"Independent my ass," Hunt spat.

"We know it was anything but. However, that's what his state-controlled media is feeding to the public. He needs to maintain status quo until he can legally destroy them."

"He doesn't even need them for that long," Schlager said. "Give it a few more weeks, maybe a couple of months, and the public will have moved on. People are already losing interest."

"Right." Connelly tapped on the table, pointing at the lone road leading to the storage facility. "Before we discuss how we smoke them out, I'd like to mention that we have a slight advantage. We know where they would be going."

"You want to ambush them the moment they are outside of the range of those miniguns?"

"No. Engel's guys are as aware of this road's vulnerability as we are. They'd be on high alert. This is also too close to the facility and if they feel threatened, they'll retreat under the cover of mortar fire and Phalanx systems. But we have a piece of information they don't have. Rovinsky got his hands on the contingency plans. And there is a Plan B. There's another fortified storage facility near Langley in Virginia. Our best chance is to hit them somewhere in the middle of the transit. The initial adrenaline will wear off by then. They'll be tired and starting to relax."

"Do you have a particular place in mind?"

"Yes." Connelly swiped his palm over the glossy surface of the computer screen. "Here. It's a bridge over the Susquehanna River. Technically there are two bridges, but since they'll be going down I-95 South, they'll take this one. Millard E. Tydings Memorial Bridge. One way in and one way out. We can create a diversion, block the traffic, and hit them right on that bridge."

"All right." Hunt walked around the table to stand next to Connelly and looked at the aerial view of the narrow bridge. "Say your plan works. We get them on the bridge. We're able to overcome their defenses and capture the truck with the ballots. Then what?"

"We'll decouple the container from the truck and get two choppers in. One for air support and one to airlift the container away, hopefully before the reinforcements come in. It's a continuous deck truss bridge. There's no steel structure above it that would create issues for the birds. It's all wide open."

"That's great," Hunt said, still looking at the picture. "We got the ballots and got away with it. What do we do with them?"

"I have an idea," Connelly said. A hollow pang twisted his guts, and he took a deep breath, trying to push it away. "I used to know this woman, who worked for the *New York Gazette*."

"The *Gazette*? Guardian's mouthpiece?"

"It wasn't Guardian's anything, until they forced the sale of the paper."

"Oh." A shadow crossed Hunt's face. "Sofia McAllister. I remember now. I'm sorry. I did not connect the dots before."

"Thanks." Connelly collected himself. "There was a lot of pressure on the paper to get acquired. Sofia didn't know at the time from whom. Her boss, Brian Sorkin, abruptly resigned because he feared for his life and moved out of New York. He advised Sofia to do the same."

"I take it she didn't listen," Hunt said softly.

"No. But recently, I tracked him down and he's back in New York."

"Does he know?"

"Yes. The guy's been through hell himself. His family was killed in a traffic accident—as far as I know, unrelated to any of this. But regardless, he says he's full of guilt about how things worked out for

Sofia. He doesn't work for any news outfits at the moment, but he still has a lot of contacts. He could help us disseminate this and give it legitimacy. There are still small independent papers throughout the country that aren't bought by Engel and his ilk."

"All right." Hunt's bionic fingers rapped on the smooth surface of the computer glass. "Tell us how we get them to move the ballots."

19

The limo pulled up in front of the building, and Jason Hunt stepped out on the sidewalk. The boutique hotel was perched above a restaurant at the very end of the famed Wall Street, its stepped facade cascading toward the East River. The sun was still low, and Hunt screwed up his eyes as he glanced at the sparkling water.

"Mister Hunt?" A burly man with a crew cut stepped out of the hotel's double doors and headed toward him, only to be stopped by Connelly, who seemed to have materialized out of thin air between them.

"It's okay, Mike," he called out to Connelly and then turned to the man. "Can we come up?"

"Yes." If the man was displeased by Connelly's intervention, he didn't show it. "Mr. Price is ready to see you."

"Great."

The man opened the double doors and ushered them inside the art déco lobby. They crossed the marble floor without slowing down by reception and headed straight for the elevator. A few moments later, Jason stepped inside the suite as Connelly and Price's man stood guard on the outside without as much as glancing at each other.

"Mister Hunt." Darius Price put a paper he was reading down on a coffee table and got up from the chair to offer Jason a hand. He wore a pair of dark-gray slacks and a crisp white shirt that contrasted the deep black of his smooth, clean-shaven face. Even without wearing shoes, he stood at least an inch taller than Hunt. The man gestured to another chair facing him. "Take a seat. I trust you had no trouble finding the hotel?"

"Despite its great influence," Hunt said, shaking the man's hand and then taking a seat, "Wall Street is only six blocks long."

"Very true." Darius Price took a seat, crossed his legs, and rested his hands on his knee. "To what do I owe the pleasure? I have to say I'm a big fan of yours, Mr. Hunt. I've been following your work for quite some time. The technology your company produces is fascinating."

"Thank you." Hunt reclined in his seat and studied the man. In his internal vision, the outline of the man's body pulsated in green, signaling that he was relaxed and not a potential threat. "I wish I could spend more time working on that, but alas, I don't always have the time. I'd like to discuss with you the results of the election."

"There's not much to discuss, I'm afraid." The man chuckled and his foot clad in a black sock gently kicked the corner of the newspaper. "Didn't you hear? The election is over. I'm a private citizen now. Don't get me wrong, I'm disappointed, of course, but it's the nature of the game. Someone wins and someone loses."

"I'm here to tell you that you didn't lose the election," Hunt said, "and maybe if you—"

"Stop." Price held up his hand. "I appreciate the sentiment, I do. But there was an investigation and the independent commission determined that those votes were fraudulent."

"They weren't. And if you challenged—"

"Mister Hunt," Price interrupted him again. "Do you have any proof?"

"No, not yet."

"Well then." Price took a deep breath. "It doesn't even matter. At some point, one candidate has to throw in the towel and let those on the opposing sides to come together again for common good. For the sake of the nation. Let's face it, we are living in dark times. We have been, and I know you share the sentiment because I've listened to more than a couple of your speeches about the future of the human race. And I wish I could do more—that's why I decided to run—but it looks like it was not meant to be."

Hunt rubbed his chin with his bionic hand, his metallic fingers running against the short stubble of yesterday's shave.

"Is it true?" Price asked. "That you can actually feel with your artificial hand?"

"Yes." Jason opened his palm, closed it into a fist, and then opened it again. "Better than the hand I was born with."

"Amazing." Darius Price leaned forward, as if trying to see it better. "Your tech is bringing many amputees back to their normal lives. People with ET and Parkinson's. It's a noble quest."

"I might not have the proof that you won the presidency." Hunt steepled his fingers and looked Price in the eye. "Not yet. But I'd like to tell you a story that might put what you know into perspective. In return, I'd like only a couple of things. One, I'd like you to keep what you're about to hear to yourself and never share it with anyone else."

"And two?"

"I'd like you to consider postponing conceding the election for three days."

"I can promise you the first. You have my word. As for the second, it will depend on how compelling your story is."

"Fair enough." Jason stood up and walked across the suite to the window. The sun had climbed higher and the sparkles on the surface of the river were gone. He turned back to Darius. "My father, Andrew, worked for the CIA as a consultant for many years."

Price raised his eyebrows but said nothing.

"One day back in 2007," Hunt continued, "his handler asked him to come down to DC for a meeting. They met at a Ronald Reagan Airport parking lot, and the man told my dad about a vast conspiracy spanning across the entire globe. It was a tale fit for a movie—a secret alliance of corporate interests trying to take over the world. Buying their influence, killing people who stood in their way. They called themselves the cabal. According to my father's boss, their plan was entering the final stage. They were consolidating influence and were moving to override the last safeguards that were still keeping them in check."

"Sounds improbable," Price said.

"That's what my father thought. But his handler was adamant. He proposed to start an organization to counter the cabal. Something effective that could operate completely off the books. The man offered my father to head the new agency. It never had an official name, but between themselves they referred to it as the Unit. Unoriginal, I know."

"What happened?"

"It started well," Hunt said. "They partnered with the International Serious Crimes Directorate, ISCD for short, and landed a few serious blows to the alliance. But then my parents died."

"I'm sorry," Price offered. "I read it was a tragic accident—a gas leak."

"That's what I thought. But it was no accident. The cabal killed them. The head of the organization employed an assassin who was a master of making his hits look like accidents. The murder of my parents was one of them."

"I'm truly sorry."

Hunt glanced at the river again. There was surprisingly little traffic on the water. A tugboat was pushing an empty barge up the stream and a small yacht was bobbing in the shadow of the Brooklyn Bridge. He turned around and walked back to his chair.

"Do you know what happened after your father's death?"

"The Unit was decapitated. Political winds changed, and the people in charge disbanded it. Some of the personnel went to work undercover for the ISCD, some went back to active service duty. I didn't know any of that. I was young and grieved for the loss of my parents. My wife and I moved down to Florida, where I intended to stay."

"I see it didn't quite work out that way?"

"No." Jason looked at his hand again. "My wife got a job in New York, and I reluctantly moved. But that was only a part of my motivation. The other part was my friend stumbling over some email trail that for the first time made me think my parents' death wasn't an accident. Before I knew what was happening, I was on the collision course with the same people who went after my father."

"You took on the cabal?"

"Yes." Hunt looked Price in the eye. "I have *de facto* resurrected the Unit a few years ago. Remember the failed coup?"

"It's hard to forget."

"That happened because of the pressure we applied on the alliance. They accelerated the timetable and things didn't exactly work out the way they had hoped."

They sat quietly for a few moments as Hunt studied the man. The contours of Price's body glowed orange now. Hunt's internal system still didn't consider him a threat, but the man, despite his cool appearance that would have fooled most observers, was agitated.

"That's a fascinating story," Price finally said. "I don't know why you are telling me this, but knowing your reputation, I find it hard to believe the story isn't true. What I don't understand is what does it all have to do with me? And, more specifically, with the recount?"

"That's simple." Jason stood up and headed for the door. "The coup may have failed. Some people went to jail, but contrary to what had been fed to the general public, those people hadn't been in charge. They were figureheads. Puppets. The man who was at the head of the cabal was never caught and after the coup had failed, he decided it was time for the organization to come out from the shadows. The name of that man is Alexander Engel."

"You can't be serious. I wasn't sure what to make of your visit. My initial guess was that you'd invite me to work for Orion. The thought excited me and made me anxious at the same time. But then I thought that if it was about a job, you wouldn't come to me in person. You'd invite me in. This story of yours," Price paused, as if looking for the right words, "I don't know what to make of this."

"Three days, Darius." Hunt pulled on the handle and looked over his shoulder before exiting the room. "Just three days. That's all I ask."

20

"Thank you, gentlemen." Engel waved to the two Secret Service agents outside the door as he retreated into the room and turned to Victor Ye. "I have to say, I had some serious reservations even after agreeing with you. But your sentinels are top-notch. Yesterday, I watched the ones that your boys will deliver to the White House grounds and they look like they can bring some serious heat."

Victor nodded without saying a word. He was sitting in a plush, burgundy leather chair, his black hair uncharacteristically pulled back into a ponytail. Seeing Engel in good spirits put him in a foul mood.

"Something on your mind?" Engel kicked off his shoes, walked across the shag rug, and climbed into another chair. "They counted the votes. We are on the cusp of victory, but you rather look troubled. I'm sure Darius will make some noises, but it's a battle easily won."

"The greatest victory is that which requires no battle," Victor said, still without moving. "I say we should heed the wise man's words."

"Are you suggesting we should take care of him?"

"Absolutely not. At least not now. If you're planning on maintaining any pretense of legitimacy, he must live long enough to see you sworn in."

Engel looked Victor up and down, as if trying to decipher the meaning of his words. "I don't understand, then. That's what's happening, anyway."

"For now, yes." Victor reclined deeper in the chair and crossed his legs. A deep drone of a passing helicopter vibrated the window. "But I'd like to make sure that should things change, we have a plan."

"I see." Engel's fingers tapped a muted staccato on the soft leather. "It sounds like you have an idea already."

"I do. My sources tell me that Price had a visitor recently. None other than your friend Jason Hunt."

"So I heard."

"I'd say it's a reasonable assumption that Hunt and Price might work together to undermine your plan. I took the liberty of taking some steps to make sure even if they succeed somehow, which right now doesn't seem probable, we have some alternative options."

"Say you're right. If Price somehow overturns the results and gets into the White House, it'd be difficult to eliminate him. The best time to do that would be during his inauguration."

"Not here in DC." Victor stood up and walked to the window. H Street NW below was blocked by the blue police barricades as far as he could see. Apart from a small group of policemen, there were hardly any people at this hour. The lights of the White House were visible through the bare trees of Lafayette Square Park. He could see the roof of his black limo with a running engine parked next to the intersection. "Security here would be too tight. And eliminating Price is only a part of the issue. What I suggest is a two-prong attack. One in the real world and one in the digital realm. I have a talented team that could create a deepfake, which would be released at the same time."

"I don't follow. Where would you suggest we attack him if not during the inauguration?"

"Oh, I agree on the timing," Victor said, turning back to the other man. "The inauguration is the only public event he cannot skip, no matter what risks. But we'd need to force him to change the venue. We are used to seeing presidents being sworn in at the Capitol building, but it hasn't always been the case. George Washington took his oath up in New York. Price was born and raised in Manhattan. Maybe if we play the cards right, we could arrange he does it there as well."

"That's because New York was the capital of the United States at the time." Engel got up as well, went to the bar, and poured himself a glass of water. "Last time I checked, that is no longer the case. And since it's no longer a capital, to show this kind of favoritism to one state—regardless of the reason—would be politically impossible."

"Let me worry about that—"

"More importantly, though," Engel interrupted him, his voice rising. "This is a waste of time. I'm all for being cautious, but there's simply not enough time for Price to challenge the results now."

"The polling shows people aren't convinced—"

"Who gives a shit about polling," Engel interrupted him again, now visibly angry. "I have a million important things to take care of, and this isn't one of them. I'll tell you what. You want to take some precautionary steps, be my guest. But I don't want to be bothered with far-fetched scenarios."

"Fair enough." Victor turned back to the window in time to watch as a group of cops passed his limo. "I'll do what I can and won't bother you with details. I have some good news, however. We just took a shipment of new-gen tech. It arrived last night in New York. Daimyo is here and some other toys that I'm anxious to test in action. Some of it needs last-minute tuning, but it should be ready for a live presentation in the next few weeks. I think by the time you take office, everything will be fully operational."

"Good enough to take on Jason's pet?"

Victor shrugged without turning. "I think we'll find out sooner rather than later."

He left the room and nodded to the two men in black suits by the door as he headed for the elevator. He crossed the bright-lit lobby of the hotel and stepped out into the brisk morning. The cops who camped out next to his car had moved on, and for the moment Victor was the only person on the block. He stood there for a few seconds looking through the trees of Lafayette Square Park, and then made his way to the limo.

Squeezed into the side of the backseat next to Mute, his giant bodyguard, was a skinny man who jumped at the sound of the opening door. He wore a pair of dark-green flannel pajamas and was shivering despite the warmth of the car. His hands were bound behind his back and he nervously shuffled his bare feet as if trying and failing to find a comfortable position. A black hood was covering his head.

"Please," he said, his voice muffled by the hood. "I don't know—"

Mute struck him with an open hand across the face, and the man yelped from pain and stopped talking.

Victor looked through the window as the car sped up, heading east on H Street, turned on Fourteenth Street NW, and then merged onto I-395 South toward Richmond. Finally, he turned back to his captive.

"Matthew," he said in a soft voice, and the man sat straighter at the sound of his name. "I apologize for your experience, but we are going through some troublesome times in this country and sometimes it requires certain sacrifices. Do you understand?"

"Yes, sir." The man feverishly nodded his head a few times. "Whatever you say, sir."

"Good," Victor continued as the limo passed a sign for Reagan National Airport. "I have a simple task for you, which you might not even have to complete. But if the time comes, I'll be watching you and your family closely. Make sure not to disappoint."

"Whatever you need, sir."

"If..." Victor paused and leaned toward the hood covering the man's head. "If, for whatever reason, Darius Price becomes the new president of the United States, I want you to make sure he is inaugurated in New York City."

"But—" the man started, only to gurgle as Mute slapped him again.

"Let him speak."

"Nobody's been inaugurated outside of DC since—"

"Lyndon Johnson on Air Force One," Victor said. "I know. And it was under some rather unusual circumstances. But it's not important.

What is important, is that if Darius Price somehow won back the votes, he takes his oath in New York City. Price is a decent man, but like any man in politics, he has a big ego. Exploit that. George Washington took his oath in New York. For any politician to be compared to Washington is great praise. I'm sure Darius is no exception. Do we have a deal, Matthew?"

"And if I cannot deliver? I will do anything in my power to make that happen, but what if I can't?"

Victor remained silent for a few moments as the limo passed through the gate into the parking lot of the airport and came to a stop.

"That would be unfortunate," he said. "I'll tell you what. I'm about to get on a plane and you're going to take a nice long ride back to New York with my friend here in the backseat. You should be there in a few hours. What I want you to spend those hours thinking about is this: those who fail me end up in a dark place, where very skilled people slowly remove their skin over the course of a few days. Sometimes it takes weeks. Maybe, if I'm particularly unhappy, I'll have your family keep you company there as well. Are we clear, Matthew?"

"Yes, sir," the man said, hanging his head. A few quiet sobs escaped through the hood. "I will make sure it happens."

"Cheer up, Matthew," Victor said, opening the door and stepping out of the car. The sun was climbing higher, and the wind felt pleasantly warm on his face. "If everything works out well, we might not even need your services. Then you'll go on with your life and forget about this trip as if it was nothing but a bad dream."

21

Schlager took an exit off the highway and in a few minutes, the black minivan pulled into a parking lot of the warehouse. The long L-shaped building was in the past painted in white paint. But there was no evidence it happened any time recently, and the walls had a patchy, grime-covered appearance. A dark outline of a sign that read Westore could be seen above a single window.

"You've been here before?" Chen asked, getting out of the van and looking across the parking lot.

"Yeah." Schlager produced a chain with a key. "I know the way."

"Do we need to sign in or anything?"

"Nope," he said as they walked to the building. "It's one of those *don't ask, don't tell* kind of places. People store all kinds of stuff in here. As long as you pay the rent and don't bother anybody, nobody's asking questions."

The man sitting behind the desk glanced at them for only long enough to assess if they were going to be trouble. Satisfied with his observation, he went back to the game on a handheld computer.

"This way." Schlager pointed, as he led Chen down a long hallway with identical vertical gates on both sides. Faded four-digit numbers were painted at the bottom of each door. "Here it is."

The gate of the storage unit clanged as it rolled up, and Schlager glanced up and down the hallway to make sure nobody could see them. He ducked under the metal edge and waved Helen to follow him. Then he flipped the light switch and rolled the gate back down.

"Hello, beauties," he said, looking at the two five-foot-tall cubes covered by tarps, sitting on wood pallets in the center of the storage unit. He walked to one of them and pulled the tarp off, revealing neat rows of one-hundred-dollar bills wrapped in plastic. He ran his hand over the bundles, feeling the bumps where the bills' ends met. "This doesn't get old. Like a scene from a movie, isn't it?"

"Hopefully not the scene where the feds bust in and put us in handcuffs," Chen offered. She walked closer and tapped her finger on the plastic covering the banknotes. "Unreal. I've never seen this much cash in my life."

"It doesn't get any less spectacular, no matter how many times I see this. The first time Mike brought me here, I had a hard time keeping my jaw off the floor. You know what else I saw in the movies featuring so much cash?" Schlager jumped up and sat on top of the cube, opening his hands wide.

"Dream on," Chen said. "And you can wipe that smirk off your face. I'm not having sex with you on top of this."

"Oh well." Schlager hopped off the cube and shrugged. "It was worth a shot."

"Although," Chen said slowly and then burst out laughing, looking at Schlager's face. "Nope, still not doing it. You should've seen your face."

"That's not nice," he said, joining her. "Way to go, crushing a man's dreams. Anyway, do you have any ideas?"

"How to launder all this? No clue. You?"

"Well," he walked around the cube, tracing his fingers on top of the bills, "the hardest part is going to be depositing all this cash. Once it's in the system, we can shuffle it to a million places to create a plausible provenance of the money."

"Thank you, Captain Obvious," Chen said. "The question is—how do we deposit it into the banking system in the first place?"

"Fair enough. Maybe we shouldn't re-invent the wheel. Take a page out of the drug cartels' book. Buy high-value items—say, diamonds or precious metals—with cash. Then move them across the border and sell them there."

"We'd need a team."

"Yeah." He looked at the stacks of money. "We'd have to do it in multiple cities simultaneously. This is too much cash to spend in one place. Even in New York. At least we don't have to fly it commercial. I can put Kowalsky on it. But it's going to be hard even with a team if we want to keep it under the radar with relatively small amounts. Ideally under ten grand."

"We are talking about thousands of transactions. Tens of thousands, actually. That's going to take months. We should have done this a long time ago."

"We didn't need it a long time ago."

A phone vibrated in Schlager's pocket. He fished it out and, seeing the caller ID, put it on a speaker.

"Max?" Jason Hunt's voice echoed through the small space.

"Hey. I'm at the storage place here with Helen," he said, laying the phone down on top of the money pile. "Strategizing. Are you in a car? You sound like you're driving."

"We are. Let me give you a nice incentive," Hunt said. He paused as a sound of an angry blaring horn filled the room for a moment. "All our DOD contracts have been pulled. You were right, Helen. Engel is doing exactly what you said he would."

"Shit," Schlager said. "He's not even in the White House yet. How the hell is he doing this? Like, all contracts?"

"Yes. Effective immediately. No explanation, nothing. *Until further review*, the letter said. We'll sue, but it will not matter. Our accounts will run dry in three months and he'll be in the Oval Office by then. We won't get them back. Mike is taking me back to the tower now. I need to figure out what exactly we are working with."

"I don't want to sound pessimistic, but we won't be able to do this in three months," Chen said. "Or six. I just don't see how."

"I might be able to help," Connelly's voice said. "Though it might cost us a nice chunk."

"Go on."

"Awhile back, when I still worked undercover for Engel, I flew down to Bolivia. Engel was trying to strike a partnership with Diego Flores, the self-proclaimed Prince of Cocaine. At the time, Engel's drug side business was already in full swing but he was too dependent on the triads. He sent me down there with one of the corporate heads to get Flores as a new supplier for Guardian."

"How did that go?" Schlager said.

"Not very well. The problem was Flores wanted to become the sole supplier, and that was precisely what Guardian was trying to get away from. But to make matters worse, the guy I was with was an ass who had no idea how to negotiate and told Flores he was not interested in whatever the man was proposing."

"Ouch."

"Yeah. They put us in the rooms and before long, two ladies showed up pretending to be part of the hospitality package, only to try to kill us both."

"I take it they weren't successful." They heard Hunt chuckle.

"Not with me," Connelly said. "But the other guy wasn't so lucky. I barely made it out of there and while doing this, totaled Flores's favorite Bentley. Let's just say the guy probably doesn't have a lot of fond memories."

"What would you suggest?"

"I can fly down there and try to convince him to clean our pile for us."

"That is a bad idea," Schlager said. "He'll kill you at first sight."

"Maybe," Connelly said. "But maybe not. He wasn't happy about his beloved Bentley, I'm sure. But he hates Engel's guts. He might take this as an opportunity to stick it to him. And he's a businessman first; I'm sure he'll see this as a big opportunity and try to charge us an arm and a leg."

"It's your arms and legs I'm concerned with," Hunt said.

"Wait," Schlager said and laughed. "Did you say you wrecked a Bentley?"

"Yeah."

"I remembered something," he said, laughing harder and doing his best to ignore Helen's quizzical look. "Didn't Engel buy a rare Bentley few years back? I don't remember the name. It was Blue Train or something. They made only a handful, and he got one?"

"Now you're speaking my language, Max," Connelly said.

"I like it," Chen said. "We steal Engel's car and give it to Flores to stick it to Engel. This is poetic."

"Christ," Hunt said. "I guess we're stealing Engel's car."

22

"Are you sure about this?" The helicopter pilot craned his neck to look at her. "It's dark as hell and if your helmet malfunctions, you'll be flying blind."

The bird's blades were cutting cold air at five thousand feet above the island. Jill Cooper looked over the edge—the pilot was being dramatic, but not by much. Thick clouds were covering most of Manhattan in uneven patches, with lights shining in between the gaps. Farther north, the large rectangle of Central Park loomed as dark as an ancient forest.

Getting a 3D image of Engel's eye turned out to be easier than she had thought. There were a few places throughout Guardian regularly visited by Engel that had a retina scan. Soon she found the weakest spot—a private elevator in the Sherry-Netherland hotel that would carry Engel to his penthouse. After that, it was just a matter of being patient. At the first opportunity, she clipped a skimmer—a thin, transparent rectangle—to the retina scanner and then, a week later, retrieved it filled to the brim with multiple scans of her target.

What turned out to be an unexpectedly difficult part of her plan was finding anyone willing to fly a helicopter. Doing it at night for a sole passenger with a wing suit and an apparent death wish seemed to be not high on the to-do list for most people with access to aircraft. It was even harder to convince the pilot to keep the flight off the official record. It wasn't clear if it was a brown paper bag with a few stacks of hundred dollar bills or the visible pistol tucked in her side holster that did the trick, but it didn't matter. She was here now.

"I'll be fine." She pushed a button on the palm of her glove a few times, switching between different screen modes projected on the inside of her slick black helmet. A bright path seemingly hovering in the air stretched between the helicopter and the building at the southeast corner of Central Park—her final destination. "Thanks for the ride."

She grabbed the side of the door and pushed herself off into the black void. The drop was immediate and terrifying. Cooper spread her arms and legs out, stretching the ripstop nylon surface of the suit, but it was a few seconds before she was traveling fast enough for the suit to generate lift. She was gliding now, but as she risked a quick glance up, the shining dotted line showing her optimal path to the building was hovering high above her actual path. She clicked through the view images on her screen—the wind was working in her favor, but it wasn't strong enough to carry her to where she needed to be. At this rate, she was going to smash into the side of the building. Cooper had a decision to make.

Unlike most wingsuit jumpers, she wasn't carrying a parachute on her back for the last stage of the flight. Nestled between her shoulder blades sat two slim, matte-black cylinders that contained hydrogen peroxide and pressurized nitrogen. When activated, the jetpack would generate a thousand-horsepower grunt that would balance her on the tip of a stream eight-hundred degree centigrade hot. The problem was, to keep it light, there was only enough fuel for sixty seconds of continuous flight, just long enough to slow her down first for the descend on top of the building, and then for the shorter flight to Central Park when her mission was done. But the current trajectory shown in bright-red dots terminated at the forty-something floor of the fifty-story building, which didn't leave her with a lot of options.

Cooper moved her limbs to flare the suit and slow down her

descent, and pushed the button, firing up the thrusters. The roar of the jet engines drowned out the rush of the wind for a few moments and the arc of her fall flattened and then went up, overshooting the optimal path to the landing spot. She hit the button again, turning off the engines.

Now Cooper could see the gray rectangle of the roof with no enhancements. She swerved, trying to align herself along the longer side of the building. The middle of the roof was a jumbled mess of air vents, water tanks, and a sprawling web of pipes. But on either long edge, there was a smooth surface of polished concrete about thirty feet wide. It was going to have to be her runway.

She flipped in the air, flaring the suit as much as she could to slow down, and powered the thrusters again. The gray mass of the building rushed toward her, and then she was tumbling down the hard surface. Cooper flipped again and ungracefully skidded the last few yards on her buttocks, coming to a stop just a few feet away from the western edge of the roof.

"This could've been worse," Cooper groaned as she got up and walked a few steps to look over the edge. The street below, separated by the black void of the night, seemed impossibly far. She looked at the fuel indicator in the lower left corner of her visor. Thirty-two percent. "Crap. It'll have to do."

She took off her gear and sprinted toward the ventilator shaft. A hand-sized crawler droid went in first, attaching itself to the security system cables and splicing surveillance of the office into an endless loop. Cooper's lips curled into a smirk—the droid was Guardian's tech she had used many times against their competitors.

A minute later, she was dangling on the cable under the ceiling of Engel's main office, ready to flee at the first sign of trouble. The office stayed quiet.

Cooper disengaged the carabiner and dropped to the floor. Then she slid behind the massive mahogany desk and pulled out two thumb-sized optical slides: one containing Engel's fingerprint and the other the man's retina scan. She held her breath as the computer processed the images. After what seemed like an eternity, the machine beeped and powered up with a soft whoosh, and Cooper plugged in the external hard drive.

There was no time to browse Engel's documents here. She'd have to figure it out once she was in a safe location. As the progress bar ran across the small pop-up window on the screen, Cooper kept glancing at the strip of light under the massive door. At last, the screen blinked, and the window disappeared.

She powered down the computer and climbed back out through the ventilation shaft, replacing the gate back to its place and retracing her steps back to the roof. Then, she recalled the crawler, and strapped back into the jetpack. Her next destination was Sheep Meadow, a fifteen-acre sprawling meadow between West Sixty-Sixth and Sixty-Ninth Street.

Her flight computer estimated a twenty-four hundred feet distance.

She sighed. There was no way to make that flight without propulsion. Cooper's suit gave a four-to-one glide ratio, meaning that for each foot dropped, she would gain four feet. But that ratio would only work when she was getting a full lift from the suit. Starting at the height of seven hundred feet, that didn't leave a lot of room.

Cooper walked around the building's perimeter to get to the northern side and walked back, giving herself a small path. It was going to be close.

"Here goes nothing," she said, and broke into a hard run. She leaped off the side of the building, activating the engine at the same time. It roared, giving her a hard push as she streaked across Grand Army Plaza and then over the black surface of the Pond. The path in her visor pulsated amber—she was losing altitude too fast. She swerved, doing her best to ride the light breeze. Another red alert popped on the inside of her helmet. Fuel at ten percent.

Cooper shut off the engine as she zoomed over Center Drive and shot across the trees separating her from the relative safety of Sheep Meadow.

"Ah shit." She flipped feet-first and put the thrusters into overdrive as she crashed through the top of the trees, barely missed the fence separating the baseball diamond from the sidewalk, and crash-landed into the wet sand. Cooper rolled a few times before coming to a full stop and then stayed on the ground, motionless, assessing damage.

"I'm getting too old for this shit," she said, looking up into the dark sky.

Nothing seemed to have been broken, and she gingerly picked herself up, wincing from the pain in her back, unzipped the wingsuit, and removed her jetpack.

She looked around. The park was quiet. If anyone had witnessed her dramatic landing, they were not eager to investigate. It suited her fine. Cooper folded her suit and jetpack into what reasonably resembled a medium-sized suitcase and headed toward the road. She was itching to see the contents of Engel's hard drive.

23

"I know you're not supposed to speak badly about the dead," Kowalsky said, looking at the storage space. "But what in the actual hell?"

"What's wrong?" Watkins asked.

"What do you mean, what's wrong? This." Kowalsky stuck his finger and pointed at the clutter. "When a dying man tells me, *everything is there* and points me toward his journal, I expect it to have, you know, *everything*. Not to send me on a wild-goose chase, deciphering coded texts and rummaging through a pile of junk."

It didn't take long for Chuck and his partner to crack the simple Caesar cipher. All they needed to do was to take one word from the text and start shifting letters to the same number of positions until the result made sense. First, they would shift letters by one, then by two, and kept going. They didn't have to go far—the key was number seven: letter *A* became *H*, letter *B* became *I*, and so on. But the text didn't give Kowalsky what he had been looking for. If anything, it created more questions than answers.

The text was divided into two parts. The first, bigger part had a fairly detailed description of the factory. There were two main buildings. One of them Nikko cryptically called "the energy building," and the other "the assembly shop." The site was also surrounded by a cluster of small warehouses and support facilities, and it had its own power plant. Kowalsky recalled from the journal that the place extensively used solar power as well. That and the fact that Nikko's notes mentioned a specialized system that helped to keep the sand away was in itself a clue.

Considering that Nikko fled through the port in Morocco, it stood to reason that the factory was hidden somewhere in northern Africa, and placing it in a desert made sense. The Sahara was the logical choice. The only problem was the Sahara was the world's largest desert that covered *most* of northern Africa. Without knowing where to look, finding something hidden in the area almost as big as the entire United States would be impossible. Even assuming that Nikko didn't travel too far before he got to Tangier, it left too much territory to cover.

The second, smaller part of the text contained an address for a storage unit in the industrial part of Brooklyn and the code for the combination lock. Irritated, but still hopeful, Kowalsky, with Latham in tow, drove to the address the next day first thing in the morning and opened the storage unit. To their dismay, the small place was filled to the brim with a random collection of books, documents, trinkets, housewares, toys, and other knickknacks. A few posters and signs hung on the wall, giving the place the feel of a college dorm room.

"I don't think this is his stuff," Kowalsky said, looking around the small cubic space. "Look at all these things. It looks like somebody robbed a flea market."

"But the code worked," Latham protested. "Who else can this belong to?"

"I don't know." Kowalsky shrugged. "Maybe somebody asked him to look after this. The guy hasn't lived in New York six months and came here with just clothes on his back. There's no way he'd accumulated this much junk in such a short time."

"What do we do?"

"The only thing we can do." He sighed. "Methodically comb through this pile until we find something."

"All right." Latham walked into the center of the room and looked around. "Any idea on how to sort this?"

"Start with housewares and all the little things," Chuck said and pointed his chin at the few boxes in the corner that had papers sticking out of them. "I'll go through the documents first, see if anything shakes out."

They set to work. While Watkins was doing his best to find some order in the number of seemingly unrelated items, Chuck got acquainted with the contents of the boxes.

The work didn't bother him. It wasn't the first time he had to go through a pile of junk, looking for the proverbial needle in a haystack. If anything, leafing through the pages of old family albums, casserole recipes, and teenage love letters was not much of a chore. He had to dig through much less pleasant collections of items early in his career as a cop.

After two hours, they sorted through the entire contents of the storage space, which was now neatly arranged on the floor in a few long lines, but found nothing of value.

Kowalsky took a wooden stool from the corner, put it in the middle of the room, and sat down on it, looking at the rows of items like a general inspecting his troops.

"Now what?" Watkins said. "Looks like a dead end to me."

"Perhaps," Chuck said as his eyes scanned the storage space one more time. He felt his lips stretching into a smile. "Perhaps not."

"No?" Watkins turned around on his heels. "Did I miss something?"

"What did I tell you when we came here?"

"That you don't like chasing wild geese? I don't know, I don't walk around writing down everything you have to say."

"I said that if the man tells me I can find *everything*, then that's what I should be able to find."

"Still don't get it."

"There." Kowalsky pointed to the wall. Between the poster of a punk-rock band and a framed picture of a vintage motorcycle hung a small rectangular sign. It was a pink window plaque from a lingerie shop, with a naked woman holding a bundle of strategically placed shopping bags. On the right side of the woman, it said 50-70% OFF in bold, black letters. On the left, in the same font, the message read EVERYTHING MUST GO. "You get it, Latham? Everything must go."

"No way."

He got up from the stool, walked to the wall, and took off the sign. Then he slowly turned it around, showing his partner the back side of the plaque. A small USB drive was secured to the corner with duct tape. "Jackpot."

24

The two vehicles were parked across the street from the massive garage that straddled the entire block between Edward L. Grant Highway and Cromwell Avenue. The U-shaped three-story building housed the bulk of Engel's prized car collection, including the Gurney Nutting Speed Six coupe, a 1930 Bentley commonly known as the Blue Train Bentley.

Helen and Max drove a minivan to the location first, taking their spot right after midnight. An hour later, Connelly brought in the semi-trailer and squeezed it in at the hydrant behind them and shut off the lights. Martin, who couldn't fit in the cabin, stayed in the container box.

"The last crew is leaving now. There are four guys. I can see them heading for their cars in the employee lot. Two of them are getting in one car. You should see three cars coming out." Chen's voice sounded in Connelly's earpiece. "There's still going to be one guard on the first floor, but the rest is empty. Just alarms."

"Sounds good," he replied. "Keep the channel open."

He slid lower in the driver's seat to make sure his silhouette wouldn't be spotted by chance. A minute later, the garage door, wide enough to let through three cars abreast, slid open, offering a view of the rows of vintage cars.

A bright-red Ferrari Enzo came out first, followed by a black Audi RS 6 Avant and a white Honda NSX-R. The street for a moment sounded like a racetrack and then the cars sped away, roaring through the neighborhood.

"I'm sure the neighbors love them," Schlager said on the radio. "How much longer should we sit here, Mike?"

"Let's give them ten minutes. After that, it's your show. Are you sure we'll be able to start it?"

"We are," Helen said. "There's a wall with keys in the guard's office, and all cars are fully loaded and operational. I skimmed the video recordings from the security cameras. They take them for small drives now and then, including the Bentley."

"All right then, let's wait. By the way," Schlager said. "It's fantastic."

"What is?"

"The story behind the car."

"I did not know there was a story," Connelly said.

"You've never seen the painting by Terence Cuneo?"

"No," Connelly sighed, "I don't even know who he is. If there was an art class between calisthenics and the demolition class, I must have missed it."

"He was a prolific English painter," Schlager said. "Painted all kinds of things, but most people know him for his pictures of engineering projects, especially the railway. And at some point, he started adding a small mouse to all his paintings, sometimes difficult to find. Some people enjoy looking for them in his works. Anyway, there was a famous painting of a neck-to-neck race between a Bentley and a train."

"Nope, haven't seen it, but go on."

"There was an overnight express train that shuttled between Calais in the northern France and the resorts along the Cote d'Azur. The train was called *Le Train Bleu*. A lot of Brits used that train, most of them wealthy, and some car manufacturers started racing the train and then if they beat it, use it for ads."

"I take it this car won the race?"

"Legend has it that Bentley didn't want to do it the way everybody else did. They wanted to prove, once and for all, that there was no competition worthy of the manufacturer. Instead of racing the train along the same route, they would start at Cannes and make it all the way to London before the train would arrive in Calais."

"How would it get across the Channel?" Helen asked.

"A ferry. Which took over an hour to get there, putting them at a disadvantage from the start. And there was another almost eighty miles to drive from the port to London. They got a flat tire, but they made it to London on a spare right before the train pulled into Calais."

"Nice."

"Yeah." Schlager laughed. "The French got pissed and fined the company for racing on public roads and even banned it from the next year's auto show in Paris."

"Now I feel good about stealing it from Engel," Connelly said, "but I guess I'll feel bad about delivering it to Flores. That guy doesn't deserve it. All right, people, let's do it."

"Helen," Schlager said. "Do your magic."

Connelly could hear keyboard clicking as he watched the garage door, waiting for it to open. A minute passed and then another.

"What's going on?"

"Not sure," Chen said. "I overrode the system, but the gate doesn't respond and I can't see why."

"Something is happening," Schlager said. "The guard stood up and is staring into the monitor. Something's wrong."

Connelly opened the door, jumped off to the sidewalk and jogged across the street, keeping behind the cars parked on the other side of the street.

"The guard is definitely onto something," Schlager said again. "He's up and out of the office and going for the garage door. We are missing something."

Connelly pulled one earpiece out and listened. There was a grinding sound coming from the building across the street. "Shit. You are opening the door, but something must be blocking it, because I can hear the motor straining and that's probably what the guard is hearing too."

"He's by the door now and is placing a call. And now he's running back to the office. I think the op is about to be blown."

Another sound caught Connelly's attention and as he turned, he saw Martin climbing out of the back of the trailer. "Where are you going? Go back in the truck."

The cyborg ignored him and headed for the garage, his heavy metallic steps loudly echoing through the empty street. Two flashes, one split second after the other, came out of his shoulder weapons slots and two giant holes appeared at each lower corner of the gate. A moment later, it screeched as the mechanism pulled whatever was left of the door up, opening the entrance to the garage. Martin turned around, moved his shoulders up and down, and walked back to the trailer at the same measured speed.

"Did he just…shrug?" Schlager's voice came through Connelly's earpiece. "Holy shit. I'm pretty sure he shrugged."

"There were deadbolts holding the door," Chen said.

"Let's go," Connelly barked. "We don't have all day. Max, go get the keys. I'll take care of the guard."

He ran across the street and positioned himself by the corner of the entrance, its scorched concrete still warm after Martin's blast.

"Don't shoot and you won't get harmed," he yelled as he moved into the garage, swinging a .50 caliber rubber bullet Walther T4E revolver. Two shots rang out from the garage, barely missing his head. Connelly rolled on the ground and moved behind the rear tires of a sky-blue Shelby Cobra 427 Roadster. "Stop shooting, I said."

Another shot dinged the floor a few inches away from the tire, sending sparks in all directions. Connelly swung out of his shelter and shot the guard in his stomach before he could pull the trigger again. The man grunted in pain and collapsed to the floor.

Connelly ran to him, keeping him in his sights, and kicked the Glock out of the guard's hand. Then he placed him in the cuffs from the guard's own utility belt. "All clear."

"Is he okay?" Schlager ran past him, heading for the office.

"He's fine," Connelly said, propping the man up and sitting him against the wall. "I'm fine too, thank you for asking."

He heard a revving engine and a moment later, a dark-green coupe with slick helmet wings rolled into his view, a pair of large round Zeiss headlamps illuminating the road ahead of it. Schlager, his mouth open in an ear-to-ear smile, waved to him from behind the wheel.

"So much for *Le Bleu*," Connelly said to himself, looking at the car. "It's green."

"Isn't it a beaut, though?"

"Roll it." He stepped aside, letting Schlager through. "We have to get it out before Engel's boys return."

He jogged behind the car as it drove out of the garage and then watched it roll up the ramp that Martin had lowered.

"Can we keep it?" Schlager said, cracking the door open and looking up at him. "It's gorgeous."

"No, and make sure it's secured to the floor, so it doesn't slide into Mr. Inconspicuous here," Connelly said, nodding at Martin.

"Can I sit in it while we are driving it to the plane?"

"No."

"Please?"

"Get out." Connelly laughed, patting him on the shoulder and heading for the cabin of the truck. "Pull up the ramp and lock the door. We have to go. But when Engel is no longer around, I'll bring it back to you, I promise."

25

"Who the hell are these guys?" The radio crackled into Connelly's ear. Another explosion shook the building. The three-story base of covert operations for Orion that personnel christened Langley was under another attack. "We haven't even moved in yet. I've never seen anything so brazen."

Connelly ran down the long hallway, trying to stay away from the windows. The thick bulletproof glass was holding up against small arms fire, but judging by the sounds, small arms weren't the only things hitting the building.

"Meyers, sitrep," he barked into the mic as he reached the stairwell and bounded up the stairs, skipping two steps at a time.

"Two teams. One APC is hitting us from the north. And what looks like a dozen fighters on foot are laying cover on the eastern entrance. One more thing."

"What is it?"

"They are all wearing Black Arrow uniforms. I can see the same markings on the APC, too."

"Wait, what? You've got to be shitting me. Hang in there. I'm going to the roof. I have a few toys up there."

Connelly reached the top of the stairs, climbed the ladder terminating at the ceiling, and slammed his palm into a biometric reader. Steel blades rotated out, revealing an opening to the roof, and he climbed out, keeping his head down. The two security domes on the roof stored some of the heavy equipment Connelly had saved, and the one on the farther side had an eight-point-four cm Carl Gustaf recoilless rifle. Its armor-piercing rounds could level the field against the armored personnel carrier.

He was halfway across the roof when the shooting stopped.

"Hey boss?"

"What's happening, Meyers?" Connelly headed for the concrete barrier and risked a glance outside. The armored vehicle was heading away from the building and a few seconds later, disappeared behind the trees.

"They are retreating," the voice said into his earpiece. "Unclear why."

"I can see that." Connelly stood up and looked at the parking lot in front of the eastern entrance. There was no sign of enemy combatants there either.

"I don't hear any chatter on any frequencies either. They all went silent. Total blackout."

"It doesn't make any sense," Connelly said, looking around the perimeter and still not seeing any movement. "Unless—shit."

"Boss?"

"Everybody down, now," he yelled, switching his radio channel to general broadcast, and sprinted back to the roof access door. "Incoming."

He saw a silver streak across the sky in his peripheral vision and then a giant hand picked him up, threw him across the roof, and planted him face first into the barrier on the other side of the building.

The power of the impact knocked the wind out of his lungs. Connelly sat up and spat blood as the world around him dimmed. He blinked hard a few times and the colors gradually returned to his vision. Something creaked underneath and the ground beneath him shifted, sending Connelly sliding back across the roof. He spread his arms wide, looking for something to grab onto, but his fingernails only scraped on rough concrete without slowing him down. He slammed into the barrier, bending his knees to lessen the impact when the roof stopped sliding.

"You okay, chief?"

"Peachy," he said. It came out hoarse. "How's everyone else?"

"Still assessing. Are you still on the roof?"

"Yep."

"Can you get down?"

Connelly looked up. From the place where he was sitting, it looked like a part of the roof was perched at almost a forty-five-degree angle. "I don't know, but I'll give it a shot. Have you called the tower?"

"Yes sir," the man said. "Two birds are already inbound and there's a ground team on the way."

"Good. Get everybody out as soon as you're able. The building is unstable and I have no idea how much longer it'll keep on standing."

"Roger."

Connelly shifted his weight without making sudden moves. It didn't seem to upset the balance of the slab. The top of the plate, where it buckled after the explosion, was cracked and the gap looked wide and rough enough for him to grab on to. He planted his feet into the barrier and catapulted himself, running up the tilted block. As his feet started to lose grip with the surface, he pushed harder, jumping and stretching out his arms as far as he could. The tips of his fingers gripped the rough edge, sharp rocks painfully digging into his skin.

The slab shifted.

"Meyers."

"Yeah, boss."

"Make sure nobody's standing outside on the north side of the building. Some big chunks of concrete are about to go down."

"Are you okay, boss?"

"I don't know yet." Connelly pulled himself up as the slab moved faster under his feet. Then, as soon as his right foot made contact with the top of the rugged edge, he jumped.

A large chunk of the roof disappeared from under his feet as

Connelly seemed to hang in the air for a moment before falling into an office space below. He fell on top of an empty workstation, crashing through plastic walls of an office cubicle and knocking monitors to the ground.

"Boss," Meyers's voice came through, "everyone is accounted for. We are outside in the parking lot. The birds will be here in two minutes. Looks like we dodged a bullet on this one."

"More like a missile," Connelly quipped, standing up and assessing the damage. "I'll be out in a moment."

By the time he made it to the parking lot, the two helicopters sat in front of the building and a convoy of four Suburbans was blocking the entrance. A small group of office workers huddled around a medic van with Orion's markings. One man was on a stretcher but the rest seemed to have gotten away with scrapes and bruises. Among the newcomers, Connelly, to his dismay, recognized the tall figure of Jason Hunt heading his way.

"You shouldn't have come," he said, shaking the man's hand.

"Are you okay?"

"Never better." Connelly looked back at the building. The missile had hit the east side of the complex just above the first floor. Most of the east wing was missing and large cracks snaked their way through the entire facade. "I can't say the same about the base, though. By the looks of it, we might have to tear it down."

"We have bigger problems than one building," Hunt said. "Let's step away."

"What's going on?" Connelly asked when they were out of everybody's earshot.

"There are two developments that are newsworthy today," Hunt continued. "Engel appeared on TV earlier today and called for prosecution of Darius Price. It's unclear if there's a will in the Department of Justice to do that, but Engel seems to be hell-bent on punishing his presidential rival."

"Why?"

"I think part of it is about kicking his opponent while he's down.

Revenge. But Engel does nothing without a long-term goal. I think the bigger reason is that he wants to send a message."

"As in, *don't screw with me or else?*"

"Exactly."

"What was the other news?" Connelly asked.

"There will be a disbandment of the US armed forces."

"Say what?"

"POTUS himself announced they are laying the groundwork. Something about the most peaceful time in our civilization's history nonsense. Won't fully happen until next spring."

"That's when Engel will be in the White House."

"Right."

"And what will happen to everybody in the service?"

"I'm glad you asked. There's a lot of speculation in the media, but Rovinsky is telling me there's a brilliant plan for that as well. It will be contracted out by a few corporate outfits to, and I quote, 'preserve the technology and maintain order.'"

"What corporate outfits?" Connelly said, tasting bile in his mouth.

"There are four or five names. But Black Arrow is at the top of the list."

"This," Connelly made a sweeping gesture, "was Black Arrow."

"I know." Hunt craned his neck to look at the top of the building. "They are loyal to Engel and company. And privatizing the armed forces under their umbrella solves a giant problem. Engel wouldn't want to have over a million combat-ready individuals pissed off at the government and out of work. What will happen is the opposite. He'll be seen as the savior who will swoop in and save everybody's jobs from the incompetence of the previous administration. Gives people who thought they are about to lose their jobs a secure future and better pay."

"Subsidized by the US government, I take it?" Mike said.

"Of course. Nobody else has that kind of money. It's genius really —he created a fake issue out of thin air and immediately offered a solution. The army isn't being disbanded, Mike. It's effectively being converted for his personal use. Once that happens, it's game over."

26

A simple upright headstone with a concrete base marked the grave. When Alexander Engel first saw the design, he didn't think it appropriate. Had he had any say in it, he would have done it differently for his late father's final resting place. But now, looking at the clean, straight lines of the honed marble that sat at the edge of the lot of Trinity Church cemetery, the sparks of Hudson River glimmering on its surface, it looked as if it was in the right place. It belonged.

"It is very serene here," he heard Susan say. She wore a smart black pantsuit under a three-quarter cashmere coat, and her hair was tied back in a ponytail instead of her usual layered look. "He picked a great place."

"He did," Engel said. "You can't be buried here anymore. You can offer a billion dollars and no one will take it. It doesn't matter how much money you have or who you know, there are simply no more spots."

"How did he do it?"

"Foresight, as always." Engel laughed. "He was good at it. On many levels, personal and business. I've never told anyone, but it was his idea to move into weapons manufacturing covertly at first. When

Guardian officially entered the arms race, we'd already had a massive head start. But as for this place… He reserved this plot before I was born. I don't know if it's true, but legend has it he had spent half of his net worth at the time to buy this spot. I asked him a couple of times, but he would only smirk and stay quiet."

"Sounds very much like him." She smiled. "And he's in good company here. Congressmen, mayors, entrepreneurs, dignitaries. A proper company."

"Yes."

"Have you…" She trailed off. "Forgive me if I cross the line, reserved a place for yourself?"

"No." Engel looked around, reading engravings on stones nearby. "Partly in defiance. It's stupid, but a lot of things that I did or didn't do in my life were to show him I wasn't just following in his footsteps. I wanted to be my own man. Forge my own destiny."

"You *are* your own man," she said, touching his forearm.

"I thought about it," he said. "You know who changed my mind?"

She arched her eyebrow, without saying a word.

"Jason Hunt."

"Oh."

"I watched him giving that speech, when Orion went public. It made me furious. I remember pacing back and front of the TV, yelling and cursing and making promises to destroy the little shit who stole from me. But I had to admit he knew how to sell. The way he talked. The way he showed off his bionic arm at the end."

"I remember." She removed her hand from his arm. "It was an excellent speech."

"And the bit about immortality didn't sound like a schtick. It was sincere. And that's when I thought—what if he's right? What if it's possible? Wouldn't anyone want to do that? Wouldn't you?"

"I don't know," she said. "It depends."

"On what?"

"I'm sure you're aware that not everybody is in the same situation as you are. For someone who does manual labor, the prospect of doing it forever might not be as appealing as you think."

"I guess that's true." He turned to face her. "You've been working for us for a long time."

"Since college. My first and only real job. I was fortunate."

"How long has it been?"

"I'd rather not say." She laughed. "My job might be to make sure you remember the important things, but I can live with you not remembering my age."

"Ah." He smiled. "I see. I remember your birthdays, though."

"You are always thoughtful."

He studied her face for a moment. "Can I ask you something, Susan?"

"Of course. Anything."

"A few days ago, something occurred to me. I don't recall what it was, but you did something that I wanted without me telling you it had to be done. And I thought you must know me better than anyone."

"You flatter me." Her lips smiled but her eyes didn't. He could tell she wasn't sure if she liked where he was going.

"Not at all. Over the years," he smiled, "though I won't mention how many, you've witnessed my every aspiration, every victory, and every defeat."

"So have many."

"True. But you've also witnessed my every desire, every sin, every atrocity. Haven't you, Susan?"

She stayed silent, her smile disappearing, but her eyes never leaving his.

"Do you think I'm a monster, Susan? Do you think I'm evil? Jason Hunt would want you to."

"Do *you* think you are? I think it's more important than whatever opinion I might have about you, Alex."

"You didn't answer my question."

"No," she said quietly. "I don't believe you are. You've made some hard choices, but you can't be judged by the same standards as regular people. When presidents and generals give orders that cause death and destruction, we don't consider them monsters as long as their overall goal is noble. Quite the opposite. If they achieve success, we call them heroes. Even though it might come at the cost of many lives."

"I guess that's true. History is written by the victors. Walk with me." He stuffed his hands deep into his pockets and started to walk. "You've been loyal to me, Susan. In fact, after his death, you're the only person left who I can talk to without having to watch what I say. I'd like to return the favor."

She hooked her arm through his as they walked, the muted sounds of the city getting louder as they headed toward the parking lot. The bodyguards who had given them space while they had stood by the burial site now drew closer, forming a protective perimeter.

"I owe you," he continued.

"You don't owe me anything—"

"Listen," he interrupted her. "You can make your own decision later. We are on the precipice of something that has never happened before. I've been putting things in motion for a long time, but now, when the ship is finally about to sail, I realized something."

"What is it, Alex?"

"There'll be no turning back, Susan. There are certain decisions you can't come back from. It's like unleashing a nuclear weapon. Once you've hit that button, you can't undo it. You either emerge victorious or perish in a nuclear holocaust."

They approached the limo. The bodyguard opened the door, letting Susan and then him into the car. She kicked off her shoes and curled her feet under her. If he didn't know her any better, he'd say she was scared.

"In the coming weeks and months, if I lose, everything and everyone who was connected to me will become toxic. Radioactive. They'll be hunted down like animals and thrown in jail or worse. I'd like to make a proposal. I've set up a trust fund."

She tried to say something, but he waved her off.

"There's a beautiful villa in Malta that sits right on a private beach. You can take a stroll whenever you feel like clearing your head. Or take a swim. There's full staff and expenses are paid in advance far enough for your kids to grow old before the money runs out."

"What are you saying?"

"I'm saying," he leaned over and took her hands into his, "that I'm giving you an opportunity to walk away before it's too late. Take it and enjoy yourself for the rest of your life, regardless of what happens to me or the company."

"You want me to leave you at the most difficult moment? To be a mere spectator when any day can bring the biggest victory or the biggest defeat of your life? Why?"

"Because the risks are too great," he said, squeezing her hands. "If I win, you can always come back. There's going to be a place for you no matter what. But if I don't, then there'll be nothing tying you to me or the company. You'll have unlimited funds, a new name and a new life. A chance that few people will get."

"Oh, Alex." She freed one of her hands and stroked his cheek. Her fingers were smooth and cold. "There's always been a chance that what you were trying to build would fail. You say the stakes are at their highest right now, but they have never been low. And had you lost before, I'd be in danger too. But I've stood next to you all these years without fail. That's why *when*—not *if*—you win, I want to be standing next to you as well."

"And if I don't? There will be no second chances."

"Then," she pulled back and crossed her arms, "I will go down with the ship. Just like you will."

27

The screeching alarm and a flashing light in his internal vision shook Jason Hunt out of deep slumber. He shook his head and tried to focus on the floating numbers of the digital clock.

2:30 AM.

He sat up in his bed, pulling the blanket aside, cool, fresh air washing his body and stealing the last remnants of sleep away. A flashing amber in the corner of his vision persisted and Hunt took the call. A holographic projection of Rovinsky's face appeared to be floating in the air a couple of feet away.

"Jim. What's going on?"

"I'm afraid I have some bad news. Tomorrow morning, at nine o'clock, the president is going to make a televised speech. I've seen the draft. He'll be designating Orion and its management as enemy of the state. A terrorist group. Your bank accounts will be frozen, assets seized, and anyone with the connection to the company will be placed under arrest without bail. But the speech will be post-factum."

"Christ." He stood up, chills going down his spine. "How?"

"I don't know the details," Rovinsky said. "But I'm assuming Engel is pulling the levers somehow."

"Great," Hunt said, pulling a shirt over his head. "He's been on a warpath for the last two weeks. I guess I shouldn't be surprised. How much time do we actually have?"

"They are planning on raiding the tower at three in the morning. I'm sorry for such a short notice, but that's the best I could do."

"How did you come across this information? Are you going to be suspected when we flee?"

"Don't worry. It hasn't been disseminated to us yet. You know me —I have my sources. I should be okay for now. I have to go. Good luck."

Hunt stared at the space where Rovinsky's projection had been floating a moment ago and then dialed Connelly. The man answered on the first ring, fully awake.

"We are bugging out," he said, scrambling through his room and putting some clothes on. "Engel's about to designate us as enemy of the state."

"Roger." Connelly's hologram shook rhythmically as the man started running. "How much time do we have?"

"They'll be here at three, so ten, fifteen minutes tops."

"Got it. I'll meet you at the station in ten."

"Thanks. I gotta go. I'll need to call Poznyak—"

"I've taken care of it already." Connelly cut him off. "He's acknowledged. I've alerted everyone in the tower as well. We've trained for this."

"You're the best, Mike. Are you feeling all right?"

"Never better."

"Okay. I'll see you in a few."

He disconnected the call and looked around the room he'd been calling home for the past few years. It was almost empty, save for a few articles of clothing on a chair by the window and a small, framed photograph on his nightstand. A large suitcase sat next to the door, its handle already extended.

They had been preparing for this exact scenario for a while now— Rachel had been moved to a new location and while some of the infrastructure was still being built, a lot was already in place, either fully operational or ready to be switched on with a click of a button.

All the key personnel had been prepared for the relocation as well. Chen and Schlager, who were in charge of the relocation and development teams, performed nothing short of a miracle, retrofitting the new site for their needs. Still, as Jason was about to execute on his own plan, it didn't seem real. He grabbed the photograph, picked up the suitcase, and headed to the elevator. There would be time to reflect on this later, he decided. For now, he needed to get to safety.

Connelly was waiting for him on the underground level when the doors opened.

"I thought we'd meet at the station."

"I know." Connelly smiled, taking the suitcase from him. "But I thought you'd enjoy my company."

"Max and Helen?"

"They got lucky. They were supposed to come back from the site yesterday, but ended up staying for one more night. We'll see them when we get there," Connelly said, walking between the rows of parked SUVs to the electrical panel on the wall. He opened the door, flipped a few switches and a section of the wall slid sideways, revealing a hidden hallway. They walked in, the door closing shut and momentarily plunging them into complete darkness. Then, a moment later, the lights turned on along one side of the tunnel, illuminating the way. "Come on."

As they walked, the walls of the tunnel changed. Polished concrete and slick OLED lights disappeared, giving way to rough brick and flickering lightbulbs. After a few hundred yards, they came to a large vault-like door. Connelly leaned the suitcase against the wall and turned the massive wheel.

The door opened into a T-junction—an abandoned service train station with an arched cathedral ceiling. Two teenagers—a girl and a boy in dirty coveralls and oversized jackets who had been sitting by the edge of the tracks—stood up as they approached.

"Meera." Connelly nodded to the girl, and then turned to the boy. "Sandy."

"We got your message," the girl said. "The tunnels are clear for now. We will take you to the old City Hall station. From there, Sandy will take you all the way to Myrtle Avenue."

"Thank you," Connelly said.

"It's a hike," the girl said, spitting on the floor. She pointed to the suitcase. "This shit won't slow you down, will it?"

"I don't think so. But you said the tunnels were clear?"

"You know how it is." The girl shrugged. "It's clear now, and five seconds later it's crawling with feds."

"Don't worry," Hunt said. "We will move as fast as you can lead us. And thank you. Can we go now?"

"She says you're even now," the girl said, looking at Connelly, without moving. "After this, if you need favors, you'd need to earn them."

"I understand."

"Okay then." She turned around and headed toward the end of the station, her silent companion in tow.

"What was that all about?" Hunt asked as they followed their guides off the platform and into the tunnel.

"A twist of fate, if you will. I don't know if you remember but the city had a problem with cannibals a few years back."

"I saw some headlines," Hunt said, "but I assumed it was bullshit. Yellow press being yellow press."

"Oh, it was quite real, I can assure you. I had a run-in with them when they tried to jump me in front of my building. That's when I saw one of them wearing a human phalanx on a chain around his neck. Like a trophy. I called him Bones. At the time, I needed help squaring off with some of Engel's guys without raising too much suspicion, so I came down here to see the Rats."

"The Rats?"

"That's what they call themselves. They see themselves as a guild of thieves. They have a code and follow it." Connelly chuckled. "Mostly follow it."

"What happened?"

"I offered a trade. I'd take care of the cannibals and they would help me with my problem. Turned out I was about to bite more than I wanted to chew. First, I tracked down the crew of Bones to an abandoned train station in Midtown. They had a camp there and kept their victims there in cages. Kids."

"Holy shit."

"Yeah." Connelly stayed quiet for some time as they continued to walk. "I killed the entire gang and let the kids out. But it turned out that wasn't the only camp in the city. There were several. I ended up doing some cleaning, and the Rats ended up owing me a big favor."

"It must have been awful, Mike. I'm sorry."

"Yeah. It wasn't pretty."

"Who's the *she*?"

"The Queen of Rats. She's the lady in charge."

"We're here," Meera said, interrupting them. They were standing at the fork—a smaller, completely dark tunnel was heading down at a steep angle. "Sandy will take you now. He's deaf. Don't bother him with questions. And try not to get lost."

"Thank you, Meera," Hunt said, but the girl was already walking back without as much as a glance in his direction.

Sandy took out a small flashlight that produced a surprisingly powerful wide beam and headed down the slope.

"Let's go," Connelly said, and started after the boy.

"Mike?"

"Yeah."

"If they owed you a huge favor…" Hunt paused, searching for the right words. "Why are you even now? All they did is walk us through some tunnels."

"Not quite." Connelly chuckled. "The US government is about to designate us as the most dangerous fugitives since Osama bin Laden. I'd say helping us is a pretty big favor."

2 8

Helen Chen strained her eyes as she watched the H-92 Superhawk Sikorsky helicopter make the final approach to the clearing. In the moonless sky, the bird, with its lights off, looked like a prehistoric predator circling in search of a prey. A few moments later, it touched down on the improvised helipad. Steven Poznyak was the first one to exit, followed by the rest of his lab staff. He jogged toward her, keeping one hand on his baseball hat and bending in the wind as the blades above him slowed down.

"Hey, Steve," she said, embracing the man.

"Hey, yourself," Poznyak shouted over the roar of the rotors. He looked around as they walked away from the helicopter. "This is how it feels to be a fugitive, huh? It doesn't look like much, which I guess is the point. I have to say, being whisked away on a fifteen-minute notice in a helicopter without running lights is kind of depressing."

"Hopefully it's temporary." She shrugged. "We are trying our best. I just hope it's going to be enough."

"I'm sorry I couldn't come earlier," he apologized. "I wanted to be here, especially when they were moving Rachel."

"It was better that way. You were the best person to figure out what to move here and what not to. You couldn't be in two places at once." She switched on a small flashlight and set it on its lowest setting. It did little to illuminate the ground in front of them, but seemed to plunge the rest of the world into an almost impenetrable shade of black. "Come on, I'll give you a tour."

They walked across the field covered in brown wilted grass, that in the light of her torch looked almost black, toward a few domed structures raised a few feet high above the ground.

"You could drive by this place and not notice it," Poznyak said. "At least at night."

"Watch where you step. The surface is not very even. There's not much to see above the ground, even during the day. Ballistic missile silos weren't supposed to be noticeable. And no major roads lead here anymore either. They used to, but not for some time. There are three silos—this one here. One more over there," she pointed at a dome looming farther away, "and one more on the other side of this field, but you can't see it from here behind that shed which is the only aboveground structure that is higher than me. The system of tunnels connects all three of them and we have been retrofitting the place to suit our needs."

"You've rebuilt all three silos? Helen, you're a magician."

"I wish." She chuckled. "These two are only half finished and I haven't even touched the one on the other side yet. It also has less coverage from the trees. It made sense to develop it last, when we expand the tunnels and can work on it from inside rather than spending too much time on the surface. But regardless, we had to do the essentials first. I had the crews install two new generators and a battery pack to make sure we had no issues with power. Silo 1 is going to be all yours. It's seven floors. Not nearly as much space as you had at Asclepius, but it'll have to do. Rachel and the computers are all the way at the bottom. The rest is all your wet-wire and augmentation tech. Sorry I couldn't find the place for all of your projects."

"It is what it is. We had to prioritize." Poznyak shrugged. "What about the living quarters?"

"That's Silo 2," she said. "It's also closest to the control center, which has three levels. But they are small."

"That one is for the big shots, I assume?"

"Yes, and you are one of them. I gave the top floor to Jason, which I'm sure is going to double as our war room. One went for Schlager and his gadgets, and the one on the bottom is yours."

"Why, thank you."

"You might be happy to know that the escape hatch that leads to a ladder in the fresh air intake shaft is on your floor." She smiled and patted him on the arm. "Should you get claustrophobic, just think that you have a direct route to the surface if the main entrance is compromised."

"I wasn't claustrophobic until you said it." He laughed. "Now I won't stop thinking about all the possible ways the main entrance will cease functioning. And I can promise you, none of them will be good."

"It gets worse, I promise." She chuckled. "Max was suggesting once we are past the crazy scrambling stage to install faux windows in living quarters. We could simulate the natural day and night cycle to help us with the circadian rhythm and improve morale. The lack of windows gets on your nerves real fast. But I don't know when that will be possible. Once everybody's here, helicopters will be camouflaged and there'll not be a lot of flying for some time. We've been camouflaging the entire area. Mike is going to have to go to Bolivia, but that's a separate matter."

"Bolivia? Why does he need to go to Bolivia?"

"Long story."

"All right," Poznyak said. "What are those things?"

"What?"

"Those metal poles with ears." He pointed.

She shined her flashlight in the direction he'd shown. "Those are TIPSIES. Something that we are also trying to repurpose."

"That sounds like the state I'd like to be in right now." Poznyak chuckled. "Very tipsy."

"You and me both. Those are territorial protection systems. You could say it's a sophisticated house alarm, based on the Doppler effect. They used to guard the silos. Extremely sensitive to any movement, as you can imagine. Not operational at the moment, but my engineers are telling me we could use them."

"That's great."

"Anyway, here we are." She stopped by the entrance and looked back. Another helicopter without running lights was coming in for a landing. "Looks like Jason's here. Follow the signs as you go down. It was confusing to most people in the beginning. One of the first things we did was put up the signs so nobody would get lost."

"Thank you, Helen. For everything."

"Don't mention it. Let me know if you need anything when you get settled." She turned around to walk away but stopped as he placed a hand on her forearm. "What is it, Steve?"

"Look," he said. "I know it's been tough the last few weeks and it'll probably get worse before it gets better, but we can do it. I'm not saying it in a fake, cheerful way. Not my forte. I'm saying this because we have people like Jason and Max. And most importantly, because we have you. I know if those two lose sight, you'll set them straight."

He let go of her arm and, before she had a chance to reply, disappeared into the belly of the bunker below.

She turned off the flashlight and looked around. A few wobbling lights were moving her way as the new group of people departed from the helicopter. She could recognize the tall, slim figure of Jason Hunt. Despite the circumstances, his posture was straight, and the wind carried the cheerful tone of his voice. She wondered how much of it was genuine and how much was a projection of confidence to keep the rest of them going. To show them that while the battle might have been lost, the war was far from over and in the end, they would come out victorious.

She rubbed her eyes, fighting back tears, grateful for the darkness. By the time Hunt and the crew reached her, she was again in control of herself, giving hugs, saying hello, and calmly directing the newcomers around the camp she'd become familiar with in the last few weeks.

When the last person descended the stairs, she stood on the surface for a few more minutes, looking up at the dark, cloudy sky. Then she went down into the hatch and closed the door shut.

29

$\mathcal{J}$ ill Cooper glanced over her shoulder as she passed a locked for the night bodega and approached the high-rise residential building at the end of the block. The sidewalk was empty as far as she could see, and she quickly ducked into the service entrance and went down the concrete steps leading into the basement. She took the long, heavy bag off her shoulder and leaned it against the wrought-iron door, fixed the straps of her backpack, and then kneeled in front of the lock. A few seconds later, the gate squeaked and Cooper made her way past the rows of black trash bags, a discarded TV set, and a broken massage chair to the service elevator.

This was the weakest link of her plan, she thought, pressing the button, and winced as the clanking of gears echoed through the empty shaft. It was past midnight, and the sounds seemed loud enough to wake up half of the tenants. She knew it wasn't likely that she would encounter anyone inside of the service elevator at this hour, but the fact that she had to rely on chance was driving her mad. She was never fond of "fire and fury" operations. Sometimes those were inevitable, just like the one she was about to undertake. A rush job. But she much preferred to work on her own schedule, when she could create a scene that even the most skillful investigators would write off as an accident. An unfortunate turn of events. Now, as she stood waiting for the metal cage to descend to the ground floor, all she wanted to do was to scrap the entire plan.

It wasn't an option. Engel had made it clear enough and the building, perched at the southern tip of Bay Ridge, was the only structure tall enough to give her a commanding view of the bridge straddling the Narrows, the strait separating Brooklyn and Staten Island.

The secretary of defense, whose behavior troubled Engel enough to send Cooper into action, was going to be crossing the Verrazzano Bridge in a motorcade in thirty minutes. The man was notoriously cautious about his security and traveled mostly at night in a limo that would give the presidential Beast a run for its money. The ten-ton monster, with five-inch-thick windows and hermetically sealed cabin, would have easily repelled sniper fire.

The small window on the elevator door lit up as it finally arrived and the door slid open, revealing a gray metal box. Bright spotlights blinded Cooper after the twilight of the basement and she stepped aside and pulled her baseball cap lower, making sure she didn't accidentally appear in the view of the single camera. The elevator, a standard residential model by EZLift & Co., had only one wide-angle camera mounted in the left upper corner. Cooper pulled a small rubbery ball from her jacket pocket and squeezed it hard between her thumb and index fingers. Then, while remaining out of the shot, she stuck her hand in and threw the ball inside the metal box. There was a small popping sound that was followed by a loud hiss and when she entered the elevator, the camera lens—along with most of the corner—was covered in sticky black resin.

Cooper pressed a button for the top floor and tried to focus on her breathing as the elevator started its ascension.

A few seconds later, the door slid open again and Cooper sighed in relief as she stepped out into a dark, empty hallway. According to the landlord records, the apartment of the corner unit was unoccupied, but before she tried to pick the lock, Cooper leaned her ear against the door and listened. The place was empty.

It was a small one-bedroom apartment with rooms in a line like a train, all except a small kitchen opposite to the tiny living room. There was no furniture, except an old coffee table by the window, and the squeaky parquet floors were covered in a thick layer of dust. Nobody had been here for quite some time.

Cooper wiped down the table and then placed the long, heavy bag on it along with the backpack. She rolled her shoulders this way and that way, getting the knots out. Then she unzipped the bag and got to work. The FGM-148 Javelin missile system didn't look nearly as elegant as the name suggested. But a fat tube about one meter in length with a detachable command launch unit, or CLU for short, was a perfect weapon for the job.

After Cooper assembled the system, she checked the time. Nineteen minutes left—so far, so good. She unlocked the double-hung window facing the bridge, pulled it up an inch, and then depressed the latches on the lower sash. She pulled the lower window out and down, and repeated the operation with the top window, giving herself an unobstructed view of the bridge. Then she set the timer and relaxed while watching the flow of cars on the top deck.

The timer beeped and Cooper glanced at the watch—two minutes. She picked up the Javelin and took a knee in front of the open window, peering into the magnified, green-lit thermal vision screen. A few moments later, there it was—a cavalcade of vehicles crawling on the top level of the bridge. Two police motorcycles were rolling approximately fifty feet in front of the line of cars. Then there were two Suburbans carrying protection, and right after them, the long silhouette of the limo. The system beeped as the infrared seeker locked onto its target and Cooper pulled the trigger.

A soft launch ejected the missile a dozen feet into the air, its back blast thundering through the empty apartment and whipping up the dust in the air like a small tornado, which pushed Cooper in the back, almost causing her to lose balance. The missile flew horizontally a few feet and seemed to hover in place for a split second, and then the main engine ignited, its bright flame illuminating the street below. It streaked away, gaining altitude as it went. The infamous curveball shot.

Cooper turned around on her heels and removed the CLU from the launch tube. *Fire and forget. Gotta love the concept.* A fireball blossomed on the upper deck of the bridge as she stuffed the unit inside of her backpack and closed the zipper. Then she packed the tube inside of the duffel bag and headed out of the apartment. There was no need to clean up after herself. The neighborhood had plenty of CCTV cameras that would catch the launch. Once the cause of the explosion was clear, she had no doubt that any investigator worth their salt would triangulate the precise position of the missile launch in a matter of minutes. It didn't matter. By then she'd be long gone.

She closed the door, careful not to touch anything with bare skin. Then she hurried down the hallway to the elevator. Without the heft of the missile, it was easier going. A police siren went on down the street outside the building.

The window on the elevator door was dark—she could see the cables dangling in the empty shaft and the outline of the brick wall behind them. Cooper pushed the button and tensed as she heard the gears clank somewhere deep down. Someone must have used it while she was up in the apartment. For a second, she contemplated taking the stairs, but there was no other way to access the basement but by the elevator, and taking the stairs would mean going out through the main entrance. The lone camera there wouldn't capture her face, but it would reveal her gender and build. Cooper moved the duffel bag to her left hand and patted the small of her back, making sure the handgun was accessible as the door of the elevator slid open.

"What are you doing here?" A tall, skinny man in a dark-blue building uniform was standing inside of the metal cage, his eyes scanning her up and down with suspicion.

"Friends," she said, stepping inside. The wail of the sirens was louder now.

"There's nobody on this floor," the man said. His accent was heavy, Eastern European.

"Sorry, I thought I pressed the ground floor, but must've hit the wrong button and ended up going up."

"I'm going to have to call the police." He moved to block the exit out of the elevator. "You took something. What did you steal? What's in your bag?"

She hit him in the solar plexus and as he stepped back, bringing his arms up to his chest, hit him again in his throat. As the man fell, his back hitting the wall behind him, she stepped closer, pressed the gun against his rib cage, and squeezed the trigger twice.

Even with the suppressor, the shots were deafening.

Cooper tensed as the elevator continued its slow descent, but after what seemed an eternity, the door opened, letting her out and into the dimly lit basement. She hurried past the garbage bags and up the concrete steps, pausing only for a second to make sure there was nobody to see her exit the building. As she walked back to her car, she glanced at the bridge—a fire was still raging on its top level, illuminating the thick tension cables in a hellish amber glow. A tall column of smoke was rising into the sky, blotting out the stars. At the intersection, Cooper pulled out a burner phone and typed a brief message.

It's done.

A smile emoji appeared on her phone a split second later. She glanced at her car parked across the street, then turned around and walked north. Two blocks away, she found the BMW motorcycle she had parked two days ago under a linden tree. She straddled the seat, put on a helmet and then opened the app for her car. For a moment, her thumb hovered over the button unlocking the doors and then touched the screen. A massive blast shook the ground, smashing the windows in the nearby buildings. A hot shock wave hit Cooper in the back a split second later, throwing litter and small debris down the street.

She broke the phone in half and threw it on the side of the road, ignoring the chaos erupting around her. The information she had found on Engel's computer was accurate—this was intended to be her last mission. The flames consuming her empty car two blocks to the south were supposed to kill her. Instead, Jill Cooper just bought herself freedom.

30

A pickup truck took a sharp turn off the main road and climbed up a muddy hill, its powerful high beams shining over the splotches of wilted brown grass. The engine whined as the vehicle went deeper into the forest until the spacing between the trees made it impossible to go any farther. Connelly turned the truck around, pointing its mud-splattered grille toward the road below, stopped the truck and shut off the engine. As the lights went out, the night seemed to have swallowed them whole. The cabin shook and squeaked as Martin jumped out of the cargo bed in the back, and then the truck rose a few inches as its coil springs expanded, unburdened from the cyborg's massive bulk.

Connelly jumped out of the cabin in time to see Martin pull two large cases off the cargo bed and place them on the ground behind the vehicle. Then, together, they pulled a camouflage net over the pickup.

"Twenty clicks," Connelly said, looking at a tablet with a satellite view, his face illuminated by the blue glow of the screen. "What do you think?"

"On this terrain," the cyborg's voice was flat, matter-of-fact, "I can do sixty, maybe sixty-five miles per hour."

"We are talking five, maybe six minutes before you get within the range of the Phalanx systems. These babies," he nodded at the cases, "will be there about ninety seconds before. Should give them plenty of time."

Martin nodded without saying a word, making Connelly's reflection on his shiny liquid-mercury-like helmet surface jump up and down.

"Remember," he continued, "those are twenty-millimeter multi-purpose tracer self-destruct rounds we are talking about. Coming from four systems at once. We stick to the plan. If I can't overwhelm them remotely, you fall back."

"I can withstand their fire for at least sixty seconds," Martin said. "Probably more. I've done it before."

"From one of them, yes, but let's not tempt our fate with all four. And you're going to have to deal with the mortars and at least one machine gun."

"The machine gun is irrelevant. I can avoid mortar fire, too," the cyborg said. "But I'll follow your instructions. Let's get set up."

"Okay." Connelly craned his neck as he looked up. A thick, impenetrable layer of clouds stretched as far as he could see.

"Visibility is low," Martin said, as if reading his mind. "Should help your birds."

Connelly picked up what looked like a bulky motorcycle helmet from one case and suppressed a shiver as he glanced at the few rows of sharp needles gleaming in the faint light of the moonless sky. The surface of the soft goggles glistened with moisture and the two organic audio cables were moving like two fat white worms in search of fresh food. "I hate this bit."

He pulled the helmet on and tried to relax as the apparatus came to life. For a couple of moments, he was entirely blind and deaf apart from some whirring and scratching noises coming from the inside of the device. Then the goggles sucked onto his eyes, wet tentacles slipped into his ears, and a series of sharp prickles ran down his neck from the top of his head. Another moment later, the night exploded in sounds and colors as Connelly's view expanded in every direction, giving him a three-sixty-degree field of vision. He focused on Martin and the system automatically zoomed in, opening what looked like a multilayered 3D-model of the cyborg. He could see the power coursing through Martin's wiring and hear the buzzing of the energy that held together the armor.

"Ready?" he heard Martin ask, only to realize a half-second later that the message came via electromagnetic wave rather than sound.

He focused his attention on the two cases. His internal systems paired to the six remote-controlled drones that rose from their charging cradles like a fleet of lethal UFOs. The disks, about a foot tall and four feet in diameter, were covered in a thin layer of radar-absorbing matte-black polymer and bore no identifying markings or lights. They hovered above the two men for a few seconds as Connelly accessed his controls and then disappeared into the sky with a barely audible whoosh.

"Go," he said. The projection of the cyborg lit up in Connelly's enhanced vision. A moment later, Martin took off, plowing through bushes and small trees like a hot knife going through butter. As Connelly returned his attention to the drones, he briefly wondered if they made a mistake, assuming they wouldn't be able to defeat the defenses of the facility. Watching Martin in action, it was easy to think the cyborg was indestructible.

By now the drones had climbed to their service ceiling of ten thousand feet and continued on their path toward the target. The black expanse of the unsuspecting forest lay quiet under the unblinking eyes of drone cameras. A minute later, the building came into view as the lenses zoomed in on their destination. Quiet and inert a few moments ago, now it looked like an angry beehive. The sentries on the roof rotated, bringing the multi-barrel systems online. The thermal imaging picked up a few human silhouettes running across the roof of the building. Judging by the way the Phalanx systems were positioned, they had detected Martin's approach but hadn't opened fire yet as the cyborg was still out of range. So far, the drones seemed to evade the radar of the defense perimeter.

"Let's crash this party," Connelly whispered, sending the command to the drone fleet. The firing bay windows opened on the sides of each drone and the machines spun around their own axes. As each open slot aligned with the target, the drones spat a swarm of self-propelled laser-guided projectiles. Thousands of tiny tungsten-tipped missiles, each carrying a small explosive, rushed toward the building. A second later, the close-in weapons systems on the top of the building swerved, looking for the new threat, and roared to life, the angry dashes of tracer rounds racing across the sky to meet their targets halfway. The sky illuminated in orange and red glow as the ordinance collided in the air. Each Phalanx system was spitting four and a half thousand rounds per minute, and combined they were disintegrating most of the missile swarm above the forest.

But it wasn't enough.

The miniature missiles zigged and zagged in defensive maneuvers, and a few seconds later, the compound lit up like a Christmas tree; a series of explosions decimated the front two Gatling guns and then a split second later the two in the back. The bodies on the roof were still visible in Connelly's thermal vision, but they were no longer in motion. The four mortar sites flashed fire and Connelly briefly glanced at the silver streak moving through the trees. Martin dashed this way and that, easily dodging the incoming shells, and picked up speed, closing in on the target.

"Sentries are down," Connelly said into the mic. Another second later, Martin burst into the clearing around the compound. A series of bright flashes came from the cyborg and four missiles streaked in a low arc across the field, terminating at the mortar sites. Four explosions blossomed simultaneously and the filters inside of the helmet darkened Connelly's view, protecting his eyes. A bright amber alert appeared in his vision and a loud alarm went off as one of the drone's cameras identified a new threat.

"Shit," he said, "there's a bird inbound. Actually, make it two. Fall back now."

"Roger." The cyborg rolled into a ball and came up facing away from the building. Another moment later, he sped away from the clearing, ignoring the angry staccato of a large caliber machine gun.

The camera zoomed in on the incoming helicopters. It was still too far to identify the type, but the stub wings jetting out on the sides of the crafts left little doubt about the military nature of the vehicles.

Connelly pulled the camouflage net off the truck and, straining, heaved the empty drone cases back onto the cargo bed. Another amber alert pulsated in his vision as the computer identified the threat.

"Those are two Longbows," he said, climbing into the truck, referring to the helicopters. "That's thirty-two Hellfire missiles. They are still out of range, but you better pick up speed. Cut across to the interstate. I'll pick you up there. I don't think they'll have the cojones to fire on us there."

"Roger." Martin's voice was flat, without a trace of emotion.

If Connelly didn't know any better, he could have thought that the cyborg was resting, rather than smashing through the woods at almost seventy miles an hour.

He revved the engine and let the truck roll down the hill, gradually picking up speed. It was tempting to floor it, but on a muddy surface the risk was too high. He would not help Martin by getting stuck here.

Finally, the tires screeched as they gripped the asphalt of the main road and Connelly stepped on the gas.

"I don't think we are going to make it." Martin's voice came through. "I'm going to be in range of the missiles before I get to the interstate."

"I know," Connelly said as the pickup truck sped up through the night, pieces of dirt flying off its rear tires. "We need to buy you thirty seconds, and I might have an idea."

He didn't want to lose the drones, but they seemed to be out of other options. The swarm swerved in the air and headed toward the helicopters. As Connelly merged onto the interstate, Martin jumped in the back, almost tipping the truck over. As the last drone disappeared from his internal vision, Connelly accelerated, heading back to the city. At least for the moment they were home free.

$\mathcal{A}$lexander Engel was lying in a bed that was propped up for the moment to keep him comfortable as the men and women around him were getting ready. He would never admit it to anyone, but the surgical lights hanging off booms affixed to the ceiling intimidated him. But not as much as a silver sphere, six feet in diameter, that was suspended off a rail running on the ceiling parallel to his bed. Several video lenses and multiple slender, multi-jointed arms made it look like a monstrous cybernetic spider ready to devour him. The serial number RD-24, etched on its side in golden letters next to a pair of stylized wings, stood for Robo Dynamics, a new subdivision of Guardian Manufacturing.

He let his eyes wander away from the machine. The blinds on the window were drawn, but the light of a setting sun was seeping through the gaps on their sides, coloring the wall in a cheerful shade of orange.

"Are you comfortable, Mr. Engel?" The woman with gray hair, neatly tied into a ponytail, walked up to his bed and bent over him. The wrinkles around her eyes deepened as if she smiled, but since most of her face was covered by a blue surgical mask, Engel couldn't tell if that was the case.

"I'm fine. Not too happy about the restraints." He pulled on the belts securing his feet and arms. "But I guess I'll have to get over it."

"I'm sorry about those," the wrinkles around her eyes appeared again, "but we have to make sure that you stay absolutely still. Once you are sleeping, they won't bother you anymore."

"How long did you say it will last?" He looked at the table next to his bed. Now that the procedure was about to start, the view of glistening metal and wires laid out on the surgical table covered in a blue cloth was making him nervous.

"We are hoping to be done in twelve hours," she said. "It's not an exact number, of course, but I don't expect it running much longer than that."

"Good."

"And here's your team," she said. "You know most of them. I've selected Doctors Guevara and Schwartz to assist me today. There are also four nurses. And Rodin, of course."

"Rodin?" He looked at her with surprise.

"This guy right here." She pointed at the spherical machine with her chin. "As in Auguste Rodin."

"Touché."

"Miss Martinez here is the circulating nurse; she'll keep track of time and will get you ready. She'll also be in charge of the other three nurses who will come at various stages of your procedure. Messrs. Petrov and Bernard are your surgical technicians. Doctor Acharya is your anesthesiologist."

"Don't break anything," Engel quipped. "If you break it—you buy it."

"Doctor Acharya will take it from here." The surgeon stepped aside, letting a short, slim man step forward.

"Mr. Engel." The man walked around the table, lowered it into a horizontal position, and looked at the monitors to check his vitals. "Don't worry, you're in excellent hands. Your surgeon is the best in the world."

"I know. I hired her."

The needle seemed to appear out of nowhere and there was a

blunt pain as it went into the vein on his left hand. The pain grew stronger and as Engel was about to complain to the doctor, it disappeared as quickly as it came. Then the room went out of focus.

He couldn't see at first when he came to. He was cold, groggy, and nauseated. There was a garbled noise, too, but after a few moments of panic, it dissipated without a trace.

"Can you see me, Mr. Engel?" he heard the nurse say. "How many fingers am I holding up?"

A dark, shapeless silhouette floated in front of his face. He blinked and then, without a warning, it looked like a woman's hand, her index finger touching her thumb in what resembled an okay sign.

"Three," he said. It came out as a croak. His throat was raw and when he tried to swallow, it ended up in a painful heaving somewhere down in his chest as he couldn't produce enough saliva. He was in a large suite with walls painted in gentle blue, lying on a bed fitted in a starched white linen. A heavy blanket covered him almost all the way to his chin. The bed was facing the window, and the curtains were open, but the outside was completely dark—all he could see was the reflection of the room. "I need something to drink."

"There you go," the nurse said, bringing a small plastic bottle to his lips.

The liquid sloshing inside had a noticeable blue tinge and smelled like a cheap soap, but he greedily downed it in a few gulps. The pain in his chest became dull but didn't disappear.

"That should get you on your way."

"How long was I out?"

"About thirteen hours," she said. "The doctor and the technicians will be here shortly, and they'll be able to answer all your questions. Rest now."

With that, the nurse hurried away, leaving him alone before he could say anything else. He tried to shift the blanket down, but his hand wouldn't move—the restraints were still attaching him to the bed. Engel tugged on it harder, but they wouldn't bulge.

"They have to stay on for a little while longer, I'm sorry," he heard the doctor's voice and a moment later, she walked into his field of vision. Instead of the scrubs, she wore a gray checkered wool pantsuit and a black turtleneck, and this time he could see her smile. "Everything went smoothly, but we need to run some diagnostics first, to make sure the parts fused and are functioning as they are supposed to. Then we will switch on the power and remove the restraints. This is for your own protection."

She waved and a team of four technicians rolled in two tables stacked with a few devices—most of them unfamiliar to Engel—a large, curved monitor, and a thick bundle of color-coded cables hanging off the side the table next to him.

"Mark here," the doctor nodded toward a burly man with thick, hairy hands, "will activate your main CPU and cranial implants."

"Relax, sir," the man said in a deep baritone. "Let me know if you feel any discomfort."

"Okay."

The man brought one of the thicker cables closer, lifted Engel's head, and placed the cable at the base of his skull.

There was a mild vibration and then a prickling sensation, as if someone pressed a wiggling hedgehog to his skin.

"How is it feeling?"

"Weird," Engel said, "and my neck feels hot."

"That's normal." The man nodded, flipping a few switches. "Let me know if you see anything."

"I see you—" started Engel and stopped, as his internal vision populated with a row of icons and symbols. "I got the interface up."

"Fantastic," the man said. An identical row appeared on the large monitor in front of the man. "Now, it'll take some practice, so take it slow. Let's start with the basics. I want you to concentrate on the big wheel in the middle. That's your primary access point. Try to rotate it and see how it opens up different applications. Imagine yourself doing it. Think of it in terms of depth of view. When you look at something in the distance, the objects right next to you become blurry and vice versa."

"Okay." Engel tried to focus on the big wheel. At first, it was like trying to turn a crown on a watch while wearing thick skiing mittens.

But after a few attempts the wheel responded faster, turning this way and that as he willed it to go in different directions.

"Good. Now let's try something different. You see that symbol of a running man? This is where you will see some real magic happening. Activate it, but, and listen to me closely, do *not* move your limbs. It'll be disorienting at first."

"Okay." Engel turned the wheel until the icon of a running man popped up. "I got it up now. How do I activate it?"

"Imagine it's a physical button. Visualize yourself touching it with a finger."

The hexagon with a symbol on it depressed, and then time slowed down to a crawl. Engel looked around the room in wonder, noting as people around him seemed to be frozen in place: their limbs without any motion, their eyes staring in the same direction. The effect lasted only for a few moments, and then he was surrounded by warm-blooded people instead of statues again.

"Fun, wasn't it?" Mark said. "This thing is a dual-action shotgun. It floods your system with over two dozen stress hormones and also stimulates some part of your neural network. For obvious reasons, you're not fully loaded yet, and it's not a button you want to press too often, but I'm sure it could come in handy."

"That was great," Engel said. "What's next?"

"Now," the technician rubbed his palms together, "let's do some fun stuff. Let's activate your weapon augs."

32

The rain hitting the windows of the luxurious cabin of the Mercedes-Benz EC145 Eurocopter completely hid the view of the lowlands below them. Michael Connelly and Helen Chen had landed in Santa Cruz de la Sierra an hour ago and were picked up by a small, plump man who escorted them to a helipad. Connelly was expecting to see more armed guards, but the man helped them load into the helicopter, and left them alone with the pilot.

"I wish you hadn't come," he said to Chen as they made their final approach to the landing site. "I still don't understand how Max agreed to let you go."

"I've never been to Bolivia." She smiled. "And I'm very persuasive."

"Right."

"Looks like we are landing right next to the house."

"Yeah." Connelly peered through the windows. The rain stopped as suddenly as it had started and he could see the landing site that was built into the clearing at the foot of a yellow cobblestone road. "This helipad is new, and so is the transport choice. Last time they brought me here on a coke-coated Cessna and we had to drive here from the landing strip. There was a bunch of guards with us, too."

"Not this time," Chen said. "You think it's a good sign or a bad sign?"

Connelly shrugged, wondering the same thing. There was a chance Flores was going to shoot him at first sight before he even had a chance to explain why they were there.

The Eurocopter bounced softly as it touched down.

"Just a moment," the pilot said in a perfect English. "Ernesto will pick you up."

A four-passenger golf cart appeared on the road, heading toward the helipad. A single guard accompanied the driver, an older man with a balding head and full gray beard.

The guard strip-searched Connelly, loaded their bags onto the golf cart without saying a word, and a minute later they were going through the main gate and into the front yard of a massive Spanish Colonial with a red-tile roof. A few young men and women were lounging at the pool, seemingly unperturbed by the recent rain.

Ernesto made a loop around the multitiered fountain in the middle of the yard, drove past a fleet of collectible cars and parked in front of a silver 1996 Bentley Rapier.

"Is it?" Chen whispered, leaning close to his ear.

"Yep."

"Way to make a point."

"Michael Connelly." Diego Flores appeared on the top of the stairs of the house. He looked older than Connelly remembered. Instead of a clean shave, Flores was sporting a trimmed goatee, and his short hair was streaked with gray. He walked down the steps to meet them. "I have to admit, I didn't expect to ever see you again."

"I didn't expect to be back," Connelly said, getting out of the cart and helping Chen out. "But, as they say, sometimes life is stranger than fiction."

"And who is this lovely lady?"

"Helen Chen," she said, shaking the man's hand. "It's nice to meet you."

"You fixed the car," Connelly said.

"Oh yes." Flores walked to the Bentley and traced the outline of the wings on the hood ornament. "I had to. They say a Bentley is the nearest a car can become to having wings."

"I'm not as sophisticated as you are when it comes to cars," Connelly said. "But I've heard a good story lately about a car that raced a train. The 1930 Blue Train Bentley."

"Did you now?" For the first time, Diego Flores produced a genuine smile. "I was hoping what I read in the papers was related to your visit. But I don't want to be rude. Come on in. I'll have Ernesto show you the rooms and then the help will serve you dinner."

"Just one room, please." Chen leaned on Connelly, startling him. "You wouldn't want to stay away too far from your girl, right, darling?"

"Of course not." He placed a peck on her cheek. "One room is all we need."

"As you wish." Flores waved them in. "Rest, eat, and we'll talk business in the morning."

They followed Ernesto up the stairs to the second-floor guest bedroom, where the man left their bags and hurried away. Connelly looked around the airy room with arched windows that opened onto a balcony and facing the front yard.

"And this is the same room," he said. "Flores doesn't let grudges go easily, it seems."

They took turns taking a shower and were unpacking their luggage when there was a light knocking on the door. Connelly signaled to Chen to get behind him and positioned himself next to the doorframe.

"Come on in," he said loudly.

The door slowly opened, and he yanked it back, moving in for a strike when he saw a frightened face of a teenage boy.

"Your dinner, señor," the kid said, pointing at a rolling tray with a few plates covered with silver cloches and a pitcher with a drink.

"This is Chicha de pina," the boy said, pointing at the pitcher. "It's very refreshing. There's also a peanut soup and Pique Macho."

"Gracias," Chen said, coming to the door.

"And this one," the boy opened another tray, "is cunape. A bread made of cheese. Delicious."

"That's kind of you, thanks."

The boy bowed and hurriedly retreated into the hallway, closing the door behind him.

"Scared the kid half to death," she said.

"Last time people showed up in this room ostensibly bearing gifts, they were trying to stab me," Connelly said. "Forgive me for being wary of local hospitality."

"It smells delicious," Chen said. "Let's eat."

As they sat in wicker chairs around a small round table, enjoying the host's meal, Connelly felt Helen's foot striking his shin. He looked up at her from the bowl.

"My bag," she whispered. "Pull a tablet from there and put it under the blanket. Don't make it obvious."

He glanced in the window's direction and dropped a fork on the floor.

"There's good news and bad news," she said as he made a show of picking up the fork while simultaneously stuffing Chen's tablet under the covers behind him.

"Okay."

"The good news is there're no bugs in the room."

"And the bad?"

"There's no access to the net from anywhere in the suite except this room. Some kind of dampening system. And we are being watched from the room in the guesthouse across the yard."

Connelly put his elbow on the table and rested his cheek on the fist. He moved his head around as if stretching his neck. The room across the yard was dark, the drapes drawn, but one corner of the curtain was askew, and when he risked another glance again, he could see a glint of the lens.

"Good observation skills," he said.

"Excellent food," she said, moving the chair away from the table. "Are you finished?"

"Sure."

"Here's what we are going to do. Go sit at the edge of the bed and move the covers."

He did as he was told and watched as she got up, took a last sip of Chicha de pina and then stretched. Then, she turned to him and pulled her blouse over her head.

"What are you doing?"

"Don't look away," she said as he tried to turn his head. "Undress, lean back, smile, and look at me. Put the pillows on the window side. That way, they will block most of the view when we lie down."

He did, his heart suddenly pumping at one hundred beats per second, as she removed her shorts and the bra, leaving her in a black thong.

She walked to him, placed her hands on his shoulders and leaned in for a kiss.

"They are watching," she whispered. "I don't think Diego Flores likes to be lied to."

They locked lips and he let his hands move down her back and cup her buttocks as she climbed on top of him. Then, she pushed him down on the bed, drew the blanket over their bodies, and slid under.

Connelly held his breath as he felt her climb down his body, her soft breasts brushing against his stomach and then resting on his thigh. He stayed still, his mind racing in search of something to think of. Anything that would distract him from reality.

He thought about a trip he took with his uncle and two of his cousins when he was thirteen. They rented a cabin by the river and went ice fishing in the morning, but the weather had been warm for a few days and when he tried to drill the hole, the ice gave. Connelly fell through, almost bringing all of them under, but his uncle was fast. He splayed himself on the ice, sprint-crawled to the edge of the hole and grabbed him by the jacket before Connelly got pulled under. He spent less than a minute in the freezing water, but he could still remember the bone-chilling cold. He could use some of it now.

"I'm done," Chen whispered a few minutes later, coming out from under the covers, her forehead damp with perspiration. "I'm on his server and installed a back door access. We shouldn't try to use it here; his systems are too sophisticated. But I can exploit it once we are back in the States."

"Great," he said, finally finding his breath.

"I'm sorry," she said, resting her head on his shoulder. "I didn't mean to make you uncomfortable, but I don't want to give Flores yet another reason to kill us."

"It's fine," Connelly said, trying to keep his voice level. "I know how to keep a cover. We should get some sleep. A big day tomorrow."

"Yes," she said, putting her arm around him and closing her eyes. "We should."

Connelly watched her drifting asleep as he stayed immobile, afraid to wake her up. He sighed and stared at the ceiling fan. It was going to be a long night.

33

"Thirty-five percent is a hell of a haircut," Schlager said, as the helicopter took off from the JFK private jet terminal and started the climb, heading across Jamaica Bay. They had chartered the flight back to the US under a shell corporation, and the helicopter was registered under the same company and bore the markings of a nonexistent agricultural consortium.

Connelly shrugged. The trip to Bolivia was a success. Despite the obvious lack of love after the last encounter, Diego Flores softened once he learned the reason for their visit. A gift, a mint-condition dark-green 1930 Bentley, that was delivered to the Prince of Cocaine after their meeting sealed the deal. Flores would launder the giant cash pile that had been sitting in storage in Staten Island for a hefty fee of three hundred million dollars and funnel the rest to Orion through his European bank intermediaries. The irony of where a large part of the money would end up didn't escape Connelly. In the end, he and his squad mates had risked it all to take the cash from the drug lords in Afghanistan, only to give it to a drug lord in Bolivia a few years later.

"We wouldn't be able to clean it fast enough to make it useful," Chen said. "I think a thirty-five percent fee is not a terrible deal. I don't like one bit that we had to hand so much money to Flores, but beggars can't be choosers."

Connelly glanced at her and turned back to the window. The helicopter was flying over the farm lands. Neat squares and rectangles ran up to the forest line, which then continued as far as the eye could see. Soon, they'd be back at the base, and life would go on and suddenly he wished he could have stayed in Bolivia.

They hadn't discussed Chen's cover story before the trip, and in hindsight it was a mistake. Operationally, posing as his girlfriend made sense. Had something gone wrong, staying in separate rooms would've been a tremendous disadvantage. And yet, the cover and the need to play the part threw him off-balance. He hadn't been with anyone since Sofia, not in a serious sense, anyway. There were occasional one-night stands, and a few short-lived flings, but every time, he broke it off at the first hint of commitment.

Helen Chen was different. Until the night in Bolivia, he hadn't even looked at her that way. She was beautiful and whip smart, but after all she was Schlager's girl, and Connelly had never been interested in anyone already in a relationship. And yet, when the Bolivian sun had colored the tulle on the arched windows of their room in the lightest shade of pink of the morning, he was still wide awake. It had been warm at night and Helen pushed away the covers in her sleep despite his best efforts to keep them on top of her. She slept without a care, her arms spread wide, her chest rising and falling gently with each breath, her bronze skin glistening with sweat.

She was all business as soon as they were out of the prying eyes of Flores's entourage and he played the part as well, but now, occasionally glancing at her silhouette against the bright window, Connelly wondered if the trip was a corporate success but a personal failure. He couldn't afford to be distracted. Not now. Rovinsky had intercepted a report that Engel was about to move the ballots from the stronghold in New York to the location in Virginia, as Connelly had predicted. That meant they only had a few days to prep an assault on the convoy.

It was going to have to be flawless. Once the ballots were moved, they'd never see the light of day again and come Inauguration Day, their fate would be sealed.

The shadow of the helicopter crossed a river and then they were coming into a camouflaged clearing with blinking lights of the helipad. They touched down and moments later they were heading toward the entrance into the silo complex.

"See you later, Mike," Chen said, giving him a smile as she disappeared down the hatch, Schlager carrying her bags in one hand, his other holding her hand for balance. "Thanks for everything."

"You did good," he said. "I'll see you at the meeting. I'll see you later, Max."

Connelly watched them go and then headed for his tiny unit at the top of Silo 2.

He had just enough time to splash some water on his face, shave, and grab a quick bite when it was time to be back at the control center, doubling as Jason Hunt's quarters. The man himself was already there, talking to somebody on the communication implant. By the time he finished the call, Schlager and Chen joined him at the table as well.

"Good to see you," Hunt said as he disconnected the line. "I hear the trip went without a hitch."

"More or less." Connelly shrugged. He thought he caught a shadow of a smile on Chen's lips. "Flores is still no friend of ours, but he'll do what he promised. And what's even more important is that Helen installed a back door onto the cartel's servers. Hopefully, when we no longer need them, we can right some wrongs."

"Hopefully," Hunt said. "I know it must've been hard to agree to hand over the money to a drug lord, but we need to stay afloat. And it sounds like your plan is working, Mike. Engel is about to move the ballots, and even sooner than we'd thought. It'll happen in three days. They'll be leaving the current facility at four in the morning on Monday, which means they'll reach the bridge sometime before six o'clock. Knowing Engel, he'll have some flashing lights clearing the traffic in front of the convoy. They'll be traveling fast."

"We'll account for that. My team is prepped and Martin is at full charge. We are as ready as we'll ever be."

"Not quite," Hunt said. He stood up and leaned on the table. The wood creaked under his weight. "There's something I'd like to propose. We are about to enter a new phase of our confrontation with Engel and his minions. Rovinsky is convinced we are on the brink of civil war. I'm not as pessimistic as he is, but the man's got a point—we've had more shootouts with Engel's forces in the past month than in the entire last year. We are on the run, for crying out loud. There are riots all over the country. The entire system is close to a breaking point. Over the past few days, Max here is aware, I've installed over a dozen new implants and weapon systems. I'm suggesting you get upgrades as well."

"I agree," Schlager said. "Although the idea creeps me out—no offense, Jason."

"None taken. And I don't suggest you install the same mods as I did. To each their own. We all have different roles to play. But I think it would make sense to enhance our strengths. Max and Helen, for example, would install supplement CPUs and remote network penetration mods and you, Mike, should consider weapons augs. I have a few suggestions you can look at, but at the very least you should consider installing EMU."

"When would we do it?" Chen asked. Her face was neutral and Connelly couldn't tell if she was agreeing to the suggestion or not. "If we only have three days before the attack on the convoy, we won't be able to recover in time."

"You and Max would. We wouldn't have enough time to calibrate your new mods to their full potential in this time frame, but the procedures themselves are minimally invasive. For Mike, of course, that wouldn't be possible as wet-wired mods would take a few weeks' recovery time. Once you've built the chassis like I have, any new upgrades are much easier. Plug and play. What do you say?"

"I'm game," Schlager said. "We need an edge and at this point I'll take what I can. Helen?"

She stayed quiet for a few moments, her eyes looking somewhere in the distance. Finally, she nodded. "I'm game, too."

"You, Mike, should do it after the raid," Hunt said. "We'll take our time, make it as little invasive as possible so we don't derail you—"

"I think I'll pass, Jason," Connelly said, interrupting him. "I'd like to stay as is."

"Look, it's ultimately your decision," Hunt said. If he was surprised, he didn't show it. "We've been lucky. We know, well, *you* know Engel has been trying to create a new generation of cyborgs. No one has been able to replicate Martin yet. But it's only a matter of time. And when that time comes, no human—even an elite soldier like you— would stand a chance in a battle."

"I understand," Connelly said. He looked down at the palms of his hands. His skin was rough and callused, and there was a long scratch at the base of his right thumb. He touched it and it stung. He couldn't remember where he scraped it. "I used to have a friend. When we were in Afghanistan, a few times as we were going through some rural areas, I saw him taking a piss in the open. Just standing there doing his business without a care in the world. It grated on me, to be honest. One time I asked him if he wasn't afraid of getting shot."

"What did he say?"

"He said that if a 7.62 round was going to find him a few clicks away, it was his time and there was nothing he could do about that. I feel the same way. For now, I'd like to continue pissing in the wind."

34

"I can see it, boss."

Connelly's radio crackled in his ear. He was lying prone on top of the short hill at the foot of the Millard E. Tydings Memorial Bridge that carried Interstate 95 over the Susquehanna River. The six-lane highway—three in one direction and three in another—was empty at this hour save for an occasional truck. It looked like a chain of islands floating in dark sea under the miniature moons of the light poles.

"Go on, Lee."

"Two SUVs with flashing lights in the front," the man continued. "A semi with the trailer and another two SUVs in the back. I read two signatures in the big truck and four in each SUV. You've got eighteen hostiles, all heavily armed. Two minutes out."

"Any civilians?"

"Negative. Black Arrow mercs."

"Roger," Connelly said. "Stay close."

Lee was circling the bridge in the Killer Egg, a nickname given to the Boeing MH-6M Little Bird helicopter, fitted with outboard benches that carried three soldiers on each side.

Connelly looked at the remote-activated spike strip at the entrance to the bridge that he had installed a few minutes ago. Colored in asphalt-gray with a sloping edge on both sides, it looked nothing more than a slight bump on the road in the poor light of the lamppost. But at the push of a button, three-inch-long spikes, sharp as a razor, would deploy at the forty-five-degree angle to the oncoming traffic. Another strip was positioned two hundred yards farther on the bridge.

"Martin?" he called into the microphone. "Are you ready?"

"Yes," came the laconic answer. The cyborg was hanging off the concrete Jersey barrier on the outside of the bridge. His camouflage systems were online, and unless the convoy was looking at the specific spot with some sophisticated equipment, he would remain invisible.

"Thirty seconds. I'm heading for the other side."

Connelly could now see the flashing lights of the front SUV speeding down toward the bridge. A few moments later, the convoy came into view: two Black Suburbans in the front, a Volvo truck pulling a white box trailer about twenty yards behind, and two dark-gray Range Rover Defenders another twenty yards back.

He let the Suburbans and the Volvo pass the first strip and then hit the button. A row of steel teeth rose from the trap, biting into the tires of the Defenders. The two SUVs swerved, trying to regain control, one of them failing and flipping on its side. The other slowed down, and Martin flung his massive body over the barrier, opening up a torrent of fire on both vehicles while he was still airborne.

The Suburbans and the Volvo, seeing commotion behind them, pulled away, and that's when Connelly activated the second strip. The front SUV flipped over a few times, coming to a rest at the barrier long enough for the second SUV to ram it, sending up a fountain of sparks and coming to an abrupt stop.

The driver in the Volvo truck slammed on the brakes, coming to a screeching halt in front of the strip.

As if on cue, the Killer Egg dropped out of the dark skies, blocking the truck's escape route, six commandos jumping off the benches.

Automatic fire erupted for a moment, and then the night was quiet again.

"Brian, sitrep."

"Hostiles neutralized. We didn't detect any outgoing transmissions. Decoupling the trailer now. It'll be sling-load ready in sixty seconds."

"Roger." Connelly stood up and looked up in the sky. "It's your show, Simon. Take Martin. He's coming with you."

A minute later, the low rumble of the CH-53E Super Stallion heavy-lift helicopter filled his ears and, in a few seconds, he saw the massive machine coming over the bridge.

Connelly brought up a pair of binoculars and watched Martin hop on top of the trailer and connect the cables to the cargo hook. Then the bird lifted the trailer, made a turn, and headed north, slowly gaining altitude as Martin sat down on the edge of the container, his feet dangling over the void below. As the Stallion passed over Connelly's hiding place, Martin raised his hand and saluted.

"Show-off."

Another moment later, the Killer Egg, its engine sounding like an angry bee after the low roar of the Super Stallion, jumped into the air and disappeared into the night.

Connelly climbed down the hill and took the camouflage net off the Ducati Panigale bike. As the short-stroke two-hundred horsepower engine screamed east on the interstate, he dialed Jason Hunt.

"Cargo is en route."

"How did it go?"

"Without a hitch." Connelly zoomed past a small minivan and kept accelerating. "The guys did an outstanding job. We hit the support, but the truck was undamaged. The trailer is being transported as we speak. We will rendezvous in ten minutes like we discussed."

"You still want to split up? It seems like we will have more protection if we stay as a group."

"Yes, but we will also stick out like a sore thumb. Let's stick to the plan. We'll keep Sorkin company until we cross into New Jersey, and from there he should be safe."

"All right, I'll see you in a few."

Connelly revved the engine, shifting into a higher gear. It was still dark, but it was no longer pitch black, and when he took the MD 272 exit following the signs for the interstate, the sky in the east changed from monochrome to full color.

A minute later, he took another exit to a local road and soon was pulling into an abandoned truck stop. The large parking lot next to a boarded-up truck shop and a crumbling Denny's that once used to serve long-haul truckers was empty save for the two rusting carcasses of eighteen-wheelers. But now, in front of Denny's, there was a Ram pickup truck with a container hitched to it and two Ford F-150 trucks. A group of people stood next to the vehicles, the immense bulk of Martin towering over everyone else.

Connelly rolled next to one of the F-150s and killed the engine.

"Hey, Mike." Brian Sorkin stepped forward from the group, shaking his hand. "Thanks for letting me be a part of this."

"Good to see you."

"This old geezer here is Chris." Sorkin nodded at the older man leaning on the Ram's cabin. "He'll be helping me out to process the ballots. He used to work for the *Gazette*. It was way before my time, but he knows the drill."

"How long do you need?" Jason Hunt asked.

"Forty-eight hours. I've already prepped two semi-major papers and a whole slate of bloggers and online news outlets. We don't need to scan all of them. Just enough to sort through the data and show that they are fake in a compelling story. Hopefully, it ignites enough fire for the story to go viral."

"Did you tell them what it was?"

"Of course not," Sorkin said. "But I still carry enough weight in a few places to be taken at my word when I say I've got a major scoop."

"We should move," Connelly said. "Somebody could have heard the bird. Was it here long?"

"It was here less than five seconds," Hunt said, "just long enough to unhook the trailer and then they were gone, but you're right. We shouldn't push our luck."

"We'll get going then," Sorkin said and climbed into the cabin of the truck. He started the engine. "I won't contact you unless something urgent comes up."

"Hang on one second," Chen said. "Let me grab one box. Just in case."

Connelly watched her run to the back of the trailer and then a few moments later she emerged with a bankers box in her hands.

"You know what?" Hunt walked over to her and looked at the box. "I think it's a good idea. Mike, since we are splitting up anyway, can you take Helen back to the base? We will make copies of these and then reconnect with Brian and give the ballots back to him. I'll stay with Max and Martin. We need to pick up a few things."

"Sure." He glanced at Martin loading up the Ducati in the back of his pickup truck. "You are not going back to the city, are you?"

"No," Hunt said. "Don't you worry. It's on the way. I have a small stash of things in a storage near Albany. It's under a shell name. No one knows about it."

"Okay then." He helped Chen put the box into the truck and climbed into the driver's seat. "Brian, you're ready?"

"Yep."

"We'll shadow you until we cross the Delaware River and then you're on your own."

"We'll be fine."

"Famous last words." Chris chuckled and waved through the open passenger window. "See you later, fellas."

They waited as Sorkin's truck pulled the trailer out of the parking lot and climbed on the road. Jason Hunt's rolled out next, the springs of the back wheels compressed under the cyborg's bulk. Connelly released the brakes and started after Hunt. There was a long road ahead of them.

35

$\mathcal{A}$ bath bomb was sizzling at the surface of the bathtub as Jill Cooper watched the sunset over the Hudson River. With no access to her place at Park Slope after Engel's people's failed attempt to kill her, she had a decision to make. Cooper had been a firm believer in doing the opposite of what most people thought was a good idea in dangerous situations. Most, in her shoes, would try to lie low in some inconspicuous motel, pay cash, and avoid meeting anyone unless absolutely necessary.

But Cooper didn't feel like feeding bedbugs and watching pay-per-view on a twenty-year-old television. Hiding in plain sight was more her forte. She accessed her emergency account in the Cayman Islands and paid a visit to a forger who owed her a favor. Then, as Alison West, a jet-setting socialite, she checked into the Hudson room at the Standard Hotel. The swanky place in the Meatpacking District sitting on giant concrete stilts above the High Line, the famed elevated park built on a former New York Central Railroad spur, was the opposite of inconspicuous. But that was precisely the point.

She thought she was ready to do a deep dive into the trove of information that had been sitting on the small drive in her purse. And yet, when she locked the door, connected the drive to her laptop and opened the copy of Engel's computer, she looked at the long list of files and then closed the laptop shut. The truth was—she feared what she could find. What thread was she going to pull in her search for Elizabeth? Was it going to be her location? A place Cooper could actually find? Or a small note with a message from an anonymous killer, reporting on a completed assignment? A contract fulfilled at the same time Cooper was supposed to be blown to bits?

Instead of being relieved and ready to look for clues, she felt like a giant coiled spring, ready to explode.

She needed to unwind. For three days, she did nothing but shop, drink wine while watching traffic on the Hudson, and twice a day went down to the bar to pick up someone to distract her.

"Bring me another glass," she shouted without bothering to look. "Make sure it's full this time."

She couldn't remember his name. *David? Don? Danny?* It was something that started with a D, she was pretty sure of it.

"Here, princess." He appeared in her view, nude as the day he was born, a glass of white wine full to the brim in his hand.

She accepted the glass from him and took a sip, her eyes wandering up and down his muscular frame. She couldn't decide what to do with him. He smirked and went down on one knee next to the tub, his right hand going under the water and touching her foot. Then slowly moving up. By the time his fingers reached her thigh, she had made up her mind. "Thanks, um, David. You can go."

"It's Zach."

So much for the D.

His hand froze in place. He didn't pull it away and his lips were still curled into a smile, but she could see it was now a facade. He tried to play it cool, but she wasn't buying it.

"Is something wrong?"

"Nope. Just time for you to get off the train, that's all."

"But I thought—"

"Get the fuck out of my room," she said without raising her voice.

"Bitch."

She ignored his angry mumbling as the man shuffled around the suite, getting dressed. A few moments later, the door slammed and the room was quiet again. It was her and the sunset.

But now the colors had lost their magic. The body had taken care of its needs. The itch that she felt now was all in her head. Cooper pushed aside the pieces of the bath bomb, turned on the shower to wash off the foam, and stepped out of the tub. She wrapped herself in a soft bathrobe, sat down on the couch, and opened her computer again.

The folder had two big parts. One opened into a complicated file system that looked like a three-dimensional family tree, with cubes at each junction signifying multiple pieces of Engel's empire. The biggest of them all, right at the top, was Guardian Manufacturing itself, with a multitude of branches splitting away from it and connecting it to other businesses, both legal and illicit. Each cube was color coded. She quickly learned that the green ones were profitable, and the flashing yellow needed attention. And there was a whole subsection of the tree with gray cubes—the companies and illegal enterprises that weren't connected to Guardian on any reports, but were part of the empire, nonetheless. The other part was a spiderweb of folders connected to each other with color-coded lines.

Mesmerized, she wandered through the diagram, clicking on different cubes and watching them disassemble into a swarm of diagrams, charts, profit-and-loss statements, contracts, and spread-sheets. She chuckled—if Engel ever found out that she was alive and stole this from him, he'd definitely kill her, and this time for real. If there ever was a treasure trove of information, this was it.

But for now, none of this was of particular interest to her. She launched a crawler program, populated it with a dozen words and word combinations she thought would be relevant to start the search, and let it loose on the disk. A moment later, it started printing the matches in its gray-colored window.

The word she had the highest hopes for, *Elizabeth*, produced nothing useful. It made her heart jump when the crawler started spit-ting multiple files with the word in it, but the exhilaration quickly faded into angst and disappointment. All the hits had to do with a city in New Jersey, where Guardian apparently had a quite extensive operation. There was a large, legitimate pharmaceutical plant producing a line of a profitable cancer drug, a smaller factory producing even more lucrative street drugs, and a few warehouses storing them both.

Cooper scrolled through the results and, finding no leads, started to erase them when something caught her eye. There was a file titled *SCL* and when she clicked on it, it opened into a simple text document. The text was coded, but Cooper's pulse jumped as she looked at the long strings of letters and numbers.

Could it be so simple?

Her mind wandered to the windy road to Sa Calobra village on the northwest coast of Majorca, the peaks of the Serra de Tramuntana touching the clouds in the far distance. Was Elizabeth kept all this time in the very place Cooper thought she'd never be able to go back to? Was it what the letters stood for—*Sa Calobra, Liz?*

She drew a sharp breath and lifted her hands off the keyboard, her fingers trembling. She had spent years begging and pleasing and manipulating, trying to pry the secret out of Engel's hands. Thinking that Elizabeth was held in a place she couldn't possibly find.

Instead, Engel had been hiding her in plain sight. Cooper, it seemed, wasn't the only one capable of cutting against the grain.

She'd need to decode the message to be sure, and for that she was going to have a specialist. But she *knew* she was right. She also knew she couldn't act on an impulse. Cooper looked through the coded file. Twenty-six pages of scrambled text. That was a lot of pages. Before she hopped on a plane and jetted across the ocean, she needed to know exactly what she was getting herself into.

She went back to the laptop and looked through the gray files. A lot of them were password protected, and she skipped them for now, fascinated by the depth of Engel's empire. She opened the Guardian master file again, and poked around, reading reports, looking at spreadsheets, and scanning stored emails. One folder opened up into a series of gray cubes, also password protected, to her dismay. The name on one of them caught her eye. *Project Daimyo.*

She stuck her thumb into her mouth and bit on the nail, a habit from her childhood that never went away. She was safe for now, but while Engel and his minions thought she was dead, Cooper needed to move fast. The files on this laptop were her leverage that one day might save her life. It was her "get out of jail" card, but a big part of it was useless. The best part of it, anyway. Someone was going to have to help her open it up.

Cooper had been in her line of work for a long time, and to survive and thrive for that long in her field, one needed to develop a network of trusted professionals. Specialists on top of their game. Mistakes didn't get you fired when you were a hitman for hire—they got you killed. Over the years, she had established relationships with all kinds of people who supported her trade: bankers, forgers, arms dealers, smugglers. But there was a weak spot in her network—cyber specialists.

She had used black hats before, of course, but it was all for low-level jobs. Ironically, her specialty—making a hit look like a coincidence, an accident, an act of God—prevented her from relying on technology too much. For this job, she thought, looking at the coded file, she couldn't afford any mistakes. She needed to know *precisely* what the documents said. And not just the one that could finally lead her to Elizabeth. All of them.

To do this, she was going to hire the best hacker there was.

Cooper thought about it for a moment. She might not have used many hackers before, but in her line of work, she knew the underworld. And when it came to hacking, no one had more legends created about them than one person in particular. Cooper didn't have much to go on yet, but she was good at finding people who didn't want to be found. And she had a small clue.

A name.

The Witch.

36

"How's the upgrade?" Hunt asked.

They stayed in the right lane of the highway, just under the speed limit. The husky voice on the radio over a country tune was singing something about a long way home and forgiving without forgetting. The sky in the east had already turned from black to pink and now was turning pale-blue. Jason had allowed Sorkin to pull ahead—at this hour there were still too few cars on the road and a convoy traveling together would attract unnecessary attention. He could see the Ram truck with a container hitched to it about a quarter mile and a few cars ahead of them. Without an entourage, it blended in perfectly. Brian and Chris could have passed for a father and son traveling the country, or two working men, hauling some equipment. The chances of them being pulled over were slim.

"I'm getting used to it," Schlager said. "It's still weird and the controls feel clunky, but I'm getting better at it."

"It gets easier. When I first fitted my arm, I thought I'd never be able to get over how weird it was. It felt foreign, and even though it was exactly the size it was supposed to be, it felt three sizes too big. Every time I went through a doorway, I thought I was about to smash it into a frame. It took forever to calibrate, too. It's a strange experience when your eyes tell you one thing about something and your sensors feed something different to your brain. Trippy."

A radio station hissed, the country boy band disappearing, and then the sounds of a light rock song filled the cabin.

"At the very least, I'm capable of changing the music channel." Schlager smiled. "I can camp out by Engel's building and drive him crazy. Play for him the cheesiest radio station in the tri-state area twenty-four-seven. That will show him."

"Impressive." Hunt chuckled. "In all seriousness, though, I'm glad you gave it a shot. I only wish I could convince Mike to do the same. He's risking his life for us almost daily. If anyone could benefit from proper defensive upgrades, it would be him. But I understand why he doesn't want to."

"If I were him, I would be hesitant, too—no offense," Schlager said. "It's one thing to agree to get a tiny chip under your skull that no one can see. It's quite another to be visibly augmented."

"That's what I think we should work on once we have the opportunity. It would be the next logical step. For now, it's proven to be an elusive goal, but I think we'll get there sooner rather than later."

"What?"

"To make our tech indistinguishable from what Mother Nature gave you. That will break down the hesitancy. Don't you think?"

"I don't know." Schlager scratched his chin. "Maybe? I'm conflicted about this. On the one hand, I would be reluctant to get any augs that would look like augs, but when I see them on you, or Martin, they don't bother me at all. That's part of the package. But I can see how artificial limbs that look like real ones would weird some people out. That can lead to prejudice against augmented people. And we had tried this. What was it—two, three years ago? It all came out like Barbie parts. That was terrible."

"We did. We'll have to keep on plugging away until it works. And there's already prejudice, Max. I am in a privileged position, but I know when people stare and act weird around me. Hell, I was biased against the tech when Rachel worked on it. I thought unless someone needed a part, it was not unlike plastic surgery. A fad. And to be frank, if circumstances didn't force me into getting an artificial arm, I don't know if I'd ever come around on this. Most people are ossified in their beliefs. For certain things, it might take generations to challenge the status quo. Sometimes people need to see it in front of their faces long enough before they accept it."

They rode in silence for some time, the sun steadily climbing in the east.

"I wanted to ask you something," Hunt said. "Do you think JC is alive? I'm having a hard time processing this. So what that it sounds smart? Most commercial house controls sound almost as smart."

"I do." Schlager chewed on his lip and threw a glance at his friend. "It's not about what she said that convinced me she was self-aware. It's the ability to think in abstract terms. Think about it. Computers, even the most sophisticated ones, are at their basic level still making binary decisions. Ones and zeroes. That's all there is. Of course, as you get more processing power, you can create enough forks on the logic tree that it would *appear* as if the machine is thinking. NPCs in modern games are good at this. But that appearance stays there only as long as you don't stop for a moment and dig deeper. And when you do, you are left with a simple logic tree that you can trace with a finger. If this happens—you do this. If that happens—you do that. And so on."

"And you don't think JC is like that?"

"No." Schlager became animated. His gestures were more pronounced and there was a glint to his eye. Whatever he saw in the program that Helen Chen brought from across the ocean clearly made an impression on him. "JC can think like us. I've never seen anything quite like it. She contemplates life and death and beyond. She can operate in hypotheticals. If that's not the sign of intelligence, then I don't know what is."

"And you think we need her for Rachel's procedure?"

"Yes and no." Schlager leaned back again, took off his sneakers, and pulled his feet onto the chair. "If you want that to happen soon, then yes. I'm sorry if this is blunt, but it's the truth. She'd be capable of doing it in no time at all. The only issue is for us to make sure she doesn't somehow escape."

"If she's truly alive," Hunt said, "keeping her confined sounds kind of bad."

"Perhaps." Schlager shrugged. "But I've seen too many movies to risk it."

"Touché. Do you think we can use her against Engel? To hack him?"

"Probably not." Schlager shrugged again, almost apologetically. "I don't see how we can let her hack things in the real world without risking her running away. Speaking of hacking. What did you think of Chuck's intel?"

"Which part? About Otomo's factories?"

"Yeah."

"I don't quite know what to make of it. It's a compelling story but Otomo's bankrupt and as far as I know the assets have been nationalized. At least whatever was in Japan. But I guess it's possible some of their factories abroad could have fallen into other people's hands. I'm not too worried, though."

"How so?" Schlager said. "If Victor Ye is building something new, we should be worried. Especially if he got his hands on a technology that wasn't available to him before. We should send somebody to investigate. Maybe Chuck would go. He knows more about it than anyone else."

"If I had to guess, they are building sentinels. I've read some reports that they had delivered some to the US already. Those don't scare me. If anything else, hearing this makes me happy. Engel's been trying to replicate Martin's tech for years, but hasn't been able to. To be fair, we haven't been able to replicate it either—that's why our sales to the DOD have been limited to alloys, protective current generators, and energy weapons. But cyborg tech is where the edge is. And not just from the technology perspective. It's the combination of human mind and lethal machinery where you get the advantage. Drones are great, but they still need operators. We are closer to a true symbiosis than any other corp out there, Engel included."

"If I didn't know any better," Schlager said, "considering that we are on the run, hiding in a retrofitted nuclear missile complex and have been designated to be enemies of the state, I'd say you sound optimistic."

"It's always darkest before dawn, my friend. Isn't that what they say?" Hunt smiled. "Call me a fool, but I think once Sorkin disseminates the information about Engel's foul play, the tables will turn. He won't go down without a fight, I presume, but if enough people believe he cheated his way to victory, his support will wane and die. Once that happens, the rats will abandon his ship. Black Arrow, Victor Ye—do you think they support Engel out of ideology? Because they think he's a nice guy who will lead them to a better future?"

"He's a means to an end," Max said.

"Exactly. They are riding what they think is a winning ticket. Once it becomes obvious it's no longer the case, they'll turn their backs. Then we'll pick them off, one by one."

"I hope you're right."

"Have some faith, my friend." Jason smiled and turned the music louder. "I know things look pretty gloomy right now. But I think we are about to turn the page."

37

"Three miles till we hit the bridge," Jason Hunt said over the open radio. The traffic had been building up as they got closer to the Delaware River and now it slowed down almost to a crawl. Connelly's truck was now traveling in front of their group and Hunt right behind the trailer as they prepared to go different ways. "Brian, remember what we discussed. Once we cross the bridge, we are peeling off. Stay off the major roads and you should be fine. The only other point where you'll be exposed is when you are crossing into Staten Island."

"We'll manage. Look at that guy. Just going across the lanes."

"What's going on?" Hunt straightened in his seat to look over the cars in front of him, but the trailer was blocking his view. They were approaching a small bridge over Christina River, the last crossing before the monstrous Delaware Memorial Bridge. He turned to Schlager. "Can you see anything on your side?"

"Nope." Schlager rolled down the window and stuck his head out.

"Watch out," Connelly yelled. "There's—"

There was a screech of tires and a clash of metal, and Hunt watched in horror as the F-150 carrying Connelly and Chen shot out and went airborne on the side of the road as if launched from a catapult. Its driver's side smashed, the truck flipped in the air and went over the barrier into the river below.

"No!" Schlager screamed.

Hunt pulled hard left, cutting in front of a beat-up sedan and eliciting an angry torrent of honks. The front of Sorkin's truck stopped with a thud, hitting something, and then the front of the car whipped up, lifted by an invisible force, its wheels helplessly spinning in the air. It stood on the back wheels for a split second and then came crashing back down, the windows shattering on impact.

The traffic stopped. Hunt slammed on the brakes, the car shaking as Martin jumped out of the back.

"Stay in the car," he shouted at Schlager—who ignored him, got out of the car, and ran toward the edge of the bridge. Hunt swung the door open and rushed out toward the Ram truck. Sorkin's arm was hanging lifelessly out of the broken side window, blood dripping off his fingertips and puddling on the ground below.

"Jason," he heard Schlager yell. "Watch it."

"I told you to stay—" he started and froze, looking at the figure walking to him in a lurching swagger. The ugly face, the thick arms ending with disproportionately long, sinewy hands. A memory came rushing back, hitting him like a freight train. A general population holding block. A man pacing back and forth like a caged animal looking for a fight. The flurry of blows. The blinding pain of broken bones as the man's foot crushed his elbow. And then the perverted smile as those creepy oversized hands held his broken arm out and slashed his flesh with a scalpel, going in so deep the steel scraped the bone.

Johnny the Butcher walked in the middle of the lane and stopped in front of him. A burnished armor covered him all the way up to his neck. A low, almost inaudible vibration came from somewhere inside of it. A shiny helmet with an open visor pulsated with a bluish glow.

"You look like a lost puppy," the man said in a high-pitched, squeaky voice, as the visor slid closed. "I should have cut off both of your arms last time."

From the corner of his eye, Hunt saw Martin rush past him to engage someone hidden behind the bulk of the trailer, the scales on the cyborg's arm moving to reveal a snub-nosed barrel of a gun. The rattle of automatic fire snapped Hunt out of his trance.

He charged at Johnny, covering the distance between them in one powerful leap and then shooting him point-blank in the chest from a shoulder cannon as he landed. The man tumbled back from the impact, sparks flying off the front of his armor. He hit the trunk of the car behind him, an old Subaru with a woman in the backseat, her face distorted with a scream of horror. Hunt pressed the advantage, stomping on Johnny's knee to bring him down and then his bionic arm shooting out at an impossible speed, aiming for the face.

An armored arm went up, turning a killer shot into a glancing blow, and then Johnny propped himself up on one arm, kicking Hunt in the chest with both feet.

Jason rolled back, the EMU controlling his move, the armored plates in his chest vibrating, dissipating the blow but hard enough to make his teeth chatter.

A moment later, he was on his feet. He and Johnny circled each other like two prizefighters at the end of an even round: each waiting for the other to strike, each wary of making the first move. There was another torrent of automatic fire on the other side of the trailer, followed by a few powerful thuds and more shots still. A chill went down Jason's spine—he hadn't seen anyone yet who would last that long, confronted with the overwhelming power of the cyborg. Whoever was fighting Martin was giving him a run for his money. He needed to finish this dance with Johnny.

Fast.

He faked another charge, hoping to throw his opponent off his balance, but Johnny sidestepped, remaining perfectly in sync.

"Hey, asshole," Schlager's voice said. He had snuck around the row of cars while Hunt was trying to gain the advantage and climbed on the hood of the car behind Johnny, toting a pump-action shotgun in his hands. As Johnny turned to the sound of his voice, Schlager shot him in the face and then, as the man stumbled back, shot him again.

Hunt rushed forward, his bionic arm smashing the adversary like a mechanical hammer and pinning him to the ground. As Johnny struggled to get free from under his weight, Hunt pummeled his helmet again and again, his mind replaying the horror of the holding cell, the crazed Butcher's smile as he carved his flesh. Hunt wanted to flatten that ugly face—to erase him from existence. Sparks flew off the helmet, its glow growing weaker.

"Jason!"

He heard Schlager yell, but before he could turn to see the new threat, something massive slammed into his side so hard it launched him into the air. The grille of a white Mercedes SUV arrested his flight, knocking the air out of his lungs, his reinforced ribcage straining against the impact. A few scarlet alerts popped up in his internal vision, highlighting compromised systems as the world outside dimmed in and out.

"We finally meet, Mr. Hunt," Victor Ye said, stepping into view. His body was also covered in shiny scales, but unlike the Butcher's thick, burnished plates, his armor seemed thin and had a mercury-like surface that almost looked liquid.

Hunt had never seen any armor like this anywhere else except on Martin.

Martin.

As the world came back into focus, Jason looked in horror at the object that had smashed into him and sent most of his systems offline. In the middle of the carnage, a few feet away from the dazed Butcher, laid the twisted body of the cyborg. The head was almost separated from the body, sparks flying from ripped wires sticking out of the steel vertebrae. A big part of his right shoulder was missing, and his right leg was bent at the knee in the wrong direction. He wasn't moving.

Jason struggled to his feet in time to see Schlager charge at Victor Ye, shooting him at point-blank range. Victor shifted away from the blast, his movement so fast it looked blurred, his hand swatting the barrel like a tiresome pest and throwing Schlager on the ground.

Hunt yelled in frustration and charged, but before he could cover even half the distance separating him from the crime boss, Victor Ye's shoulder plates shifted, revealing a nose of a strange barrel.

It spat blue fire.

Jason Hunt's limbs seized. He fell on his back, his EMU popping another urgent message, all pixelated and weirdly colored, and then all his systems went offline, plunging him into internal silence he hadn't experienced for a long time. With no power, his chassis was too heavy to carry, and he stayed on his back, watching as Victor stepped over Martin, walked by Schlager's crumpled body, and came closer.

"I've wanted to do this for a long time," the leader of the Red Dragon said, leaning over and grabbing Jason's bionic arm. Then, in one powerful move, he ripped it from its shoulder socket.

3 8

The car flipped in the air, hitting the water upside down with a thunderous crash. The airbag exploded in Connelly's face, blinding him. He hung off the chair for a second, dazed, the skin on his hands feeling the burn of the airbag, the seat belt painfully biting into his shoulder.

"Helen?" he called, but she didn't answer. Chen's eyes were closed, a thin line of blood dripping down on the headliner below her head. It was getting dark inside the cabin as the car sunk into the dark-brown water of the river. The gurgling sound as the liquid sipped into the insides of the vehicle was getting louder. They needed to get out. Fast.

Connelly placed his left hand below his head for support and disconnected the seat belt. He collapsed onto the roof and turned around, cursing at the pain in his neck.

"Helen, come on," he called again, but she was unresponsive still. Connelly unbuckled her seat belt, catching her fall, and placed his ear to her face as the darkness enveloped the car.

She was breathing. Good.

He tried the door, but it wouldn't budge. They weren't deep yet, but it was deep enough to make the door feel heavier than anything he could move. He'd need to equalize pressure first. Connelly hit the power window switch, expecting the water to rush in, but nothing happened. He tried it a few more times and then leaned over Chen and tried hers. Nothing.

Shit.

Connelly turned around and, using the headrest for support, kicked the windshield with both legs. It cracked with a crunching sound, a long, dark line running across the glass.

He hit it again, aiming at the fault line, leveraging the weakness. It crunched again, louder this time, concentric circles radiating from where his boots had hit the glass. Water seeped through the gaps around the seal, small rivulets pulling into puddles.

"Come on," he yelled, putting his weight into another kick. The windshield gave, Connelly's feet going through the rubbery mosaic of broken glass, letting the torrent of dark, icy water into the cabin. He grabbed Helen under the arms and held her, shivering, as high as he could, giving her a few more precious seconds to breathe. When water reached his chin, he held his breath, reached out, and tried the door handle again. It worked, letting more water in and pushing the last pockets of air out.

He grabbed Chen and pushed with all his might, clawing with one hand against the brown liquid, reaching for the dim light overhead. His lungs burned, longing for a mouthful of fresh air as he kicked and clawed, and then kicked and clawed again.

He broke the surface, gasping and choking, pushing Chen's head above the water. They were a few hundred yards downstream from the bridge, the distant sounds of gunfire fading like fireworks.

He kicked as hard as he could, pushing for the shore, and soon he was dragging Chen's body out of the water and onto the muddy bank covered in sharp gravel. He brushed the rocks aside, clearing some space, took off his jacket, and laid Chen on top of it. She wasn't breathing, her usually bronze skin pale with a bluish tinge.

"Damn it." He interlocked his fingers, placing his palm on her chest, and gave it a series of quick, hard pushes. Then, he pinched her nose, placed his lips around hers, and blew air into her lungs, waiting for her chest to rise.

She coughed, spitting a small amount of water, and then rolled over on her side, retching into the mud.

He held her until the spasms stopped and then helped her sit up.

"I need to go back," he said, pulling his jacket around her shoulders. It was soaked through and held little warmth, but she nodded, still unable to speak.

He turned back to the river and, not giving himself enough time to find a reason not to, jumped back into the icy water. He fought the flow, his muscles cramping up from the cold, his lungs burning again for air. But there it was—the darker outline of the pickup truck, barely visible in the water thick with mud.

The flow had shut the door again, and he wasted precious seconds prying it open and going back inside the cabin. Then, with the bankers box in his hands, he was swimming for the surface again.

When he climbed up to the bank, he placed the box next to Chen and collapsed on the ground, not caring for the sharp pricks of gravel biting into his back. He welcomed the shivers that ran throughout his body as through pain they brought back control to his stiff muscles.

"Are you okay?" she asked.

"Yeah." His voice was raspy, his breathing ragged. "You?"

"I'm fine." She placed her hand on his shoulder. "Mike. You saved my life. I don't even know what to say."

"You don't have to say anything."

"Thank you."

He got up on his elbows and looked toward the bridge. "The shooting stopped."

"Yes. My shiny new implant can't get a signal from anyone. All I get is an extra headache. You don't have a radio, do you?"

"Nope." He tapped his belt. "It must've fallen off on impact."

"What do we do?"

"We need a car." Connelly forced himself up and looked around. There was a tree line two or three hundred yards away from where they were, and he thought he could see a road through the trees. "Let's go. It looks like a road. We follow it until we find something."

"Did the papers survive?"

"I don't know," he said, glancing at the soaked-through bankers box covered in smudges of brown mud. "But the sooner we bring it somewhere dry, the better."

The road turned out to be a railroad track running parallel to the river and as they followed it, they came up on a large L-shaped building that housed an auto parts store, a tile market, and a moving company. They sat, shivering, behind the trees and watched the parking lot in the back of the building for a few minutes and finally settled on a beat-up, white, working van that seemed to be parked there long-term.

"Stay here," Connelly said, setting the box down. "I'll try to start it and then you can join me. Don't come out if the alarm goes off."

"I have a better idea," she said. "Let me try something else."

Before he could protest, Chen walked out of the trees and headed toward the line of cars. She stopped in front of the white van for a few seconds and then pulled on the driver's door handle. Connelly tensed, anticipating the screeches of a car alarm, but nothing happened and Chen dived into the car. A moment later, the engine rumbled, and the headlights switched on.

Connelly picked up the box of ballots and ran over to the parking lot.

"Was it open?"

"Nope." She smiled and put the heat on full blast. "But it looks like my new gadget is actually good for something."

"I better make sure to never carry credit cards around you. Let's get back to the bridge," he said as they pulled out of the parking lot. "Whatever happened there is over, but I want to see the aftermath. It might give us some clues. But let's circle around so we are moving in the opposite direction. Those lanes might still be closed."

"Okay."

They looped around the shopping center, watching warily for anyone who might recognize the van, but the area was empty save for a few cars and soon they were on a local road running parallel to the railroad tracks.

"Did I imagine it was Victor Ye in some souped-up armor?" She broke the silence.

"It was."

They drove through the underpass and turned north. It was an industrial area—a chemical plant, a few rows of warehouses, a car repair shop. But then they were in the suburbs again, and before long, Chen was getting onto the highway.

"It's ahead," she said as they got closer to the crossing. "There's a fire truck."

The traffic slowed to a crawl, as the cars ahead of them slowed down to look at what was happening on the opposite lane. Connelly could see the fire truck and as they moved even closer, two ambulances and, to his surprise, an armored police cruiser.

"Martin." Chen exhaled.

He saw it too. The crumpled body of the cyborg laying in the middle of the lane, its head turned at an unnatural angle, the wires sticking out of his broken neck. The surrounding carnage was staggering. The truck with the trailer carrying ballots was missing, but the highway was littered with burned-out cars riddled with bullet holes.

"Slow down," he said as they got level with the ambulance. A man was being loaded inside of the truck. His face was caked with blood and at first Connelly thought he was dead. But he was covered with a blanket, and as the medic moved out of the way, the man turned his head ever so slightly. For the briefest moment, they made eye contact. "That's Brian. Sorkin's alive."

39

----

*D*rip plop drop. Drip plop drop. Drip plop drop.

The roof of the tent, pitched next to a tall northern red oak, was sagging under the weight of the dripping water. Jason Hunt squinted to see if there was a leak, but couldn't tell in the diffused light of the electric lantern set to night mode. He pulled on the zipper of his sleeping bag and stuck his head out. It was cold. Even in the relative warmth of the triple-layered tent, the air was biting outside of the safe cocoon of his four-season sleeper. Up here, the days would get pleasant enough to strip down to a pair of shorts and a T-shirt while he watched the bobber attached to the end of his line go up and down with the waves. But as soon as the sun went below the jagged peaks, the temps dropped fast enough you could get your tongue stuck to the spoon you were licking a moment ago.

He glanced at the bag next to him. His father was deep asleep, a soft snoring sound rolling off his slightly parted lips. White puffs of warm air rose over his mouth and disappeared in the darkness some-where under the roof.

His mother, perhaps wisely, declined to join them on the fishing trip, citing a weather report that had promised a generous amount of rain for the entire duration of the holiday dubbed by his father in advance as "the best fishing expedition ever."

He should have refused, too, but something in the way his father talked about the excitement of the upcoming trip made him say yes. High school was only a few weeks away and in some strange, telepathic way, he knew his father saw it as their last childhood trip. The last chance to spend some time with his son when he was not quite a man yet, but still a child—asking for fishing tips and relying on his parent for shelter. Perhaps his mother had felt it too, and it wasn't the weather report after all, but her desire to give them space and a chance to bond one last time, to stretch the summer of simple days, that made her decide to stay.

Drip plop drop. Drip plop drop. Drip plop drop.

He pulled the zipper lower and sat up, a shiver running down his spine. His father stirred, his snores quieting down, but didn't wake up.

Drip plop drop. Drip plop drop. Drip plop drop.

Jason reached out and touched the fabric with the back of his hand. It was wet. And cold. And it was smooth, like skin.

It was strange. He brought his face closer to the fabric, straining to see in the dim light of the lantern, and recoiled in panic. Floating above him in the darkness was a face of a woman he hadn't met yet.

No, not above. Below.

"Don't be scared," she said.

Her face was wet. Her body was submerged in a tank of glowing yellowish liquid, dense enough to make her float without moving. *Like a fly inside amber*, he thought. The chrome-colored tank was propped on a large rolling table with a snake's nest of wires coming underneath.

"I can't do it," he said. "There's gotta be another way."

"You know there isn't."

"Maybe we can steal it," he pleaded. "Steven has access to the labs. I'll go there and take the prototypes."

"You know it's not possible." She smiled. "You'd need a team to install them. Doctors, nurses, engineers, programmers. Support staff. This is the only way."

"But to save you, we'd need to kill you," he said. "*I would need to kill you. I* would have to tell Steven to stop your heart."

"Yes." She smiled again. "And when I come back, I'll be sure to milk it for as long as I can."

He laughed, but his eyes stung. It was cold in the makeshift lab, white puffs coming out every time she breathed, the steam condensing on the walls and ceiling. Dripping from the ceiling.

"You better go, Jason." He heard Poznyak's voice. "You don't want to be here when it happens."

"No. I'll stay here."

It was getting colder still. He looked up at the ceiling, suddenly concerned for those drops of water.

What if they get into the liquid? Will they screw up the formula?

"Go, babe," she said. "It's okay. I know you'll figure something out."

Reluctantly, he moved on toward the exit. Looking at her but thinking about the water condensing on every surface.

"I'll see you on the other side."

"I know you will."

Drip plop drop. Drip plop drop. Drip plop drop.

The walls were shaking. They swayed left and right. There was some shouting and cursing, and something fell with a loud, clanking noise and rolled away from his view. His body was cold, but his right arm was hot. Pulsating. Drops of bright ruby red seeping through a dirty T-shirt stuck to his ruined arm. Falling on the gray concrete floor as the gurney rolled on, marking his trail. A scarier version of Hansel and Gretel's story.

He shivered. He was colder still. But not because it was outside. No, this was the cold that came before the end. It seeped into the bones and turned your blood into a thick slush.

The gurney bumped into the wall as it turned the corner, sending an electric jolt through his body.

Drip plop drop. Drip plop drop. Drip plop drop.

They rolled him onto the bridge. Now it was time for him to go. *Could he go?*

He looked around. There was a car flipping in the air, going over the barrier. It was moving so slowly he could count the pieces of broken glass flying out of its side window. The driver was there. He looked dazed from the impact, a fresh cut above his left eyebrow. Still clean, but it would bleed soon. Jason could see the passenger there, too, her face slacked, eyes closed.

He turned back to the bridge.

A figure in shining armor was standing over the bodies, like a god who came down to Earth to smite mortals.

The bodies.

Jason Hunt looked at them. They were important to him. They used to be. The skinny man crumpled next to a tire of a car. Another man—a giant, part human, part machine.

He gave them up. He knew that now. He exchanged their lives for the life of a woman.

No.

Not for a life of a woman. Just for a chance of her life. He liked to think that it was for a bigger cause. To bring technology to the people. Defeat death itself. He said as much. But in his heart of hearts, he knew it was not what drove him. He wanted to get his wife back. To go back to the simplicity of the days where the rest of the world could disappear and he wouldn't care.

Was it worth it?

He thought it was. But he didn't know the answer anymore. Not looking at the bodies. Not looking at the carnage on the bridge. The terrified faces of people in bullet-ridden cars stranded in the middle of a battle that they wanted to have no part of.

His mind raced back to the place where he thought he'd never be able to go. To a secret lair somewhere deep inside the malfunctioning interface that sent pixelated pictures that made no sense to his weary brain. There, at the very bottom of the forbidden well, laid a solution that could give him peace. *End the struggle.* His enemies would cele-brate. Their forces would march on to claim the victory, and the world would move on. But what did he care?

A wave of cosmic lassitude was consuming him. He felt like a dying star, expanding as it cooled off, burning the last of its fuel. It was dark when he closed his eyes, and it was dark when he opened them. Nothing made sense anymore. He could hear a steady drip of water, the steady drumbeat that connected the past and the present. Sooner or later, he would have to make a choice, if there was going to be a future. Or someone else would make that choice for him.

He closed his eyes again, giving in to fatigue. He'd make that decision soon. For now, all he could do was listen to the water dripping from one invisible surface to another.

Drip plop drop. Drip plop drop. Drip plop drop.

40

Jason Hunt woke up to the sound of dripping water. It was a rhythmical drumbeat that repeated itself after each three notes that sounded slightly different from one another.

Drip plop drop. Drip plop drop. Drip plop drop.

The beat never stopped, never paused, and never changed. It was maddening.

He blinked, opening his eyes, and then fought a wave of panic before realizing he hadn't gone blind. It was pitch black. He blinked a few times, trying to adjust, and after a while he saw the outlines of things. A thin outline around the door. The gray contours of a rectangular cell.

His chassis had rebooted while he was unconscious but the energy cells were almost depleted, giving him just enough juice to keep himself upright without crumbling under his own weight. All of his systems were offline, and the visual interface looked pixelated and glitched every few moments. He couldn't tell how long it had been. His head was heavy, like after a night of hard drinking.

He couldn't remember much.

A sheen of perspiration covered his face, and he reached with his right hand to wipe it off.

Nothing happened. He groaned, and that's when the memories came rushing back in. The fight on the bridge. The explosion. Souped-up Victor Ye standing on top of him and ripping his bionic arm out of its shoulder socket.

The sensor implants in his shoulder were still wet-wired to his nervous system. Without the visual input, he could *feel* the arm, but it wasn't there.

His body ached. His left arm was shackled above his head and his feet were tied to an anchor at the base of the wall.

"Great," he said out loud. The word came out raspy and flat, stifled by the oppressive darkness of the cell.

As if on cue, bright lights came to life on the wall panel, blinding him. Blaring music of Wagner's *Walkürenritt* filled the room, swelling with each wave. It got louder and louder until it filled his chest cavity, making it pulsate with each note.

Then, as abruptly as it began, the music stopped, and the lights dimmed, leaving the cell in a harsh uniform light.

There was a clattering of keys and then the door to the cell swung open, letting somebody in. Hunt squinted against the harsh light as his eyes adjusted.

Victor Ye was standing at the entrance of the cell. Glistening armor was covering the man up to his chin. A barely audible humming sound came from the inside of the shining surface as he moved around.

"Dramatic," Hunt said. "Playing the *Ride of the Valkyries* right before your entrance. Never took you for the theatrical type."

"There's always a time and a place for the right amount of drama." Victor gave him a tight smile as he walked to the center of the room and stood there for a few seconds, looking the prisoner up and down.

"You padded your shoes? You looked much shorter in pictures."

"And you look naked and scrawny," Victor shot back. "But I'm not here to trade insults. I thought after being locked up in the dark for so long you'd appreciate some entertainment. And boy, do I have some entertainment options for you."

"Can't wait."

"However, it wouldn't be fair if you watched this alone. I brought your friend here as well."

He moved to the side, and two men wheeled a gurney into the cell. A naked man, his body covered in extensive bruises, was tied to it. Hunt's chest constricted as he saw Schlager's face. One of his eyes was swollen shut.

"Max. My God. Are you okay?"

Schlager forced a smile at his friend as the men unloaded him off the gurney and shackled him to the wall next to Hunt.

"Look at that." Victor clapped his hands and the harsh sound from the contact of his metallic fingers reverberated through the small room. "A reunion. I think the stage is set and we are ready for the main act, don't you think, Jason?"

Hunt didn't answer. Whatever Victor Ye had in mind, Jason had no interest in playing along and giving him satisfaction.

He waved his hand and the two men retreated from the cell, only to come back a minute later, rolling in a table with a large computer screen set up on it. They moved it to the wall in front of the prisoners and then pulled the wires from outside to connect it. The screen blinked a few times and then displayed a high-definition picture of a forest clearing. It looked like a live, high-altitude feed from a drone or a plane. A small timer window in the upper corner of the screen was counting down to zero.

"Do you recognize it?"

Hunt squinted at the screen. For a few seconds, it looked like any other forest clearing shot from above, but once his eyes adapted to the unusual angle, he drew a sharp breath.

"You do, I take it," Victor said, satisfied with Hunt's reaction. "There was a mothballed governmental project with a mighty name, Project Thor. Few people were aware of its existence, not even the president himself. But due to some fortuitous circumstances, I came across the project and I couldn't help but think that sooner rather than later it could come in handy. Have you heard about it?"

Hunt didn't answer, his eyes glued to the black-and-white timer in the screen's corner. There were only two minutes left before something happened. Something terrible, he had no doubt. Their missile silo hideout was discovered, and now dozens of the most loyal people —along with Rachel—were sitting ducks inside a trap without the slightest clue. But what could Victor possibly do? Those silos could withstand anything but a direct hit from a nuclear missile. *He surely wasn't going to...?*

"Of course, we wouldn't want to use nuclear warheads on our own territory," Victor said, as if reading his mind. "But Project Thor is a weapon that can generate almost as much force as a tactical nuke without generating a fallout. It's a kinetic device. I don't care to explain how it works, so I'd rather let it speak for itself."

Victor moved aside and waved his hand, as if inviting his prisoners to enjoy the opening of a show.

"He's bluffing." Hunt heard Schlager's voice.

The clock had less than thirty seconds left.

"Only one way to find out," Victor said, without looking back.

The clock counted down to zero and for a moment nothing happened, giving Hunt a glimmer of hope that it was indeed a bluff, nothing more. Then the screen went white.

"No!" A harsh scream filled the room and bounced off the walls before dying out. Hunt pulled on the shackle with all his might, nearly dislocating his arm. "You bastard. You're going to pay for this."

The bright light faded out on the screen, yielding the view to the dreaded shape of a mushroom cloud. A deadly circle of a shock wave moved deceptively slowly away from the epicenter. Then, without warning, the picture disappeared, replaced by white noise.

"I've got to say, I knew what to expect," Victor said, nodding in approval, "but even I'm surprised to see how powerful it was."

He waved to his goons and the two men rolled out the table with the screen out of the cell.

"I will kill you, Victor," Hunt said. "I don't know how. But sooner or later, I will find you and kill you."

"I'm right here." The man took a couple of steps and stopped in front of Hunt. Even in his armor suit, he had to crane his neck to look Jason in the eye. "And there's nothing you can do. Look, you might not like our methods, but this war is over. And I say it's good for everyone. We don't have to be enemies. We could work together. You've shown that you have grit, ingenuity, and you're not afraid to take chances. Alex can certainly use someone like you on the team. There's no shame to switching sides when the only other alternative is death. I'll tell you what—come work for us and help us build a better world. Don't you want to have some input into shaping the future?"

"Fuck you."

"Alex and I didn't agree on a lot of things," Victor continued, "but we've always agreed on one thing: this world is dying. It needs someone like Engel. Someone who has a vision and is not afraid to get his hands dirty. We are building a new empire, Jason. And when we are done, our power will be rivaled by none. We will be gods."

Jason Hunt said nothing, looking at the man in front of him.

"It's a shame." Victor studied his face for a moment and then turned on his heels and headed for the door, his boots clanking on the hard stone. "Suit yourself. I'll leave you with my doctors then."

He walked outside of the cell and a moment later, two other men wearing plastic aprons rolled in a large wooden table. Then one of them disappeared, only to come back with a smaller plastic table. It was covered in black felt and a large array of gleaming instruments was laid out on top of it.

"Lovely. That kind of party," Jason said and closed his eyes. "Do what you will, assholes. Just don't play me any more Wagner. Your music choices are atrocious."

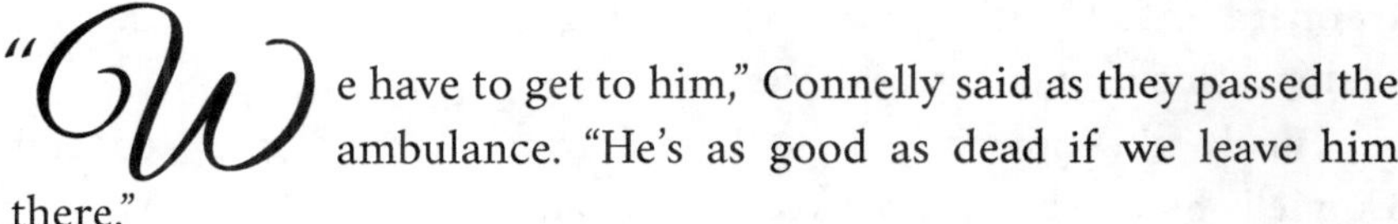

"We have to get to him," Connelly said as they passed the ambulance. "He's as good as dead if we leave him there."

He drove until the armored police cruiser was no longer visible and slammed on the brakes, bringing the van to an abrupt stop.

"What are you doing?" Chen said.

"Come on." He jumped out of the van, ignoring the angry honks of the cars piling up behind them. "By the time we get across and come back, they'll be gone and we'll never find him. Grab the box."

He hopped over the barrier separating the opposite side of the highway, not waiting for her to follow. An old sedan almost swiped him as it zoomed by, the furious honk fading in the distance. Then there was a Jeep barreling down on him, a middle-aged mustachioed man laying down on the horn as he got closer and closer. Connelly tensed as the car's grille came to a stop a few inches from his chest.

"Are you out of your fucking mind?" The man rolled the window down and stuck his head out. "I could've killed you."

"I'm sorry, pal." Connelly slid around the front of the car and smashed an open palm into the man's face. Then he reached inside the vehicle, grabbed the handle to open the door, and pulled the dazed driver on the side of the road.

The man tried to take a swing at him, but Connelly swatted his hand away and hit him in the face again. "Please don't struggle. I don't want to hurt you."

He climbed into the Jeep and opened the passenger door for Chen. She heaved the bankers box into the cabin, climbed in, and a moment later they pulled into the lane, accelerating away.

"The cops," Chen warned him as they approached the police cruiser.

"Look around at the wreck," he said. "That would be a natural reaction of anyone driving here. Don't be too calm."

They crawled past Sorkin's trailer, waiting for the drivers in the cars ahead of them to get their fill of rubbernecking. Two police troopers in full battle gear were walking around the wreckage, but there was no sign of any bodies.

Finally, the flow ahead of them started picking up speed and Connelly bullied his way between a few cars and stepped on the gas.

"I can see the ambulance," Chen said, pointing ahead.

He could see it too—a large white minivan with a red stripe across, a few hundred yards ahead of them, its bright, pulsating lights making the cars in front of it scurry away like roaches in the kitchen.

"How do you want to do this?" she said. "We can try to get to him in the hospital. You have a laceration on your forehead. We could pretend to look for help. You actually need to get it stitched, anyway."

"No." He shook his head. "Too risky. We have to assume that Engel already knows who Sorkin is. If he's in the hospital, he won't make it out. We're going to have to grab him before that."

"We don't know the condition he's in. He might be critical."

"That's a chance we're going to have to take."

He followed the ambulance, keeping a few cars behind it, and when it took the exit, Connelly sped up, overtaking the van and cut in front of it, forcing it to the shoulder. There was a mall on the other side of the road and a gas station farther down by the traffic light, but there were no cars nearby. The siren blared and died out as quickly when the driver saw the barrel of a HK Mark 23 pointed at his head.

"Get out of the car and get down on the ground," Connelly shouted, keeping the Jeep between himself and the driver in case the man tried to ram him with the ambulance. "Right now."

After a moment's hesitation, the driver obeyed and soon Connelly was tying the man's hands behind his back.

"How many people in the back?"

"Two EMTs and the patient."

"Stay here," he said and ran to the back of the van. He opened the door, dodging a fire extinguisher in the hands of a stocky technician. He trained the gun on the man and waved him out of the vehicle. "Don't do anything stupid. Get out. You, too."

He forced the two men out and down on the ground next to the driver and tied them as well.

"Is that you, Mike?" Sorkin groaned when Connelly stepped into the ambulance. "I thought you were dead. What the hell happened on that bridge?"

"We got our asses handed to us, that's what happened," he said, undoing the belts that secured the man to the gurney. "Are you okay?"

"I'll live. Some cuts and bruises." The man gingerly touched the side of his head. "My head weighs a ton of bricks, so probably a concussion, too. Did everybody make it out alive? Where's Chris?"

"We don't know. We might be the lucky ones." Connelly helped the man stand up and guided him out of the van. "We almost drowned and by the time we made it back to the bridge, everybody was gone. I only saw Martin. It's hard to tell for sure, but it didn't look like he'd made it. There was nobody else. Did you see anything?"

"No." The man moaned as Connelly pushed him inside of the Jeep. "Damn, that hurts. I was out for a while. The last thing I remember was that man in shiny armor hitting your car and you guys flying over the rails. I thought you were goners. When I came to, all the excitement was over and I saw you driving on the other side of the bridge. I hope Chris is alive. There was a lot of blood on his seat. Geez, I can't believe it was all for nothing."

"Not for nothing," Chen said as the car pulled away from the ambulance and accelerated away. "Mike saved a box of ballots."

"You did?"

"Yes." Connelly glanced back at the man. "I fished it out of the river. It's not what you might call mint condition, but it didn't spend too much time under water. I think some of it should be salvageable."

"Can I see?"

"Here." Chen passed the bankers box back to Sorkin.

"Oh boy. We need to find a place to separate the paper and dry them properly. If we keep them like this, they'll all glue together."

"You can come back with us."

"I'd love to, but no, I cannot. Despite all of this—" He stopped himself. "No, especially *because* of all of this, I need to get back to New York as soon as humanly possible. That's the only way I'll be able to put this out there before it's too late. One box of soggy ballots isn't quite the same as the entire batch, but still. But first, we need to stop somewhere and save these documents. Is there a motel around here? I don't know the area and I left my phone in that trailer."

"Can you find a place?" Connelly looked at Chen.

"I don't know. Let me try." She closed her eyes and leaned back on the headrest.

"What's she doing?" Sorkin asked.

"She has an implant," Connelly said. "Hopefully it's working."

"There's a motel about two miles from here," Chen said, opening her eyes. "I can guide you there. Do we have any money?"

"I have cash," Sorkin said from the backseat. He laughed, a bitter edge to his voice. "I don't know why, but as I was dressing this morning, I thought I had better take cash. Stupid, I know, but look at us."

The motel, proudly named Noble Inn and Suites, was a sad, oblong, two-story property painted in bright yellow. The manager, a pot-bellied woman with an eighties hairdo, gave the disheveled group a suspicious look, the crease on her forehead deepening even more after they asked for only one room. But she took Sorkin's money and then produced a key, chained to a card with the painted number of the room.

"Room twenty-two. Make a left when you go upstairs. And I don't want to see any stains on the sheets," she warned them as Sorkin took the key.

"No, ma'am," he said, visibly cringing.

"At least no new ones," Chen added when they were out of the woman's earshot.

The room, with beige wallpaper and a queen-sized bed with a faded red headboard, was cleaner than Connelly had expected. He pulled the flower-print comforter off the bed and spread it on the floor. Then they spent the next twenty minutes carefully pulling papers out of the bankers box and laying them out to dry.

"What do you think, Brian?"

"They will do," the man said. "I saw a hair dryer in the bathroom. That'll speed up the process. I should be able to get going in a couple of hours."

"All right then." Connelly threw the keys to the Jeep to him, and Sorkin caught them in the air. "Keep the car. Helen and I will find something else. Thank you for what you're doing."

"I owe it to Sofia. Now go."

They left Sorkin in the room and went outside, the manager watching them from behind the desk the entire time.

"Do you think they are all gone?" Chen said as they stepped out to the parking lot. Something in the tone of her voice made him stop in his tracks. "Max, Jason, everyone?"

"I don't know." He put a hand on her shoulder, feeling her shiver under his fingers. "I hope not. They might've been taken. We'll get them back. We need to find out what happened."

"There's something else," she said. "I didn't want to say it in front of Brian."

"What?"

"Our base has been hit. I can't get access to the direct link and the urgent message that I received is scrambled so bad, it's impossible to understand what it says. I can't tell for sure what happened. But whatever hit us was powerful."

"How powerful?"

"Could've been nuclear."

He looked at her for a moment, lost for words. Then he turned around and headed across the parking lot to the gas station across the street. "We better hurry then."

42

"At least it's only two of them at each entrance," Chen said, pointing Connelly at the two guards in front of the scaffolding surrounding the building. "And there's the truck. The other sides are too exposed."

They had been hiding in a tiny square across the street from Orion Tower for the past two hours. A steady stream of cars going for the Holland Tunnel was flowing next to it, the honks and engine noise drowning out the rest of the city. The pungent smell of exhaust filled her nostrils.

After leaving Sorkin at the hotel, they stole another car, a black Beetle that seemed to have had seen enough trips to circumvent the globe several times. Its engine sputtered and coughed along the way, but it dutifully delivered them to the city in a few hours. They ditched it not too far from the Staten Island Ferry terminal in lower Manhattan and then took a few trips on the subway going up and down the island. Finally, they got off at Canal Street and cut across the city on foot before going north to the tower.

In the few days after they had fled the headquarters, there had been scaffolding constructed around the entire building that restricted entrances to four choke points. A pair of guards clad in black combat gear guarded each entrance, openly carrying submachine guns. They picked this side of the building because the street was narrower and there was a flatbed truck with a few plastic barriers on top parked next to the curb and partly obstructing the guards' view.

"Are you sure we can't do this from anywhere else?" Connelly said. "This place is crawling with Black Arrow."

"Yes, I'm sure," she said, watching the guards at the entrance. They were chatting, occasionally throwing glances up and down the street. One put out a cigarette on the side of the building and then flicked it toward traffic. "We need to know what happened at the compound before we go there. Apart from the quant at the silo, which might not even be operational anymore, this is the most powerful machine we'll be able to get our hands on. If we want quick answers, this is the only place we can get them. Once I'm able to use the system again, I'll be able to access it from anywhere."

"And you can't access it from the outside?"

"No." She cringed. "I built it this way. The system will light up like a Christmas tree if I try. It seemed like a good idea. The irony is, I've *always* built back doors in the systems I had designed before. Just in case. Here it didn't seem appropriate. Like leaving the garage door open at night in your own home."

"I understand."

"Once we are inside the building, it'll be easier. I had paired my new neurolink with the system before we fled the tower. But since I got it installed at the silo, I haven't had a chance to try it yet. We'll have to figure some things out on the fly, but I'm fairly certain it'll work. It'll give us an advantage. Any ideas?"

"Maybe." Connelly looked around and then pointed at a white Range Rover parked at the end of the block. "That SUV looks fancy enough. It should have a modern nav system. Can you access it?"

"Yes." She pulled up the internal view of the remote neurolink and searched for the SUV's signal. Once the system established a connection, she saw a smaller window pop up that mirrored the navigation interface of the car itself. She tried the hazard lights. The car's tail-lights blinked.

"This is like magic," Connelly said. "Can you program it to drive around?"

"I can. But not for too long. It's not built for a fully autonomous drive. It'll start making mistakes and will eventually crash. I'd give it fifteen, twenty minutes tops."

"No, we don't want that. How about you make it drive a few blocks away and park itself?"

"I can do that."

"Okay." Connelly checked his watch. "But we won't get much time, anyway. These guys seem to check in every thirty minutes and the next one is due in roughly two. We have thirty minutes at most and that's only if we are lucky and nobody calls on them for something random. We should aim for fifteen minutes, anyway. Is it enough time for you?"

She thought about it for a few moments. The best point to access the system would be her own place on the twenty-seventh floor. But it was also the place most likely crawling with Black Arrow agents. Going there also meant taking the elevator that could limit their options of escape. But from anywhere else, it could take longer.

"I'll make it work," she said. "But we might run into a guy or two on our way there."

"Understood."

"Are you sure about these?" She nodded at a pouch of heavy marbles, one inch in diameter, that Connelly bought when they stopped at a gas station.

"No," he shrugged, "but the moment the shooting starts, all bets are off. We should try to keep it quiet as long as we can."

They stayed hidden until the guards did the next security check. She watched as the guard who had smoked before spoke to someone, pressing his finger into his ear. The man stood straighter for a moment as he reported his status and then relaxed again, returning his attention to his partner.

"Back up the car now and bring it to the building. Make it dramatic," Connelly said to her and sprinted across the street, keeping behind the flatbed.

She brought up the nav system again, touched the virtual ignition button, and plotted the path terminating in front of the truck. The tires squealed as the powerful engine jerked the car out of its parking spot and propelled it in rear gear toward the building. The guards snapped to attention as the vehicle sped toward them, and that's when Connelly snuck around the flatbed and struck.

Chen had never seen him in real action before. A few times she'd watched Connelly spar with Jason, when Hunt was calibrating his systems, but that was not a fair fight. No man, no matter how skillful or talented, could outpace a machine. It was like using a cheat code in a computer game. Remotely starting a car with something that had been implanted in her brain might have looked like magic to Connelly. But watching him ambush two highly trained and armed to their teeth mercenaries? *That* looked superhuman.

The guards were out before they knew what had hit them and Chen popped the trunk of the SUV, letting Connelly stuff two unconscious bodies inside. Then, with another tap on the virtual button, she sent the car into drive and watched it disappear around the corner. She'd programmed it to park five blocks away from the tower. Then she crossed the street to meet Connelly by the doors.

"Ready?"

"Let's do it."

They went through the double doors and headed for the reception desk. A lone guard in a black uniform looked up at them in surprise.

"How did you—" The man made a gurgling sound and collapsed backward and out of his chair as one of Connelly's marbles struck him squarely in the forehead.

"I'll never play bingo with you," she said, struggling to keep up.

"Are you in?"

She rushed behind the reception desk, doing her best not to look at the guard. A massive purple welt on the man's head looked like an alien trying to break through the skin. Chen opened the computer terminal and punched in her credentials. Then she navigated to the main security system and enabled access to her neurolink. A cluster of icons peppered her internal vision, and she swept them aside, leaving only a handful of security controls.

"Let's go."

They ran toward the elevator bank, the doors chiming as Chen overrode the system.

"Magic." Connelly smiled as they went inside. "Can you tap the security cameras?"

"Already have," she said as the elevator's doors closed. "There are two people in my apartment right now."

"Anyone on the floor?"

"There were," she said, "but at the moment they are investigating what's going on at the room at the end of the hallway."

"And what's going on in that room?"

"Led Zeppelin." She smiled. "Pretty loud, too."

"Definitely magic."

The elevator stopped at the twenty-seventh floor and they stepped outside. She could hear the sounds of "Whole Lotta Love" coming from down the corridor. They tiptoed their way to the door of her apartment and she raised her hand, signaling to Connelly to stop.

"There are two men, one in the living room looking out the window and one, ugh, is using my toilet," she said. "I'm going to turn on the shower vent and unlock the door at the same time. Ready?"

"Go."

The door clicked and opened, and she saw Connelly rush into her living room and strike the man by the window.

"Rob?" a voice came from the toilet. "Did you say something?"

Connelly disappeared in the bathroom and a moment later, Chen heard two quick thumps, followed by a thud of a falling body.

"Sorry," Connelly said, coming back to the living room. "I'm afraid he made a mess."

She nodded, slid behind the desk and powered her computer terminal. "Let's get some answers."

43

It was strange to be a fugitive in her own room. She accessed the server and her hands continued on autopilot as if they were some nimble animals with minds of their own. Chen glanced around the room as her fingers continued to fly over the keyboard. A man, his hands and feet tied up, was lying face down on her couch. He was unconscious, but alive. She could see the light-blue linens—*her linens*—that Connelly pulled over his head move up and down as the man breathed.

The other man stayed in the bathroom. A pair of feet in black combat boots were sticking out of the door, and judging by the fact that Connelly didn't bother to tie them up, Chen suspected the mercenary was no longer capable of being a threat.

"I don't mean to sound like a kid on a road trip," Connelly said, coming back from the door where he had been watching the hallway. "But are we there yet?"

"There's a lot to process," Helen said, pulling away from the computer terminal and turning back to him. "There's good news, and there's bad news."

"Give me the bad news first."

"They tried to break into our servers and failed."

"How's that bad?"

"That part isn't bad on its own," she said. "But it triggered our defense systems. Some of them are written in. But there's also another level of protection. It was Jason's idea. He insisted that in the event somebody was trying to hack us, our servers would get physically disconnected from each other and the outside world."

"That's smart. It flipped a switch somewhere?"

"Yes." Chen glanced at the screen. The diagram of Orion's network resembled a group of islands—a few blinking lights scattered in a big dark sea. "All twenty of them."

"Twenty?" Connelly leaned on the corner of the desk and looked at the monitor. "How do we turn them back on?"

"There are two ways." She brought up a three-dimensional blueprint of the building and expanded it for him to see. "There are four switches on each of the top five floors. They are in a hidden panel next to the stairs. They look like regular circuit breakers and act the same way, too. All you need to do is flip them back on, preferably without running into any of the Black Arrow guys."

"What's the second way?"

"I could override the system from the penthouse. That would flip all the switches back. But…" She swapped the window on the monitor and brought up the security camera view. There were no cameras inside of the suite itself, but the large double doors of the elevator were open and the high-resolution camera on its wall gave a wide-angle view of Jason's living room. Two guards were positioned at either side of the entrance, and there were what looked like at least a dozen men in black uniforms inside the penthouse. "It's a hornet's nest. I don't see how we get the servers up and running again."

"Agreed. Sounds like a lot of bad choices." Connelly stood up and paced the room back and forth. "You said you had some good news too?"

"It's sort of good news," she said. "The tower's system analyzed the hit on our silo before it was shut down. There's not a lot of information to draw conclusions from, but some things are obvious. It was powerful, but it wasn't nuclear."

"Thank God. Can you tell where the missile did come from?"

"I don't think it was a missile." She hid the building's schematics and brought up another screen. "This is one of the side projects that Max and I have been working on for some time. We initially created it for the covert communications with our assets overseas. A giant relay that bounces the message through a series of unsuspecting satellites, but we never used it. I tried to repurpose it to track a beacon in Jason's built-in chassis, but with little success. The signal is there, but it's so weak, I can't triangulate it without access to the mainframe. But the fact there's a signal gives me hope."

"We'll find them, Helen." He walked back to the desk and put a hand on her shoulder. "I know we will."

"Maybe if the silo is operational and I can tap into the quant's power, I can give it another shot. Regardless..." She paused, collecting her thoughts. "We designed the system for a specialized satellite, but it tracks almost every satellite over the planet. Some data is coming directly from NORAD. Most of this information is not even classified. They track orbits, calculate positions of weather satellites, make satellite decay predictions, and do a lot of other things. What it doesn't see is space junk and inert satellites."

"You think it was a satellite that hit us? With that much precision? How's it even possible?"

"No," she said, pointing at the map with a scattering of white dots moving over the continents. When she zoomed out, the dots merged into a shape that looked like a donut—a wide torus with Earth in the middle of it. "There's a ton of them—thousands. But all these are known objects, so unless you are looking for something specific, the system doesn't care about it. You can zoom in on it, and read what it's used for, when was it launched. The system also tracks all launches, so every time a new object appears in the sky we know where it came from."

"Okay."

"Here," she opened another window and scrolled through a seemingly endless table of data, "you can see the data on every launch. You can open each and read a fair amount of information about it. Even the classified ones have stats. When the system doesn't know something, it highlights the object, just like this little fellow in bright yellow."

She clicked on the link, and the view expanded into a generic picture of a satellite. Unlike others, the page was entirely empty, except for a large word at the top: UNKNOWN-b80.

"What's b80?"

"That's our internal classification. It simply means this rock had been launched before nineteen-eighty, but we don't know exactly when. It's not necessarily true, either. It's simply an extrapolation from available-to-us data. What's more interesting is this," Chen said and looked up at Connelly from the chair. "This is an interactive system. It stores the data continuously, but for the last seventy-two hours, I can access it right from this console. Whatever hit our compound, hit it yesterday at nineteen forty-four. Guess where our friend here was at that time?"

"Directly overhead?"

"You got that right." Chen got up and paced the room. "I think Engel hit us with some kind of orbital weapon."

"I don't understand." Connelly sat at the edge of the desk and leaned closer to the screen, as if trying to see something encoded in the empty table. "A new satellite that is not new but was launched before the turn of the century? Where did it come from?"

"I don't know for sure. But I suspect it was inert for a long time."

"You think Engel reactivated it somehow?"

"Maybe." She shrugged. "It doesn't really matter. It's there, and it hit us. Which means as long as it's out there, it leaves us vulnerable. Now that we know the silo has survived, we need to move. We need to get back to the compound and get the quant working."

"What are you going to do?"

"What I always do." Chen stood up, a roguish smile on her face. "Hack."

44

*J*ason Hunt tensed like a coiled spring getting ready to strike when one of Victor's torturers would have to unlock his arm, but the man never gave him a chance. He approached him from the side and, without saying a word, jabbed a small syringe that seemed to have appeared from thin air into Hunt's thigh. Then he proceeded to Schlager to do the same.

A warm wave spread from the site of the injection. It felt as if he had gotten a new, tiny heart that was now beating inside his thigh, sending out wave after wave that traveled through his body, one hotter than the one before. Goose bumps covered his entire body—his skin felt electrified, like a thundercloud pregnant with a charge, ready to release its power in one blinding microsecond. Even the air flow over his skin produced a sensation that was almost too much to bear. He was sure when the *doctors* started their work, he would descend to the levels of hell so deep there would be no coming back. A few seconds later, Hunt felt his muscles stiffen, refusing to answer his commands. His face seemed to be the only part of the body not affected by the poison. He squared his jaw, not to show any weakness, but a sickly sense of dread started to settle in.

The goons silently watched the two prisoners for a few minutes.

When they seemed to be satisfied that the paralysis had taken hold, they removed Hunt's restraints and dragged him to place on top of the wooden table. He bit his lip as his bare skin slid over the rough surface. His mind raced to the small corner of his neural interface. Buried deep under the multiple levels and firewalls, there was a small rectangular button. If he pushed it, if he *willed* it to be pushed, a capsule buried under the back of his cranium would release a toxin a hundred times more potent than the venom of the black mamba. He'd be dead in seconds. It surely looked like it was going to be used today.

After the two men secured him to the table, one of them turned to Schlager. "You'll be taking turns, yes?"

"Of course," Schlager slurred and spat in the man's direction. "Who'd want to miss that much fun."

Hunt closed his eyes and tried his best to concentrate on his own breathing. It wasn't working. Even with eyes closed, all he could see was the terrifying array of instruments that were about to tear into his flesh. A raw, primal panic started to cloak him like a cold, wet blanket.

He opened his eyes and looked at Schlager, a horrible truth dawning on him for the first time. Schlager didn't have an easy way out, and if Jason was going to check out early, Victor Ye was surely going to make his friend pay for it in spades.

If you can hear me, clear your throat.

The voice coming through the radio implant sounded garbled and unrecognizable, but for a second Hunt was grateful for being paralyzed as he would've jumped otherwise. Instead, he cleared his throat as asked.

Great. How many hostiles are in the room? Cough once for each person.

He coughed twice.

Okay. I want you to count down from ten and then yell at the top of your lungs. Make it loud. I need those guys startled.

He was about to follow the command as a flash of blinding white-hot pain exploded in his right foot. He had never experienced anything like that in his entire life. It was all-consuming. It had no beginning and no end, and had he had the ability, he would have reached down and ripped his own foot off his body to make it stop. A guttural wail forced its way from his lungs, filled his throat, and exploded into the small room.

There was a loud crash and then a double-clap of a silenced weapon echoed through the room a second later. Hunt opened his eyes in confusion. His foot was still throbbing with a horrible pain, but Victor's *doctors* were no longer standing next to the bed and when he strained his eyes to look down, he could see someone's foot. It wasn't moving.

Another moment later, Connelly's face came into his view. There was a freshly stitched deep cut above the man's left eyebrow, but his eyes were smiling. "Missed me?"

"Oh, you have no idea."

"You yelled too early," Connelly said as he helped him to sit up. "Threw me off."

"Sorry about that." Hunt looked at the great toe on his right foot. The nail was missing and fresh blood was trickling down on the table. "Getting your nails pulled apparently causes people to yell. Who knew?"

"Can you guys walk?"

"No. They gave us some kind of paralyzing agent. It's wearing off fast, but not fast enough. And it intensifies everything you feel. It's not for the faint of heart."

"You too, Max?"

"Afraid so."

"Okay, we can do this." Connelly moved the table with Hunt on it to the wall and leaned him against the cold, wet stone. "Stay here. I'll be right back, okay? I'll bring you some clothes, too."

"Sure. I'll just hang here," Schlager quipped, rolling his eyes at the bonds that secured him to the wall.

"Wait," Hunt pleaded. "Do you know what happened to the silo?"

"All's fine. Engel hit Silo 3, which wasn't occupied yet. And it wasn't a direct hit—it landed a few hundred yards due north. The other silos fared well. Some minor damage on the inside. No serious injuries as far as I know. A few scratches and bruises. The equipment held up too. Some broken furniture, a few cracks here and there, but nothing crucial."

"How's…" Schlager said, but then stopped, unable to continue.

"Helen's fine," Connelly said. "She's the one who found you."

"That was her on the comms?" Hunt said. "It was all garbled; I couldn't understand if I was picking up a signal from one of ours or if it was some random radio station."

"Yep. That's how we've found you. She tracked down your beacons to this general area, and then Rovinsky was able to give us the exact coordinates. But we better go. We don't have much time."

"Did you evacuate?"

"No. Lucky for us, we have Helen Chen. She wrestled control of Project Thor assets from Engel. For now, there's a stalemate. He has an overwhelming force, but we have a doomsday weapon. Nobody wants to make a decisive move first. At least for now."

"Lucky for us indeed."

By the time Connelly came back with a man from his security team, Hunt was mobile enough to climb off the table and even attempted to free his friend. The knots around Schlager's ankles proved too tight and complicated for his one hand, however, and he was happy to pass that honor to Connelly's tactical knife.

"Where are we?" he asked as he struggled to put a pair of jeans on. "I have no recollection of getting here."

"Northern Virginia. Or maybe Maryland. It depends whom you ask."

They walked out of the cell into a dark corridor, and Hunt leaned on Connelly's shoulder to step over two dead bodies near the cell.

Hunt squinted as the door opened, letting bright afternoon sun in. It seemed Victor had been keeping them in a basement of what looked like an old farmhouse. Three more dead bodies of Victor's guards were laid out on blood-splattered snow.

"Mike, you didn't tell me. How did Jim know? He might be in jeopardy, if Engel finds out we escaped."

"He said it used to be a safe house for the CIA. I don't think his position was compromised."

"Okay." Hunt shivered, the cold, hard snow crunching under the soles of his bare feet. "Now what?"

"Now this." Connelly pointed at the road leading away from the house. "Sorry about the shoes. There was no time to look."

"I'll live."

At first, Hunt couldn't see anything, but as he kept squinting against the sun, he noticed a black dot on the horizon. It grew in size and a minute later, a large black Suburban pulled up in front of the house.

"Come on," Connelly urged, and the group loaded up into the SUV. "Get in the back. I'll ride shotgun."

"Good to see you, boss." Chuck Kowalsky craned his neck from the driver's seat and gave a small wave.

"Hey, Chuck. Can you guys fill me in?" Hunt asked as the SUV pulled away from the farmhouse. "What the hell happened on that bridge? We'd never been blindsided so badly before."

He watched Connelly's face as his head of security contemplated the answer.

"I think we either have a mole, or we have been hacked," he finally said. "Not something I'm saying lightly, but I don't see any other explanation."

"We could've been hacked," Schlager said. "Engel and Victor have some top talent too. Besides, Engel now has the entire force of the NSA at his disposal. I think it's a greater possibility than a mole."

"Because it's more likely or because it's easier to swallow?"

"Not to be a Debbie Downer here," Connelly said, turning to face the passengers. "But it could be both. And I'd suggest until we know otherwise to treat it as such."

45

The new arm was integrating well. Jason Hunt looked at himself in the mirror, his left hand's index finger tracing the red, swollen fresh scar that ran around his right shoulder. The sensory input hadn't been calibrated properly yet, and from his previous experience he knew he had to be patient. It was going to take some time to dial it in. For now, he was going to have to contend with sometimes mismatching information between what he saw and expected to feel instead of the actual sensory reaction uploaded from the receptors on his artificial arm. It was jarring at first, but as time went on and the sensors fine-tuned, at some point he'd get where the flow of information would become more nuanced from his bionic arm than the one from his real arm had ever been.

There was a knock on the door and he pulled on a black T-shirt before answering.

"Yes?"

"Sorry to disturb you, sir," a man said. "Darius Price is here. His helicopter just landed. Should I bring him here, or you'd rather meet him outside?"

"Bring him in. I'll meet him in the blast lock area."

"Right away, sir."

As the man disappeared, Hunt put on a jacket, stepped out of his living quarters, and took a flight of metal stairs to the lower level that used to be the launch control center. From there, he went into the tunnel—the cableway—that connected the former control center with the actual missile silo. Sitting roughly in the middle of the cableway, behind the two sets of massive three-ton steel blast doors and a meter-thick concrete walls, was the blast lock area, which connected the outside world to the underground missile complex.

A minute later, Darius Price came through the access portal doors with two bodyguards in tow. Dressed in a leather bomber jacket, a pair of khakis, and a pair of dark-brown combat boots, he looked more like a general visiting the troops in a theater rather than a politician.

"Darius."

"Jason."

His handshake was firm, but he withdrew his hand a touch too soon, as if he wanted whatever the part he had to do here to be over as soon as humanly possible and not a second longer.

"Come on in. Your boys will have to stay here, though."

Price nodded and Hunt led him through the cableway back to the control center.

"It's smaller than I had imagined," Price said as they climbed the stairs.

"Please, make yourself at home." Hunt went around the table, pulled out a chair, and sat down. "Take a seat."

"You know," Darius Price rapped his knuckles on the steel door without moving; the sound was muted, almost too quiet to hear, "I've always wanted to check out one of these installations. I was once in Tucson, Arizona, and they have this museum built in a Titan II site. We even had the tickets, but then Henry, my youngest, got sick, and we had to cut the visit short. It's hard to imagine that at some point two people sat here with the power to launch a weapon that could kill millions."

"It is." Jason Hunt looked around the small space. It was partitioned into three sections. One doubled as his living quarters, with a

Spartan military-style bunk bed with a computer terminal on the lower level by the wall and another standing workstation built into the opposite wall. The second served as a miniature bathroom with a shower stall barely wide enough for him to squeeze in. The main room had been cleared from the old equipment and now had a slick round table in the middle, doubling as a second computer screen. The place had the feel of a miniature modern home, but the thick metal door that Price was leaning on stayed the same as a remnant of what the place was meant to be. "Luckily for us, it was built to withstand almost anything except a direct nuclear hit. Now that Engel put it to the test, we know it wasn't an exaggeration."

"I've read about them a lot. Nuclear weapons fascinate me. It's hard for us to understand, but when I was growing up, my dad used to tell me how he always had nightmares about the nuclear war. They had drills at school, you see. And watched videos about the effects of the weapon and what to do if there was a war. As if there's actually something you can do except pray for a quick and painless death.

"Did you know," Price continued, "that the operators had no idea what the actual targets were? They only knew them as Target 1, Target 2, and Target 3. Do you know why?"

"Secrecy?" Jason volunteered. He didn't think his answer mattered. Price wasn't speaking to him. It was his way of working through the problem. Distracting himself while his brain worked on it in the background. Once the solution had been found, he'd then allow himself to let it float to the surface and get it ready for dissemination.

"No." The man separated himself from the door, took two steps closer, and sat at the table, opposite to Hunt. "It was to prevent the operator from weighing the morality of the launch. That time was too important to fuck things up. The men sitting in this room couldn't be trusted with the information whether the missile they were about to unleash was going to hit a military installation with hardly a soul on it, or a city with a few million people."

"You saw the ballots," Hunt said, losing patience. "Engel doesn't belong in the White House."

"I don't know what I saw." Price slammed his hand on the table, sending a flurry of light flickering waves on its dark conductive surface like a swarm of spooked fireflies in a dark backyard. "You said give me three days, Darius, and I'll give you unequivocal proof. Those were your exact words. I gave you my word. And what did I get in return? You disappeared for a while. I can't find a single mention of a supposed massive firefight on a bridge on the news. And then, when you come back, all I get is a story in a few second-rate news sources from a washed-up journalist with pictures of blurry papers that may or may not be real."

"They are real, damn it." Hunt stood. "The firefight was real. And I didn't *disappear*. We were ambushed. One of ours was killed. Victor Ye ripped my arm out of my shoulder with an ease of an angry toddler disassembling a toy that fell out of favor. They tortured me and Schlager. And do you think we faked the giant crater next to our base with the forest turned to ash in a quarter-mile radius just to sell you on a lie? It's a miracle that all of us are still standing."

"I'm sorry for what you've been through," Darius Price said, his shoulders slumping. "And I'm sorry I have to keep asking these questions, but I feel like those men who were supposed to send that missile. And in my case, I *need* to know what's on the other side of its path. Am I about to strike a blow to the enemy's military might, or am I to unleash suffering on millions of innocent souls? There are riots all over the country. Cities are burning, Jason. Black Arrow has now established itself as the de facto controlling force of the military, with legislation to follow as soon as Engel is sworn in. And Engel is in control of Black Arrow. Even if I take what you say as gospel, agreeing to your plan will mean the bloodiest conflict on American soil since the Civil War."

"Yes." Jason sat down again and studied the face of the man in front of him. Price seemed to have aged since their last meeting, deep lines creasing his forehead, his eyes teary and bloodshot. "The balance of power seems to be in Engel's favor. And should we lose, you'll find yourself prosecuted and most likely killed. But as a good friend had told me not long ago, the war was inevitable. It will happen with or without us. The only choice you now face is to be a mere spectator or to take sides."

"Let me ask you something." Price placed both hands on the table and leaned toward Hunt. "Why do you need me? If anyone could fit the role that you're pushing me into, it would be you. People know you all over the world. The *Times* called you the Bionic Man and named you the person of the year when your company went IPO. Your tech is revolutionary. But most importantly, you are famous for beating Engel at his own game. They teach the story of the Asclepius takeover in every business school on the planet worth its tuition. If you came out against Engel publicly, people would support you. Hell, I would support you. And you have the resources I'd never be able to match."

"That answer is simple." Hunt smiled and leaned back in his chair. "If I did that, I'd be no better than Engel. For the same reason: a general of a victorious army can't stay on as the president. You turn from the liberator into an occupant. People didn't choose me to be their leader, Darius. They chose you. That's what you've got to do. Lead. And I'll help you any way I can."

46

"GIVE US ENGEL OR GIVE US WAR" the sign said. The man who held it, a bearded, pot-bellied bear of a man in a tracksuit, leaned over the police barricades and yelled something as Chen's car went through the checkpoint. She saw the spit fly off the man's lips but couldn't make out the words through the bulletproof glass. It sounded like something about *freedom* and *dying*. She didn't care either way.

"It's getting worse every day," the driver said. "There was a shoot-out in Brooklyn Heights last night. Seventeen dead. It's like a war zone."

"You should move your family to the silo," she said. "Keep them there until the dust settles. They'll be safer there."

"Safer," the driver spat, as if the word had offended him. "This is my city, Miss Chen. We've lived here for four generations. There's no way—"

A crack of automatic weapon fire rattled across the street. Somebody shrieked in the crowd, and then everybody was running in all directions. A few seconds later, the barricades toppled over with people jumping over, stumbling and falling, trampling those who weren't quick enough to get out of the way.

The driver stepped on the gas, trying to stay ahead of the crowd. Something smashed into the side of the car; there was a swooshing sound and a sharp smell of kerosene, and then the entire right side was engulfed in a roaring flame.

"Oh my God," the driver exhaled, the car screaming through the intersection and swiping a trash can as it made a turn. "Hold on, Ms. Chen. We're almost there."

Thick smoke permeated the vehicle, and Chen moved as far away from the window as she could. A few moments later, they shot through the gates of the underground garage and then a few attendants descended on them, pulling her and the driver from the car and attacking the fire with fire extinguishers.

"Step back, Ms. Chen. Stay away from the car."

Chen tried to help, but the driver and the attendants wouldn't hear it. She watched them put out the fire and then walked to the elevator.

"Are you okay?" Schlager was standing in the hallway when the elevator doors opened and scooped Chen into his arms. The swelling on his face had subsided and the purples of the bruise were now turning into shades of green and yellow.

"I'm fine." She let him plant a kiss on her cheek and then gently untangled herself from his embrace. "I need to take a shower. I reek of smoke."

"You should have called me right away. They said it was a Molotov cocktail."

"I'm sorry," she said. "It happened fast. One moment we were driving through the crowd and the next there was shooting and that's when somebody must've thrown the bottle."

"Come on. Let's not stay in the hallway." He led her to the suite and took out a clean bathrobe and a fresh towel. "Stay here tonight. I hate sleeping alone."

"I know. Just too much work, and I didn't want to come back here in the middle of the night and wake you up."

"You can work here too," he said. "I'll build the Faraday cage, so you can access JC here as well. With everything going on, I don't want you out of my sight."

"I know." She leaned into him and put her head on his shoulder. "Every day could be our last."

"Don't say that."

She sighed, stood up straight, and took the towel from his hands. "Come with me."

Chen led Schlager to the shower, dropped the towel to the floor and turned to face him. She closed her eyes as he leaned in and kissed her on the lips, first gently, and then with more urgency, like a soldier kissing a girl before being sent to the front. Unsure if he'd make it back.

She kissed him back, feeling his hands on her body as his fingers worked their magic on the buttons and hooks. And then, as they were under the warm running water, she let him take the lead, giving in to the motions, pressing her body into his. More seeking refuge than trying to satisfy her desire. Trying to find comfort in being held by someone who truly cared for her.

After the shower, she brew gunpowder green tea, as Max cooked, but not before he put Tracy Chapman's vinyl on a turntable.

They sat at the table, shoulder to shoulder, and ate almost entirely without talking, a comfortable understanding that didn't need to be filled with words. The food was good—grilled salmon and roasted vegetables, Schlager's signature, and they sipped on green tea, while the soulful sounds of "Give Me One Reason" filled the room.

Schlager was a lot of things, but he knew her better than most, and right now this was exactly what she wanted—a quiet evening and a good meal. Despite all the craziness of the past few weeks, she felt almost at peace.

Almost.

"Stay here tonight," he said again.

"Give me one reason." She smiled, echoing the song's lyrics.

"I can give you more than one." He smiled back. "And I'll make breakfast."

"I'll move my stuff here," she said. "You're right. What was the point of moving in together if we aren't always living together? But I'll do that tomorrow."

"Good."

"I'm exhausted," she said, standing up and dabbing her lips with a napkin. "I'll go down for a moment. I'll be right back."

"Where are you going?"

"I need my pillow," she said. "Sorry, but your pillows are atrocious. And I need my purse."

"I'll come with you."

"No, that's okay." She patted him on a shoulder. "I'll be right over."

"Okay."

She put a pair of shorts on and wrapped herself in Max's bathrobe, two sizes too big. Then she stepped out of the suite and into the hallway.

The lights were dimmed for the evening and she squinted when the doors of the elevator car opened, blinding her with a bright overhead spotlight.

"Helen." Jason Hunt was standing in the back. His coat was damp and his hair wet. "Turns out freezing rain isn't good for a walk."

"Hey." She smiled and stepped inside. The doors closed, and the elevator jerked up as it went to the top floor. "Needed some air?"

"Yeah." He shrugged. The door chimed as they stopped and Hunt went out, but then turned back and held the door with his left hand. His fingers were pale. "How are you holding up?"

"It's all…" She paused, looking for the right words. "Surreal. But we've come this far, right?"

"Right." He looked down at his feet and then looked up, his eyes searching her face. "We've come so far. Good night, Helen."

"Good night."

He let go of the door, and Chen leaned on the wall as the elevator descended to the twenty-seventh floor. She took a step out, and the doors closed behind her. As if on cue, the lights went out in the entire hallway, a lone red Exit sign glowing to her left by the stairway door. Chen stood there for a moment, startled. Then, when her eyes acclimated to the dark, she walked to her room. The keypad next to the door was dead too, and she pulled out a key. She couldn't remember the last time she had to use it.

It wasn't as dark in the apartment, the glow of the city below it illuminating the sparsely furnished room. She marched to the bathroom, picked up her toothbrush, a mascara, a few bottles and tubes, and loaded them into a portable bag.

Then she went to her bedroom and went through her closet, picking out a few shirts as she held them out to the window light to see. Satisfied, Chen picked up her pillow and headed back to the living room. That's when the lights came back on.

"Weird," she said out loud. Then she stopped in her tracks. In the middle of her living room stood a petite woman. She wore a black leather motorcycle jacket, cargo pants, and a pair of black military boots. There was a sleek backpack strapped to her back.

"Who the fuck are you?" Chen said, dropping the pillow down. "How did you get here?"

The woman cocked her head without answering. She had an oval face, that under different circumstances Chen might have thought lovely, and the woman's bright, dark-brown eyes seemed to study Helen. Calculating.

"What do you want?" Chen moved to the side, one step closer to the door.

"Helen Chen, I presume?" The woman's voice was soft. "I just want to talk. Something we both might benefit from."

Helen threw her bag into the intruder's face, turned, and tried to run, but the woman dodged, caught up to her, and swiped her leg.

Chen went down hard. The impact knocked the air out of her lungs and before she had a chance to regroup, the woman went down on one knee and struck a blow to her lower back. The pain was paralyzing.

"I'm sorry," the woman said, squatting next to Chen. She grabbed Helen's wrists, pulled them back, and cuffed them with a zip tie. "I don't want to hurt you. But you have to listen to what I've got to say."

47

Chuck Kowalsky sped down Sixth Avenue, cut in front of a taxi—which, to his surprise slowed down, letting him go—and turned onto Broome Street. He pulled ahead of a beat-up Nissan Altima and parked by the curb on the opposite side of Orion Tower. There was a patch of broken asphalt a car-length away from him, covered on all sides with half a dozen white plastic barricades with orange stripes. A paper sign REPAIRING YOUR GAS SYSTEM was taped on one of them. Kowalsky considered it for a second and then moved his car a few feet forward, enough to render the spot in front of him too small for most cars.

Not the most popular move in the city, always struggling with parking space that put his car in danger of being keyed, but Kowalsky didn't care. He wanted to make sure he could get out when he needed to without inching back and forth a dozen times.

His radio squawked, and he pressed the button on the dashboard. "What's up, Latham?"

"Are you at the tower yet?"

"Just parked. You?"

"I got out of the tunnel. I should've left earlier. The Belt is one giant parking lot," the man said, referring to the Belt Parkway, a series of connected highways that formed a belt-like circle around Brooklyn and Queens. "But it looks like I'm out of the woods. Should join you in ten-fifteen minutes, tops."

"Sounds good." Chuck glanced at the plastic barricades again. "Pull up at the northern entrance. I've saved you a parking spot."

"Thanks."

"Any Black Arrow guys?"

"No," Latham said. "I think they all pulled out of New York. I didn't see any of them since Price announced his plan to hold the inauguration in the city."

"I'm not sure if it makes me happy or worried."

"How do you mean? Isn't it a good thing?"

"I don't know." Chuck tensed as he watched a black SUV make its turn on Broome Street but then relaxed as the car sped by. There was a woman behind the wheel and he could see two kids in the back, strapped into their car seats. "Shit I can't explain makes me nervous. Hurry up."

Chuck disconnected the call, got out of the car, and walked back to the intersection of Broome and Sixth. He stood there next to a red, old-fashioned fire and police emergency call box and looked up and down the street. The box was weatherworn and hadn't been painted for a long time. Chuck glanced at the oversized buttons—the red one for the fire department and the blue for the NYPD—wondering if they still worked. There were only a few boxes left in the entire city, and almost nobody knew that those that remained still ran on the original technology. When the button was pressed, or, on some models, flap lifted, it would turn a coded-wheel that would send a unique box number to the dispatchers. Those, in turn, would forward it to the appropriate depot or precinct. A few mayors had tried to get rid of them, but some advocacy group sued, arguing it would take away a vital option for deaf or mute residents of the city who could not use a regular phone.

It was a moot point, anyway. It had been a few years since the city was covered with cameras that transmitted live video twenty-four-seven. The stream went straight to an NYPD-controlled center, where it was processed by a sophisticated AI. But it had also been a few years since the police responded to anything other than a major shoot-out. And even then, only if the participants didn't belong to some large multinational corporations. *Self-government* was the key phrase these days and everybody, the police department included, tried to steer clear of getting involved in anything that could put them on the wrong side of a powerful entity.

He leaned against the box and kept watching the intersection. It wouldn't be too cold, if not for the gusts of icy wind threatening to take his breath away. Chuck zipped his jacket all the way up and pulled the hood over his head. It'd been many years since he smoked but now, standing in the cold wind on the corner of a street, suspiciously scanning the passersby, brought back the memories from his NYPD days and with that the craving for a cigarette.

As if on cue, a man crossed the sidewalk, a smoldering cigarette in his hand. He went to the row of Citi bikes, flicked the glowing stub away, and unlocked the bicycle. Then, he was on his way, pedaling down Sixth Avenue, his hooded parka ballooning on his back with every gust of wind.

Chuck's right thumb rubbed across his index and middle fingers as if rolling a tube. He snapped his fingers in frustration, trying to break the spell. It was a slippery slope.

He took his hands out of his pockets, letting the cold air be a distraction, and walked west to Varick Street. The traffic was heavier on this side, a steady flow of cars going for the tunnel, but even here it was lighter than usual.

Chuck's stomach grumbled as he caught a whiff of aromas coming from the diner on the corner—a complicated mix of sharp coffee smell, smoky bacon, and sweet bread. He swallowed, for a second considering popping in and grabbing something to eat. Then, with a resigned sigh, he turned and walked back. His phone vibrated, and he took it out as he watched a pickup truck make a turn off Sixth Avenue, a large Silverado with oversized wheels.

"Where are you, man?"

"Forgot to ask you something," Latham replied, ignoring his question. "What did Jason say about the Otomo connection?"

"We didn't have a chance to properly talk about it, but I think he took it seriously. Without going there and poking around, it'll be impossible to know for sure. But I don't care if it's Otomo or somebody else. We have to do something about it." Chuck paused. The pickup truck slowed down between the barricades and Chuck's car, a driver in a bright-orange jacket craning his neck back and forth as if gauging the distance. "You won't fit there, asshole."

"What's going on?"

"Somebody's trying to take your parking spot, that's what's going on."

"I thought you said you saved me one."

"I did," Chuck said, watching as the truck turned at a steep angle and crept backward. "There's not enough room for him. But it doesn't stop him from trying."

"You think Jason will send somebody on an expedition?" Latham asked. "Normally I wouldn't be volunteering for something like this, but after the last few weeks, I could use a change of scenery. You and I can go together."

"Right." Chuck snorted. "A dream team."

"We found the connection," Latham said. "I wouldn't mind to see it through. Even if that means a trip across the pond with an asshole like you."

"If I didn't know you any better, I'd say you want to be friends."

"Fuck you."

The truck climbed on the curb with its rear tire and the driver started turning the steering wheel back, pulling the cabin into the space.

"I'll have him buy me a new car, if he scratches it," Chuck said. "Why aren't you here yet?"

"Five minutes," Latham replied. "Almost there."

Chuck cringed as the truck stopped right before hitting his car and then the cabin started to complete the semicircle. It might not have been obvious for the driver, but from his vantage point, Chuck could see that the massive bumper was about to smash into the front barricade that carried the gas repair sign. He cocked his head, expecting to hear a scraping sound, but it never came. The front of the car went straight through the top part of the stripy plastic and came out on the other side.

"What the—" Chuck said as he ran toward the work site. He stopped near the barricade and extended his hand. Just like the truck before it, the hand went straight through the plastic without touching it.

"What's happening?" he heard Latham ask, but didn't bother with an answer. Bewildered, he leaned closer, bringing his face inches from the barrier. At this distance, it didn't seem solid. It vibrated like an unstable image. Chuck stepped forward and once he was inside the perimeter of the barriers, they disappeared altogether. There were no plastic barricades; there was no sign informing the public about a gas line repair. Even the patch of the road was as smooth as everywhere else on the block.

In the middle of the space, there was a matte-black metallic cube the size of a trash can. On top of it lay a small rectangular object that looked like an old-fashioned flip phone with a small blinking light on its side. A barely audible vibrating sound was coming from the device.

He picked up the small gadget and flipped the lid closed. It gave a beep, a perfectly ordinary sound, and powered down. Judging by the expression of the truck driver, the barricades disappeared for him too. Something clanked inside of the cube, startling Kowalsky, and then four spindly telescopic legs sprouted from the bottom of it, lifting the cube off the ground. The top surface split in the middle, both sides sliding at a forty-five-degree angle and revealing a short barrel of a strange weapon. A moment later, the sentinel was pattering across the street, the barrel of its gun swiveling back and forth between two protective plates.

"Shit," Kowalsky said and ran toward the tower.

48

The fiery disk of the sun had already sunk low enough to disappear somewhere west of the Hudson River, but its last rays set the wispy cirrus clouds on fire and colored the observation deck of Orion Tower in burgundy red. A mast bearing the dark-blue flag with three shining stars was bending in the wind, its foot-thick steel joints trembling so hard Michael Connelly could feel them through the thick soles of his boots. He glanced at the flapping fabric and then looked around the room as the music flowed from the hidden speakers behind the screen above the bar. Max Schlager was holding Helen's shoulders, and for once she didn't seem to mind the public display of affection. Jason Hunt was standing closer to the bar, his face relaxed, but his body tense as if ready for a fight.

The music stopped, and Connelly returned his attention to the big screen. The TV drone, one of the many, was hovering above the cobblestone street in front of Federal Hall, catercorner to the New York Stock Exchange. It zoomed in on the statue of George Washington for a few seconds, then zoomed out and panned around, showing the crowd stretching from the exchange and disappearing down Broad Street. The row of blue police barricades was set up thirty feet away from the steps of the hall, and a row of cops in dark-

244

blue uniforms were pushing some of the overeager spectators back behind the line.

"This is happening," Schlager said out loud.

"He got sworn in," Hunt said. "Yeah, it is happening."

The cameras shifted to a tall, slim figure of Darius Price, his wife and two kids in tow, flanked by a few men and women on the top of Federal Hall's steps under the giant stars and stripes flag. The crowd erupted in applause and cheers that refused to die out even as Price raised both hands in the air asking for silence.

"Ladies and gentlemen," the announcer said, "please welcome the president of the United States, Darius Price."

"My fellow Americans," Price started, his voice amplified by the speakers rolling over the crowd.

"You rock," somebody shouted from the crowd, interrupting him. A few other voices joined in.

Price smiled and raised his hand again until the crowd grew quiet.

"Thank you," he said. "There's a reason I wanted the inauguration to take place here in New York. I know the critics will say I had no other options, but it's not true. I wanted to do it here even before the last few weeks seemed to have put everything in this country upside down. It's going to be hard, but I will try my best not to talk about the impostor who's staging a pretend play today in front of the Capitol building down in DC in a brazen attempt to hijack our future. I want to talk about you. About us. About this great country that has overcome so much. We were a young nation when the great George Washington took his oath on the balcony of this very building. Now, I didn't choose to do it here because I think history would compare me to him. I chose it because right now, like it did back in 1789, our country stands on the precipice—"

A loud, white noise flooded the room as the image on the screen disappeared, replaced by a gray static of a dead channel.

"What just happened?" Schlager said.

Connelly ignored him as his phone vibrated with an incoming message. He gripped the screen hard as he processed the information.

"Mike?" He heard Hunt's voice. "What's wrong? Oh, never mind, I see it, too."

"Everybody out of the building, now," Connelly shouted as he dashed to the elevator. "Come on. There's been an explosion. Move it."

"You heard the man," Hunt said, gesturing to his friends.

Connelly ushered everyone inside and planted his hand onto a biometric screen. "You might want to hold on to something."

A large countdown window appeared on the elevator control panel, accompanied by a disembodied female voice. "Emergency descent. Please hold on to the railing. Three, two, one."

The floor seemed to fall out from under their feet as the steel box plunged from the eighty-sixth floor, accelerating to thirty-five miles per hour. Connelly grimaced as his ears painfully popped, but that was a small price to pay in the event of an emergency. He glanced at the floor counter—twenty more to go.

A loud bang came from above and the lights inside the elevator flickered and then went out, plunging them into the dark. A screeching sound cut through the air as emergency brakes kicked in, bringing them to an abrupt halt. Someone fell on him and Connelly instinctively held on to the person, trying to prevent them from hitting the ground. Emergency lights blinked to life a moment later, revealing Schlager's embarrassed face as the man tried to disentangle himself from Connelly's grasp.

"Sorry, man," Max said, finally picking himself up.

"All good." Connelly punched a three-digit code into the panel and the doors slid an inch apart, far enough for him to see outside, without putting passengers at too much risk.

"Could've been worse," he said, looking at the gap. The elevator had stopped halfway through the floor, but there was enough space to climb out. "Jason, give me a hand."

They pulled the doors apart, and he ducked under the ceiling to jump down. He took a quick assessment of the surroundings. There was some broken glass on the floor and small pieces of debris, but the damage seemed minimal. There was a faint smell of smoke and that worried him more at the moment.

"Come on," he said, motioning to the group. "It's safe for now."

He helped Chen jump down first, followed by Schlager and then Hunt.

"Are you getting anything?" Hunt asked. "All my systems are blind."

"Nope," Connelly said, looking at the screen of the phone. "Pretty sure we are being jammed. Let's not linger here. Let's go."

He headed toward the stairwell, motioning to the others to follow. The door under the Exit sign was ajar and Connelly removed a gun from a holster before entering the stairwell.

"Hang on." Hunt motioned to him to stop. "I can hear someone coming."

Someone screamed, a terror in the man's voice coming from down the stairs, abruptly cut off by a quick tapping of an automatic weapon.

"Shit." Connelly spun on his heels and pulled the door open to the nearest office. A small plastic table and a few light ergonomic chairs around it. Nothing remotely heavy to barricade the door to the stairwell. "Let's try the other side of the building."

"I disagree," Hunt said. "I hear only four hostiles on this side coming up, and I don't hear anything fancy. We can easily take them. And we'll be much closer to the cars when we get to the garage. From the other stairwell, we'll have to go all around the building."

"But they know we are here."

"They probably do," Hunt agreed. "I think they can see where the elevator stopped, but it doesn't change much."

Connelly looked at him and then back at the door. He hated the idea of having to engage four unknown hostiles with the man he was supposed to protect, but Jason had a point.

"All right," he said, making a decision. "Helen, Max, go back to the lobby and stay behind the wall. Do not come out unless you hear from us. Jason, you go in that office."

"And you?"

"I'll stay by the door."

"Okay." Hunt walked across the hallway to the door. "But I have a better idea."

Before Connelly could say anything, he saw as Hunt shook his right bionic arm and pulled the door wide open.

"What the—"

Hunt stepped out on the landing and hopped over the handrail, disappearing a flight below. Connelly rushed after the man in time to hear a momentary burst of automatic fire.

"It's all clear," Hunt shouted, leaning over the handrail. "You can call the guys."

"Why am I protecting you again?" Connelly asked, looking at four crumpled bodies splayed on the steps below Jason.

"You keep on insisting." Hunt winked. "Come on."

"Wait." Helen caught up to Connelly with Schlager in tow. She stopped with a vacant look on her face, apparently accessing her built-in systems. "Let me check the cameras in the stairwell."

"I told you to stay behind. Does anyone… Never mind. Let's go."

"It's clear for now." He heard Chen's voice as he started down the stairs. "Garage seems to be empty, too."

"Stay behind me," he barked as he passed Jason. "And watch those two."

They ran down the stairs in a single file, with him in front and Schlager in the back. A few minutes later, they descended into a small, windowless lobby. A large double door painted in a utilitarian gray had a large GARAGE sign on top of it. An emergency box was installed by the door, a fire extinguisher and a fireman's ax with a bright-red handle hanging on the black felt behind the glass. Connelly broke the glass with his elbow, unhooked the ax, and handed it to Schlager. "Just in case."

He pushed the door an inch and entered the garage, sweeping the open space with a barrel of a HK Mark 23. The fire alarm blared in the distance, bouncing off the concrete walls. A red light blinked on the farthest wall in unison with the sound, throwing a reddish glow over parked vehicles.

"Mike." He heard Jason yell behind him, but he already saw it: a shimmering human figure was moving toward them between the rows of cars.

It was still far, almost leisurely strolling across the concrete floor, and for a second Connelly thought it was Martin. But the man was of an average size rather than the hulking bulk of the cyborg. There were no visible weapons except a scintillating blade with a long, straight hilt in the man's outstretched right hand. The sword, with a slightly curved edge and the tip cut at a forty-five-degree angle, resembled a Japanese katana.

Connelly's index finger moved to the trigger as he put the ghostly silhouette dead center in his sights. The man didn't slow down, oblivious to the gun pointed at it.

"Go back," he yelled at the group. "We don't want to engage this thing."

In his peripheral vision, he saw Jason ignore his order and move to flank the enemy. Connelly cursed under his breath and squeezed the trigger three times in quick succession, seeing as .45 ammo hit the center mass of the target. Circular ripples appeared on the flickering surface of the hitman where the bullets hit, but otherwise seemed to have no effect on the adversary.

Then, without a warning, the figure broke into a run, flicking his left wrist in Connelly's direction. All sounds disappeared as Connelly's body seemed to be ripped off the floor by an invisible force and thrown against a concrete wall. As he slid down to the ground, he saw the cars on either side of him pushed aside by a powerful blast. There was no pain, not yet, just the sensation of air being knocked out of his lungs and a high-pitched ringing in his ears that drowned all other sounds.

"No," he mouthed as Jason Hunt came into his view, his bionic arm moving at inhuman speed to connect with the assassin's head.

The man bent backward at an impossible angle and then his right hand swung the blade in a short, deadly arc, slicing through Jason's thighs. The assassin spun around, letting the momentum carry him full circle, and then brought the sword down again, cutting clean through Hunt's left shoulder. As Connelly's vision dimmed, time seemed to freeze for a moment as Jason Hunt and the glowing figure in front of him stood still. Then Jason fell backward, his legs and left arm falling away from the torso.

Like a house of cards, Connelly thought. Then everything went black.

FATA MORGANA (THE UPGRADE SERIES #5)

Enjoyed the book? You can buy the next installment in the Upgrade series here:
FATA MORGANA

JOIN THE UPGRADE SERIES

Thank you for reading SPARE PARTS, the fourth book in THE UPGRADE series. I hope you enjoyed it. The journey continues with two final books coming out soon—FATA MORGANA and DEUS EX.

If you enjoyed this book, please take a moment and leave an honest review. Reviews are important for authors and help us sell more books and thus spend more time writing new stories you can enjoy. You can do that here:

Leave a review

And, of course, don't forget to join the series to learn about upcoming releases, exclusive free content, and more. You can do it right here:

Join The Upgrade Series

Thanks again for reading and hope to see you soon!

ALSO BY WESLEY CROSS

THE UPGRADE SERIES

BOOK 1. THE BLUEPRINT

BOOK 2. VERTIGO

BOOK 3. THE LOOP

ROGUE (A short story)

BOOK 4. SPARE PARTS

BOOK 5. FATA MORGANA

BOOK 6. DEUS EX (2022)